Praise for the Pacific H

The Second Goodbye

"The Second Goodbye is a straight-ahead jolt of police procedural adrenaline. Like Michael Connelly, Patricia Smiley grabs hold of you and pulls you into the story without tricks or gimmicks. Just a great story told by a great storyteller. *The Second Goodbye* catapults Smiley into the top tier of crime writers!"

—Matt Coyle, Anthony Award–winning
author of the Rick Cahill crime series

"Seamless prose, tightly craft clues, and surprising twists make *The Second Goodbye* a memorable police procedural."

—K. J. Howe, bestselling author of *The Freedom Broker*

"Patricia Smiley tackles Michael Connelly territory and succeeds with a realistic, compelling police procedural in the badlands of contemporary Los Angeles."

—Raymond Benson, author of *In the Hush of the Night*

Outside the Wire

"[Richards] makes a dogged and determined heroine ... Readers will want to see a lot more of her."

—*Publishers Weekly*

"[Smiley] moves the plot as deftly as she moves the reader, with lots of action and just enough heart."

—*Kirkus Reviews*

Pacific Homicide

"Smiley kicks off a hard-boiled series with a bang in this fast-paced novel that sweeps readers along quickly."

—*Library Journal*

"An excellent book about the emotions that drive some of the best policemen and—women to go after their own justice, no matter the cost."

—*Suspense Magazine*

"Terrific! The classic cop story goes contemporary in this suspenseful, riveting thriller. Instantly cinematic and completely authentic—LAPD's tough and savvy Davie Richards will capture your heart. It's a page-turner from moment one."

—Hank Phillippi Ryan, Agatha-, Anthony- and
Mary Higgins Clark Award–winning author

"*Pacific Homicide* combines an insider's knowledge of the LAPD with a clear-eyed, no-nonsense heroine and an entertaining dry wit. Davie Richards is easy to fall in love with and her story is full of surprising twists."

—Matt Witten, writer and producer for *Pretty Little Liars,*
House, Medium, Law & Order, and *Homicide*

"Patricia Smiley, at the top of her form in this multi-layered thriller … writes with the authenticity of Joseph Wambaugh."

—Paul Levine, bestselling author of *Bum Rap*

"Crackling with wit and suspense, Patricia Smiley's *Pacific Homicide* is a classic police procedural told with flair, imagination and the deep authenticity of an author who knows the LAPD from firsthand experience."

—Bonnie MacBird, author of *Art in the Blood*:
A Sherlock Holmes Adventure

"Fans of the classic police procedural will love Davie Richards, the LAPD detective at the heart of this novel ... Readers will discover Smiley's nimble talents for understated wit, unsentimental affection and the emotional wounds that drive the best of cops to buck the system in search of justice."

—Kim Fay, Edgar Award finalist for *The Map of Lost Memories*

PATRICIA SMILEY

THE

A PACIFIC HOMICIDE NOVEL

SECOND GOODBYE

MIDNIGHT INK
WOODBURY, MINNESOTA

FIRST EDITION
First Printing, 2018

Book format by Steff Pitzen
Cover design by Kevin Brown
Cover Illustration by Dominick Finelle / The July Group
Editing by Nicole Nugent

Midnight Ink, an imprint of Llewellyn Worldwide Ltd.

Library of Congress Cataloging-in-Publication Data
Names: Smiley, Patricia, author.
Title: The second goodbye : a Pacific homicide novel / Patricia Smiley.
Description: First edition. | Woodbury, Minnesota : Midnight Ink, [2018] |
    Series: A Pacific homicide novel ; #3.
Identifiers: LCCN 2018020616 (print) | LCCN 2018022740 (ebook) | ISBN
    9780738755960 (ebook) | ISBN 9780738752365 (alk. paper)
Subjects: | GSAFD: Mystery fiction.
Classification: LCC PS3619.M49 (ebook) | LCC PS3619.M49 S43 2018 (print) |
    DDC 813/.6—dc23
LC record available at https://lccn.loc.gov/2018020616

Midnight Ink
Llewellyn Worldwide Ltd.
2143 Wooddale Drive
Woodbury, MN 55125-2989
www.midnightinkbooks.com

Printed in the United States of America

Dedicated to William Shakespeare,
for his prescient description of Davie Richards:
"And though she be but little, she is fierce."
—*A Midsummer Night's Dream*

————

Other Books by Patricia Smiley

Outside the Wire
(Midnight Ink, 2017)
Pacific Homicide
(Midnight Ink, 2016)

Tucker Sinclair Mysteries
False Profits
Cover Your Assets
Short Change
Cool Cache

Acknowledgments

My deepest gratitude to the people who read pages of this novel and offered advice on how to make them better: Dana Isaacson, William Solberg, my amazing agent Sandy Harding, Harley Jane Kozak, Matt Witten, Bonnie MacBird, Craig Faustus Buck, Jamie Diamond, Jonathan Beggs, Linda Burrows, and Bob Shayne.

A tip of the hat to Nicole Nugent and Terri Bischoff at Midnight Ink for shepherding the book from pages to publication, and to my law enforcement friends who helped me better understand police procedure and takedown strategy, including Michael DePasquale and Thomas Leighton. Fingers crossed they will turn a blind eye when Davie doesn't always follow their expert advice—it's fiction after all.

Special kudos to my friends Penny and David Collins for trekking to Franklin Canyon Reservoir to scout out locations for a crucial scene in the novel, and to Hannah Hempstead and Stephen Courtney for schooling me about Florida and naming the Seaglass Cafe.

My gratitude to Jane Newell for granting permission to use her mother's name as a character in this novel in support of the Anaheim Public Library Foundation. The real Kathleen Newell passed along her love of books and libraries to her daughter, just as my mother did to me. Kathleen Newell shares little in common with the fictional Kathleen except for her Florida roots and her keen sense of style.

Finally, to all the people who have championed my writing over the years. I love you all beyond measure.

KNOWING SHE WOULDN'T PASS a background check, Sara Montaine had never tried to buy a gun, but now she had no option but to risk it. For the past ten days she'd seen strange cars parked on the street in front of her house and experienced hang-up calls at odd hours. A few nights ago she'd gone outside to empty the garbage and was sure she saw a dark figure moving in the shadows. Someone was watching her. She could only conclude that after all this time and all her careful planning, they had found her, they knew where she lived, and she had no doubt they meant to silence her forever.

Two nights ago Sara had researched weapons on the Internet. A person could find anything online these days. Semiautomatic pistols with their magazines and sliding racks seemed too complicated, so she settled on a .38-caliber Smith & Wesson revolver—easy to use and deadly at close range. She watched a video on how to load the bullets—properly called rounds. It seemed easy enough: slip a few into the cylinder and the gun was ready to fire.

Her plan wasn't foolproof, but she could no longer ignore the threat. Fate had forced her hand. The gunstore was far away from where she lived, located in a strip of squat buildings in a downtrodden section of Venice Boulevard in Los Angeles.

There was a small parking lot in front of Black Jack Guns & Ammo, but Sara decided to leave her Mercedes in a nearby residential area to avoid surveillance cameras, should there be any. No use calling attention to herself. There was a two-hour parking restriction, but she would only need a fraction of that time. She just had to stay focused. No wavering.

Approaching the front door, she noticed an elderly man watering ranunculus in a planter box outside the shop next door. She avoided his gaze and peeked inside the gunstore window. The owner stood behind the counter, watching a poker competition on TV. Her hands trembled. She took a deep breath to shore up her courage as she walked inside, forcing a practiced ingénue smile.

He turned from the TV. "What can I do for you?"

He didn't appear to recognize her, but she hadn't expected him to. It had been a long time since they'd seen each other and she'd changed since then. Her hair was darker and she'd lost weight. The cosmetic surgery hadn't been dramatic, but perhaps it was enough to throw him off. He stared at her a moment and then flashed a wide-eyed look of recognition.

She glanced inside the glass case in front of her and pointed to a Smith & Wesson revolver with a brown wooden handle and a short barrel. A snubnose, she'd learned from the manufacturer's website. Not her first choice, but it would serve the purpose.

"That's the gun I want to buy," Sara said, pointing to the revolver, "but my hands are small. Could I hold it to check the fit?"

He slipped his key into the lock of the glass gun case. Before he could open it, his cell phone rang. Sara hoped the call wouldn't last long. She was in a hurry to finish the purchase and get back to the safety of her home. The man focused his attention on the caller, speaking in hushed but heated tones as he hurried into the back room. This kink in Sara's plans left her unsure of her next step—that is, until she noticed the key was still in the lock.

She scanned the area and saw several cameras pointed her way, but there was nothing she could do about that. She'd just have to make the best of the situation. Her pulse raced as she slipped behind the counter and turned the key. She reached into the case and grasped the handle of the gun.

A perfect fit.

It was early May and a wildfire in the foothills north of Santa Paula choked the surrounding air with the acrid odor of charred chaparral. Flames fanned by years of drought and higher-than-usual temperatures had already destroyed multiple buildings and forced hundreds of people from their homes.

LAPD Homicide Detective Davie Richards had lived in Los Angeles her entire life. When she was a kid, the fire season had typically started in September, whipped up by fierce Santa Ana winds, and ended in December when the rains came. But extreme dry conditions caused by climate change had stretched a four-month disaster into a year-round hell. Climate change caused drought. Drought caused fire. Fire sent carbon into the atmosphere, triggering more climate change. Chicken, egg. Cause, effect. Davie wondered if there were parallels between the damage caused by wildfires and the brutality of murder, but maybe she was just overthinking.

There hadn't been a homicide in LAPD's Pacific Area for weeks, so for the past several days she'd been sifting through two of the division's 172 unsolved murders. Her boss Frank Giordano had compiled the list of cases dating back to the 1960s, when Pacific was called Venice Division. Most of the cold case deaths had occurred long before Giordano was in charge of the Homicide table, but it was his personal mission to solve every one of them before retiring. That was unlikely to happen because he'd already started the paperwork to pull the plug on his career.

Giordano had distributed eight open cases with the most potential among his four Homicide detectives. Davie had been poring through the two Murder Books assigned to her, making to-do lists and searching for new leads—a witness to re-interview, forensic evidence that might have been collected but never tested, or some other bit of overlooked minutiae.

The first case was the five-year old strangulation death of a female resident of Mar Vista. After a quick search, Davie not only learned her husband, the only suspect, had recently committed suicide but also that several pieces of crucial evidence were missing from police storage. Not much to go on there.

The other case was the brutal two-year-old murder of gangbanger Javier AKA Javi Hernandez. The crime scene photos revealed an overweight young man covered in tattoos and blood, curled into a fetal position on a mattress in the carport of his Palms apartment building with fifteen stab wounds on his neck and torso.

Witnesses—at least the ones who were willing to talk to the police—claimed Hernandez was a drug dealer for C-Street, a Westside gang. The Investigative Officer assigned to the case believed a fellow gang member had killed Hernandez in a beef over drug sales because the day after the murder, the victim's car was found at the other man's home. He'd been interviewed but claimed he borrowed Hernandez's car with the victim's permission. Several people confirmed his story. Before the Hernandez autopsy had been completed, the suspect had been killed in a drive-by shooting. The original Investigative Officer wasn't able to gather enough evidence on the dead suspect to withstand the scrutiny of the DA's office. A short time later, the detective transferred to another division and the case went cold.

Davie woke up her computer and searched law enforcement databases for the names of Hernandez's known associates. She quickly found a man named Felix Malo. Malo was high up in the gang's hierarchy and a good friend of Hernandez's. He'd claimed to be in Texas visiting relatives on the day of the murder and knew nothing about Hernandez's death. Malo's uncle corroborated his nephew's alibi. Davie clicked her mouse on the Criminal History System. She wanted to interview him herself, but when she accessed his rap sheet she found he'd been convicted of a carjacking six months after the Hernandez murder and was now serving time.

The California Department of Corrections & Rehabilitation website confirmed that Malo was a Level 3 inmate at the California State Prison in Lancaster, which meant he was in an individual cell, inside a fenced perimeter with armed guards. If Malo agreed to speak with her, the prison was close enough to drive up and back in the same day. Davie added the interview to her to-do list. She would also talk to Malo's girlfriend, Alma Velez, who'd also supposedly been Hernandez's friend.

Detective Giordano stood to look over the gray half wall that separated their desks. "How's it going, kid? Clear any cases yet?"

Her boss towered over her in his dark blue suit and starched white shirt. He was a tough but fair supervisor and supportive of his detectives. Giordano had investigated over two hundred homicides in his career and had passed along valuable knowledge to her. Davie still had volumes to learn from him and wasn't looking forward to his retirement.

She closed the Murder Book's blue three-ring binder. "Hernandez has possibilities. I'm going to interview the victim's friend Felix Malo. He claims he was out of state when the murder went down, but I'm guessing he knows more about what happened than he claims. He's serving time in state prison, but he might talk to me. Maybe he got religion behind bars and is ready to drop a dime on the killer."

Giordano chuckled. "Good luck with that. Just remember, they have a dress code up there. No blue. No green."

There was no risk of Davie being mistaken for a prisoner or one of the guards by wearing the wrong color clothes. She'd crawled around enough bloody crime scenes to learn that black polyester pantsuits were the only getup that made sense. They didn't wrinkle or show dirt and they were washable. She had three of them, the one she was wearing, one hanging in her closet at home, and one in her locker at the station next to her uniform and running clothes.

At five-one and 104 pounds, Davie was lucky the department had no minimum height or weight limitations for acceptance into the academy. Her personal Smith & Wesson .45 looked like a cannon hanging on her small frame, which was the point, she guessed. She'd earned a Distinguished Expert Marksman and Sharpshooter medal called a DX with that gun and she wasn't inclined to ditch it for the department-issued weapon. Her size and coppery orange-brown hair had invited a fair amount of teasing over the years, but she'd long ago found the best defense to mockery was competence.

"Malo's girlfriend, Alma Velez, is local," she said, "so she shouldn't be hard to find. She was interviewed after the murder but, of course, claimed she didn't know anything."

"Start with her. If you look far enough into any homicide, you'll find a woman involved somewhere, somehow."

Davie leaned back in her chair and crossed her arms. "Yeah. Right."

"Trust me. You'll see." Giordano stepped over to the coffeemaker he'd installed on a credenza behind his desk and poured a cup. "These old cases are tough, but do what you can."

Davie reached toward the shelf above her desk and pushed aside the metal bookends Giordano had given her to keep her desk tidy. They each formed the numbers 187, the penal code for a homicide. Her finger swept down the list of telephone numbers she'd compiled in her years on the job until she located the contact information for prison intake control. There was a fifty-fifty chance of getting the interview with Malo. All she could do was hope for the good side of fifty. A man with a gravelly voice answered her call. She identified herself and told him she wanted to set up a time and date to visit Felix Malo.

"We just busted him for assaulting another inmate," the official said. "He lost his privileges at the commissary. Also, no phone calls and no visits. He's not a happy camper right now."

"Maybe he needs a shoulder to cry on."

The man snickered. "Since you're law enforcement, I'll find out and get back to you, but I'm guessing he won't be thrilled to shed tears about an old homicide."

Davie asked him to check whether Alma Velez was on Malo's visitor list. Then she thanked him and ended the call. She thumbed through the pages of the Murder Book until she found the phone number for Velez. According to the reports, Malo's girlfriend had been uncooperative during the original investigation, but that was typical. Nobody wanted to be fingered as a snitch. On the other hand, maybe she'd been involved in Hernandez's death and Giordano's joke about women was right this time.

Davie pulled a pen from the black faux-leather notebook she'd bought in a shop at the academy. The outside was embossed with a generic detective badge. Inside she kept an 8½x11 lined tablet, business cards, small evidence envelopes, and other investigative essentials. The portfolio had a zipper that kept the contents from falling out.

She called the cell number listed in the file, hoping it was still in service. "Alma Velez?"

"Who wants to know?" Her tone was surly and suspicious.

"LAPD. Who am I speaking to?"

"I'm Alma. What do you want?"

"I'm looking into the murder of Javi Hernandez. Remember him?"

There was a long pause accompanied by heavy breathing. "Yeah, I remember, but I told the cops back then, I don't know nothing."

"Maybe they didn't ask the right questions."

Velez's voice grew louder. "They asked me every kind of question. They got the same answer. I told them everything I knew."

"Is Felix Malo still your man?"

Davie waited through another long silence.

"He's in prison."

"That's not what I asked."

"I'm on my own now."

Her cagy tone raised suspicion, but Davie decided to let it go for the moment. Velez might be an important witness and Davie didn't want to alienate her just yet.

"Let's talk face to face. Can you come to the station for an interview?"

She huffed out some air to show her annoyance. "I work."

"I can come to your job—"

Velez interrupted mid sentence. "No. I'll come to the station."

"When?"

"Tonight after work. Around five o'clock."

Davie asked her to verify if she still lived at the address on her driver's license. Velez hesitated but gave her a confirmation and the name of her employer, as well. Davie hung up and leaned back in her chair thinking, *That was easy, too easy.*

Giordano rested his coffee cup on the top of the gray wall. "What's with the girlfriend? Did she confess?"

"Ex-girlfriend, or so she claims. She's coming in for an interview after work, but I have a feeling she might not show."

"Like I said before, just do your best." He grabbed the cup to leave but turned back toward her. "By the way, if you run out of leads on the files I gave you, I have another case you might want to look at."

Davie glanced up and caught him frowning. "Is it on your unsolved list?"

"It's not a murder. It's a death in a gunstore. The IO closed it as a suicide, but the coroner didn't find any GSR on the victim's hands. There was no note, no witnesses, and no evidence she was depressed or in any kind of trouble, so he ruled the cause of death as undetermined just to cover his ass in case something turned up later."

Giordano's edgy tone piqued her interest. The Investigative Officer was the detective in charge of the case, but it was the job of the Department of Medical Examiner-Coroner to test for gunshot residue. Davie knew the window for finding GSR results was between four to six hours after the weapon was fired. There were many reasons why it may not have been found, including the possibility it had been dislodged during transport of the body.

"You think there was something hinky about the case?" she asked.

He ran his fingers through his graying hair. "Her death seemed suspicious to me. The original file is archived, but I kept a copy of the paperwork. I figured one day I'd have some spare time to give it another look. Interested?"

Davie was all in.

3

THE PACIFIC DETECTIVE SQUAD room was a rectangle with rows of workstations and shared gray partition walls that looked a tad too corporate for some people. Aside from the five desks assigned to Juvenile officers, the room held approximately forty detectives from various tables—Autos, Burglary/Theft, Major Assault Crimes (MAC), Robbery, and Homicide.

Davie had occupied one of those desks in the far corner of the room for the past six months, but she'd been with the department for ten years—eight in patrol and two years as a detective, first in Southeast Division Burglary and now at Pacific Homicide.

She felt a surge of excitement as Giordano pulled a large envelope from his desk drawer and handed it to her. Inside was a dog-eared manila file folder. Written on the tab was *Sara Montaine, female, white, age 34.*

"Who was the lead detective on the case?" she asked.

Giordano rolled his chair over to her desk and sat. "Ralph Sarlos. It was his last investigation before he retired. He didn't think the case was a suicide. Suspicious bastard. God, I miss him. Only problem was he couldn't find any evidence that pointed to murder."

Davie had met Ralph Sarlos once when she sat next to him at a retirement party for a sergeant at Southeast Division. Sarlos was a tall, lanky man with sharp features. He'd excused himself several times during dinner, returning to the table reeking of cigarette smoke. Later, she'd seen him talking to one of the waitresses in the hallway. The woman had a black eye and Sarlos had zero tolerance for domestic violence. Davie figured he was asking her how she got the shiner. The guy was intimidating. Davie remembered feeling grateful they were on the same team.

"It's unusual for a female to off herself with a gun," Davie said, "especially in a public place. Women generally use something less messy—like pills."

Giordano leaned over and rested his forearm on her desk. "Half the suicides in this country are committed with firearms."

Davie knew that. She also knew that women attempted suicide more often than men, but men were more successful at it because they usually chose a more lethal method—shooting, hanging, or inhaling carbon monoxide. Women generally chose a drug overdose. That was less effective because someone could walk in and save your life. The risk of suicide rose as people got older, especially for middle-aged women, but at thirty-four, Montaine seemed too young to be lumped into that group.

"Are you still in touch with Sarlos?" Davie asked.

Giordano clenched and unclenched his fists. "He died last winter, six months after he retired. Lung cancer. Shitty way to go, if you ask me."

"Sorry. I didn't know."

13

He turned away and cleared his throat. "It happened so fast. By the time he found out, it was too late. The cancer had metastasized. I saw him a few days before he checked out. After I left him that day I sat in my car and cried like a baby."

Davie grabbed her empty cup and wandered to the coffeepot. Out of respect for Giordano she lingered before heading back to her desk, leaving him a moment to process his grief. She returned, sipping the hot liquid. "How much time should I devote to the case?"

"We've got a file cabinet full of open cases and the lieutenant is on my ass to get as many off the books as we can. Homicide cases—even old ones—take priority. If we get a fresh murder, all bets are off. Then you'll put the Montaine file back on my desk and forget about it. But if things stay quiet around here for the next few days, knock on some doors. See what turns up."

"I'll read through the chrono and take it from there."

"Let me know what you find." Giordano stood and rolled his chair back to his desk. He hefted a stack of 3.14 reports and headed across the squad room to the lieutenant's glass office.

As she opened the envelope labeled *Sara Montaine*, Davie felt the proverbial clock ticking.

4

DAVIE FLIPPED THROUGH THE Montaine file until she found the criminal history Sarlos had run after her death. It showed no arrests. Davie took her time studying the initial crime report. According to the synopsis, Montaine had walked into Black Jack Guns & Ammo on a Monday at approximately 1100 hours and asked to look at a revolver locked inside a glass cabinet. The owner, Jack Blasdel, claimed he had never seen Montaine before and had no idea why she'd come into his store. He was about to show her the weapon when he got a call from one of his vendors complaining about a missing payment check and inadvertently left the key in the cabinet. Blasdel said the vendor was upset, so he walked into the back room to talk in private. The gunshot jolted him. He returned to the showroom and saw the woman on the floor. He immediately called 911.

Blasdel confirmed the gun was his but he couldn't explain why or how live rounds had made their way into the cylinder. He claimed there was no way Montaine could have accessed his supply of ammunition because it was stored separately in a locked cabinet. He assumed the victim loaded the revolver with rounds she'd brought into the store and then shot herself with his weapon. Suicide.

That was plausible, but there might be other explanations. Davie located the crime scene photos. Sara Montaine's corpse was supine and sprawled on the tile floor in a pool of blood and tissue that had also spattered a glass case filled with handguns. The victim was a slim brunette whose blood had saturated her prim floral sundress and the double strand of pearls around her neck. The revolver lay near her right hand, a Colt .38 Special with a two-inch barrel. From what Davie could see, the entry wound was on the right side of her head, just behind the temple. It would be easy to assume she shot herself, except neither Sarlos nor the coroner had found that theory convincing.

The autopsy report revealed no underlying disease that might have led to depression or impaired judgment, nor did the toxicology report find any drugs or alcohol in Montaine's system. The only anomaly noted on the body was facial scars, possibly from cosmetic surgery. That wasn't uncommon, even for a woman of thirty-four, but Davie knew minutiae sometimes solved cases. A driver's license and several credit cards in her name were found in her purse at the scene. Her next of kin, a stepson named Robert Montaine, later identified the body from photographs taken at the coroner's office.

The head wound obscured the woman's features, so Davie turned to the printout of Montaine's driver's license. As DMV photos go, hers wasn't bad. It showed an attractive woman with an oval face and a tentative smile. She had reported her height at five-foot-three and her weight at 115 pounds. Hair—brown. Eyes—blue. At the time of her death, she'd lived at an address in central Los Angeles that Davie knew was within the tony enclave of Hancock Park in Wilshire Division.

Sarlos had interviewed Robert Montaine, the victim's stepson and sole heir, at a hotel in Manhattan where he was staying while visiting friends. He hadn't heard from his stepmother in months and had no idea what had motivated her to go into the gunstore that day. Davie jotted down *money?* and *family dysfunction?* in her notebook because either might prove to be a motive if the death turned into a homicide investigation.

All gunstores she'd ever seen had surveillance systems with multiple cameras, but there was no copy of a security video included in the file, so she looked through all the reports again for an explanation. Blasdel claimed he'd only recently opened the store and hadn't had time to activate the system. He gave the same reason for his lack of an automatic lock system to control people entering the store. Given that he was selling lethal weapons, his inaction seemed not only irresponsible but also dangerous.

Davie glanced toward the open cabinet on the wall behind her partner's desk. It was full of blue binders, each one dedicated to a victim whose life had been cut short by violence. If Sara Montaine warranted her own Murder Book on those shelves, Davie would do everything in her power to make sure the case was reclassified.

Alma Velez wasn't due at the station until later in the day, so Davie checked real estate records for Sara Montaine's last known address. The stepson Robert Montaine was listed as the homeowner. She decided to drive to the location and see who answered the door.

5

Sara Montaine's former home was on a wide, tree-lined street in the Windsor Square neighborhood of historic Hancock Park. The area was named after the oil magnate who donated the property to the city in the early 1900s and was eventually developed into homes for L.A.'s super rich. The mansions dotting the streets were now occupied by an ethnically diverse group of people who had at least one thing in common: lots of money.

The Montaine place was a three-story Spanish-style beige stucco manse with black wrought-iron railings on two second-floor balconies. A matching filigree gate barred entry to the arched front door. Davie followed the driveway as it cut through a long sloping lawn still green despite the years-long drought. She was standing at the gate looking for the doorbell when she heard a woman's voice.

"Nobody's home."

Davie turned to see a middle-aged woman of Asian descent emerge from behind a row of rose bushes that bordered the property next door, wearing a straw garden hat that exposed a fringe of gray hair. She was petite, around Davie's height, five-one or so. Looped over her arm was an open basket loaded with long-stemmed, multi-colored roses. A pair of scissors jutted from the pocket of her bibbed apron.

The woman scrutinized the badge clipped to Davie's belt and the outline of the Smith & Wesson .45 under her suit jacket.

"Is there a problem?" she asked.

Davie pressed a business card into the palm of her hand. "And you are?"

"June Nakamura," she said. "My husband and I live next door."

"I'm looking for Robert Montaine."

"He owns the house but nobody lives there. The place was for sale a while back, but there were no offers so he took it off the market. He was asking too much for it, not that he cared about my opinion."

Davie swept her gaze over the front façade. "The house is in good shape for being unoccupied."

"A cleaning crew comes once in a while and the gardener is here every Wednesday." The woman shaded her eyes from the sun and read the card. "What brings a homicide detective to Windsor Square? Is Robert okay?"

"Mr. Montaine is fine, as far as I know," Davie said. "It's just a routine follow-up on an old case."

Nakamura hesitated, but only for a moment. "You mean Sara's death?"

Davie wasn't surprised she'd jumped to that conclusion. Windsor Square wasn't exactly a hotbed of violent crime. She took it as a positive sign that after nearly a year, somebody was still thinking of Sara Montaine.

"How long have you lived next door to the Montaines?"

"Fifteen years."

"What can you tell me about them?"

"I don't gossip."

Davie nodded to acknowledge her concern. "Anything you can tell me would be helpful."

"Are you saying it's my civic duty?"

If that's what it takes, she thought. "Right."

Nakamura removed the scissors from the pocket of her apron and clipped a rose from one of her bushes. "Sara married Charles Montaine about seven months before he died of cancer."

"I understand Robert Montaine didn't have much contact with his stepmother."

"He didn't want Sara to spend his inheritance." Nakamura snipped another rose from the vine and piled it on top of the others in the basket. "Anyway, he stopped coming to visit after they married. He didn't even show up when Charles was dying of cancer. He came to the house after Sara passed, but only because he inherited everything."

"Who handled her funeral arrangements?"

Nakamura looked up from her work. "Sara didn't have any family, so there was no formal service. I heard Robert had her cremated. Not sure what he did with the ashes. For all I know, he dumped them in the trash."

June Nakamura had judged Robert Montaine as a stepson and found him wanting. Davie sensed she was probably right, but police files were full of dysfunctional family sagas. Jealousy over a parent's new spouse was a cliché. Sometimes families worked through these issues, but resentment could also accelerate into something much more sinister.

Davie gestured toward the nearby houses. "How did Sara get along with the other neighbors?"

Nakamura frowned, perhaps weighing the pros and cons of answering. "She was twenty-five years younger than Charles." She nodded toward a brick house across the street. "The Tudor thought she was a gold digger. The Colonial next door complained she left the recycling bins on the street too long. The French chateau over there called her the B-word. I liked Sara."

For somebody who didn't gossip, Nakamura was doing a lot of it. As a detective, Davie was grateful for her lack of restraint. "Did you ever see anyone confront Sara or argue with her?"

Nakamura shook her head. "They mostly trashed her behind closed doors. But after a while even the haters had to admit Charles worshipped his wife. She took good care of him, especially after he was diagnosed with cancer."

Sara the gold digger? Sara the saint? Davie wondered which Sara had died in that gunstore.

"What was Sara's name before she married Mr. Montaine?"

Nakamura shrugged. "I never thought to ask her. Robert might know."

Davie peppered Nakamura with standard questions about Sara Montaine's personal and social habits, her use of drugs or alcohol, friends or enemies she may have had, and whether she was involved in any legal problems. Nakamura claimed Montaine had an occasional glass of wine but was not a heavy drinker. Other than that, she had no other information to offer.

"You said you've lived here for fifteen years. Did you know Charles Montaine's first wife?"

Nakamura pulled her hat low on her forehead to shield her face from the sun. "Sylvia was nice enough, but ... " She tipped her hand toward her mouth to simulate drinking.

"She wasn't exactly a teetotaler, I gather," Davie said. "How did she die?"

Nakamura pointed at a second-floor window. "Up there. Sylvia swallowed a handful of Valium with enough bourbon to fill an oak barrel. Charles told me it was an accident, but who can say for sure. She wasn't a happy woman."

"You think his first wife's death was suspicious?"

Nakamura stiffened her back. Davie half expected her to pantomime locking her lips with an imaginary key. "Those are your words, not mine."

"How did Charles Montaine meet Sara?"

"At a charity fundraiser. He told me the next day he'd just met the woman he was going to marry. I wasn't surprised. His wife had been dead for some time and he was lonely."

"How long before they married?"

"Sara wasn't interested at first, but Charles sent flowers to her at a cat rescue organization where she volunteered. I think it was called Four Paws. I warned him to be careful or she'd think he was a stalker, but she finally agreed to meet him for dinner. Four months later, they were married."

"What did Charles Montaine do for a living?"

Nakamura bent her head over the roses and inhaled. "He managed other people's money."

"Was he any good at it?"

She wagged her index finger. "Windsor Square has an unwritten rule. We never talk about our money or where it comes from. Anyway, Sara closed the business after Charles died."

"How did his son feel about that?"

"Robert is an actor," she said, using air quotes around the word *actor*. "He reacted to everything Sara did with great drama."

The heavy fragrance of roses wafted over Davie like a funeral cloud. "Do you think Robert would have done anything to harm Sara?"

Nakamura paused to consider the question and then shook her head. "He's a man-child. You'll see when you meet him. And by the way, don't call him Bob. He hates that. He's a pill, but I don't think he'd hurt anyone, even Sara."

"Anything else you want to tell me that I haven't asked?"

She paused before answering. "Sara's death shocked me. She was my friend and I still miss puttering around with her in my garden." Nakamura adjusted the roses in her basket. "She was a positive person, even during her husband's illness. Shortly before she died..."

Davie looked up from her notes, sensing a new darkness in Nakamura's tone. "What happened?"

Nakamura glanced over her shoulder as if expecting to see someone lurking in the bushes. "Sara stopped working in the garden, stopped opening the curtains during the day, stopped answering the telephone."

"Do you know why?"

Concern settled into the lines of her face. "I didn't ask. It seemed too nosy. But over time I've wondered if things might have been different if only I'd said something."

"A lot had happened to Sara—her husband's illness, his death, and the bad relationship with her stepson. Maybe life finally came crashing down on her. You think she was depressed?"

"No," Nakamura said, shaking her head for emphasis. "Sara wasn't depressed. She was scared."

6

OPINIONS AND INTUITION WITHOUT evidence were of little value in a homicide investigation and, in fact, could harm any future case if Davie wasn't careful. But June Nakamura's belief that Sara Montaine had seemed frightened in the days before her death was definitely worth pursuing.

Nakamura had also given her another lead: the cat rescue organization where Montaine had volunteered. Four Paws Cat Rescue operated out of an office in nearby Larchmont Village, not far from the house in Windsor Square. Before returning to the station, Davie called to let the agency's receptionist know she would be dropping by.

The rescue group was located between Melrose and Beverly Boulevards on tree-lined Larchmont Boulevard with its upscale shops and cafes that could have been found in any quaint American small town. Davie parked on the street not far from the Village's scaled-down version of Big Ben. Climbing the stairs to the second-floor office, she inhaled the aroma of cinnamon from the bakery below.

The furniture in the small lobby was modern and tasteful. Framed photographs of cats of every breed and color covered the walls. The receptionist was keyboarding at the front desk but interrupted her work to notify the executive director that Davie was waiting in the lobby.

A large yellow tabby with golden eyes sat on the desk, squinting at Davie with suspicion. The woman nodded toward the cat.

"That's Marigold—one of our rescues. She's looking for a forever home if you're interested."

Davie felt a twinge of regret as she thought of Hootch. The cat had belonged to a murder victim on one of her past investigations and had been her roomie for a while until she'd placed him in a permanent home. She missed Hootch but knew he was better off with his new owner.

"I'll keep that in mind," she said.

A moment later, the executive director breezed into the lobby. Davie half expected to see a woman with a jovial smile and tuffs of cat hair clinging to her clothes, but instead saw a man in his late twenties, trendy in a fashionably slim suit and an even slimmer tie—an outfit that only flattered department-store mannequins and skinny young men.

He extended his hand, which she expected to be soft and moist, but was instead rough and dry. "Trevor Lofaro. Thanks for stopping by."

Marigold trotted behind Lofaro as he led Davie down a hallway into a room with a desk and walls covered by snapshots of cats and their adopted families. Attached to the pictures were personal notes of thanks to Four Paws, including one covered with hearts and in a child's handwriting—*Thank you for Tigger. He's the best cat ever!*

Marigold joined a multicolored feline pacing near a row of empty food dishes and a white cat lounging on the top platform of a six-foot carpeted tree. Lofaro fixed his gaze on Davie like an overeager sales person. If he planned to hit her up for a donation, he was going to be disappointed.

"Are you a cat lover?" he asked.

"Cats are good people," she said, hoping her ambivalence would end any adoption pitch. "As I mentioned on the phone, I'm following up on Sara Montaine's death."

He nodded solemnly. "My mother founded the organization but after she passed away, I took over. I didn't know Sara, but mom told me everybody here loved her. I'll do anything I can to help."

"What was Sara's role in the organization?"

Davie glanced down and saw Marigold weaving a curvy S around Lofaro's calves, leaving a dusting of orange hair on the legs of his skinny pants. He nudged her away with his foot, a move that failed in its attempt to be subtle.

"She answered the phone at our annual fundraising drive," he said, "but mostly she supported the organization with her donations." He swiveled and pointed toward a photo on the wall that had been enlarged to poster size. A woman sat at a table with a pen in her hand. A watercolor painting of a farmhouse and sheep in a meadow sat on a stand to her right.

"That's Sara a couple of weeks before she died, signing a check to us. It was a cashier's check, but Sara pretended to sign it because it made a better picture."

"What was the amount?"

"A hundred thousand dollars, plus the watercolor on that easel in the photo. At the time, it was the largest contribution we'd ever received. She'd always been a generous donor, but after her husband passed away, she wanted to give a more significant amount in his honor."

Montaine's face in the crime scene photos had been too damaged by her wound to get a clear impression of her looks. Until now all Davie had was her driver's license photo. This picture had captured the woman's exotic beauty in a way the DMV photographer hadn't. Montaine didn't seem frightened. On the contrary, she appeared relaxed and happy, pen in hand, smiling at the camera. Her dark hair was swept into a ponytail, highlighting the soft angles of her oval face. Her lips were full and skin translucent. Davie stared at her but found nothing to indicate she was planning to end her life in a scant two weeks.

"Her cash donation was generous," Davie said. "Did she say why she was adding the painting to the mix?"

Lofaro picked up a bag of kibble and filled the empty cat dishes. Marigold nosed this hand for attention. Again, he pushed her away. Someone had once told Davie that cats were drawn to people who didn't like them. If that were true, it appeared Trevor Lofaro was no cat lover.

"We don't question the motives of our donors, but Sara told my mother that watercolor painting was worth a lot of money, maybe sixty thousand dollars. She also made Four Paws a beneficiary in her will."

Davie's interest spiked. "You inherited money when Ms. Montaine died?"

He sighed. "Unfortunately not. An attorney for Sara's stepson called us shortly after her death. He told us we weren't eligible to inherit because it violated the terms of the Montaines' prenuptial agreement. I don't remember all the details, but he wanted the money and the painting returned. He said it wasn't Sara's to give. Mom sent back the original check. Somebody from the attorney's office picked up the painting."

"Did you challenge the decision?"

He shook his head. "Mom thought about it, but it would have cost a fortune in legal fees and it didn't create the right narrative for her. In the end, the lawyer offered a token amount for our trouble, and she accepted. Around a thousand dollars, as I recall. Mom was upset that Sara's wishes weren't honored, but, as I said, she didn't want to pursue it."

"Did you ever meet the stepson?"

Lofaro noticed the cat hair on his trousers and picked it off with his fingers. "Sara had never even mentioned she had a stepson. Mom was completely blindsided."

Marigold climbed the cat tree and settled in for a nap on one of the lower platforms. Davie stroked her back, feeling the vibration of her purrs before returning her gaze to the photo of Montaine on the wall. Standing behind her were two people, a middle-aged woman with a kind face and a man lurking in the shadows. "Is that your mother standing next to Sara?"

He turned toward the photo. "Yes, that's her. I miss her so much."

"Who's the man?"

"Mr. Royce, our accountant, but he doesn't work for us anymore."

Davie poised her pen over her notebook. "I need to interview him. Do you have his contact information?"

Lofaro laughed. "I should ask *you* that question. Mr. Royce disappeared a couple of days after that picture was taken, along with all the money in our checking account. Good thing my mom hadn't yet deposited Sara's check. We filed a police report but nothing ever came of it. I always imagined the guy soaking up the sun and counting our money on some beach in Rio."

Small organizations similar to Four Paws, with little or no oversight, were ripe for embezzlers and con artists. Davie had heard similar stories when she worked the Burglary and Theft table at Southeast Division. She took down the accountant's name and the date of the theft. When she had a chance, she'd check with detectives at Wilshire for an update on the case.

"How well did Mr. Royce know Sara?"

"I wasn't here then, but I doubt he knew her at all. His office was off-site. I'm guessing he just dropped by that day for the photo op."

"Was there anyone else in the organization Sara was close to?"

He paused for a moment to think. "Not that I know of. Mostly, she communicated directly with my mother."

While Lofaro explained how Montaine and his mother had met, a story about three abandoned kittens and his mother's savvy outreach skills, Davie shifted her gaze back to the photo on the wall. She studied Sara Montaine sitting at that table, pretending to sign that check. Something seemed out of place, but Davie wasn't sure what it was. She closed her eyes momentarily. When she opened them, she noticed the pen in Montaine's hand—her left hand. The gun she'd allegedly used to kill herself had been found near her right hand. If Sara Montaine had committed suicide, it would have been extremely awkward to hold the gun in her nondominant hand.

The discovery sent Davie's pulse racing. Everyone had assumed Montaine was right-handed because most people are. Sarlos hadn't investigated further because the evidence didn't seem to lead anywhere, so he'd accepted her death as a suicide. Davie wondered if his impending retirement or his cancer had prevented him from digging deeper.

The coroner hadn't found gunshot residue on either of her hands, possibly because the residue had been compromised. Another hypothesis was she hadn't fired the gun. If somebody had staged her suicide, they obviously didn't know Montaine was left-handed.

If that's how it went down, Davie still had to wonder how the killer had loaded Blasdel's weapon, shot Montaine, placed the gun, and left the store without anyone seeing him.

Davie pointed to the photo on the wall. "Can I get a copy for my file?"

"Sure. Mom featured that picture in one of her Four Paws email newsletters. Sara wasn't happy when she found out."

Davie glanced up from her note taking. "Why was that?"

He shrugged. "Sara said she didn't want the story to be about her. Mom thought it was odd but she apologized for not consulting her."

"Who gets your emails?"

Lofaro glanced toward a storage room filled with file cabinets. "Donors and potential donors. We buy lists of people who contributed to other charities, mostly animal lovers but other causes, too."

Lofaro headed toward the back room. The sound of file drawers opening and closing disturbed Marigold's nap. She jumped from the cat tree and skittered out of the room. Davie pulled out her cell phone and snapped a photo of Montaine signing the check. The actual newsletter could be evidence. The cell photo was just backup. A moment later, Lofaro reappeared with a stapled printout of the newsletter with the picture of Sara Montaine featured on page one.

"Would you be willing to give me your mailing list?" Davie asked.

He hesitated. "I suppose. It's on a spreadsheet, but why would you want that?"

Davie wasn't exactly sure why, but maybe it was that Montaine had been upset her picture had gone out to an unknown group of people. "It could be useful."

Lofaro shrugged. He went into the back room and returned with a USB drive. "Please respect the privacy of our donors."

She pulled a business card from her notebook and handed it to him. "Of course. Let me know if you remember anything else about Ms. Montaine."

Davie thought about that initial crime report. Shortly after Sara Montaine walked into Jack Blasdel's gunstore, Blasdel had received a call from the vendor who supplied him with cleaning products. That vendor's name was Gerda Pittman, a cosmetician who worked out of a back room in a tanning salon on Pico Boulevard, an area real estate agents called "Beverly Hills Adjacent." Davie had no time to waste. On her way back to the station, she would interview Pittman. If the woman had been on the telephone with Blasdel and heard the gunshot, she could be an important witness.

7

ONCE SHE RETURNED TO the car, Davie called the number listed for Gerda Pittman in the original crime report and found her still exfoliating at the same location. When Davie arrived at the tanning salon she was greeted by the smell of lavender room freshener, trying but failing to mask the odor of sweaty bodies baking in hot tanning beds. A young woman with a bad complexion sat on a chair behind the front counter. She informed Davie that Gerda was with a client before pointing to a grouping of chairs where she could wait.

Several tattered tabloid magazines were fanned across the surface of a coffee table. Davie considered catching up on the latest celebrity breakups, but given the stench in the room and the unknown DNA embedded in those pages, her hands remained in her germ-free jacket pockets.

Five minutes later, she heard voices and saw a young man in his early twenties exit a room in the back, a few steps ahead of a tall, well-nourished woman packed into a tight pink jumpsuit. Her short hair was red like Davie's, but less coppery brown and more traffic-cone orange. Heavy makeup only called attention to years of hard living.

"Your back might be sore for a few hours," Pittman said in a chirpy tone. "If you need anything, call me."

The guy seemed embarrassed when he saw Davie looking his way. She wondered what exactly had been going on in that room. Maybe she was better off *not* knowing the details. It could save her a call to Vice detectives.

The pimply receptionist pointed to Davie. "Hey, Gerda, somebody's here to see you."

The young man slipped folded money into Pittman's palm. She flashed a smile, half predator and half high school girl on a clandestine meet-up at the library.

After the kid left, Pittman strode across the industrial carpet in her gold ballerina slippers, her head bobbing forward like a seagull in search of a French fry.

"Love your hair," she said, pointing to Davie's head. "Who does your color?"

"Mother Nature."

The woman ignored the comment and studied Davie's face. "I have another client in fifteen minutes. You really need a facial, but the best I can do for now is an eyebrow wax." She turned and loped toward the back of the shop. "Follow me."

"I'm not here for an eyebrow wax—"

Pittman made a beckoning gesture with her hand. "Trust me, honey. You'll thank me later."

"I'm an LAPD Homicide detective. I'm here to ask you about a man named Jack Blasdel."

Pittman abruptly stopped and turned toward Davie. "What's he done now?" Her chirpy tone had disappeared.

"Nothing I know of."

"Keep digging," she said. "Come with me. We can talk in my studio."

Davie followed her to a room off the lobby that smelled of anise and the bitter sweetness of almond oil. The walls were painted the same shade of pink as Pittman's jumpsuit, and the ruffled pillows on the rolling stool next to the facial chair made it a fitting home for Boudoir Barbie. Glass jars with faux gold tops that matched her ballerina slippers were loaded with cotton balls and swabs. Pittman flipped a switch on a stainless steel wax warmer.

"Just so you know," she said, stripping off the used sheet from the chair. "I haven't seen Jack in a while. I'm not happy about you showing up here, bringing back bad memories."

Davie leaned against the pink wall next to a glass shelf lined with beauty products. "I'm investigating a death in his gunstore about a year ago. I understand you were on the phone with Mr. Blasdel when he heard the shot. He said you were one of his vendors. Is that right?"

She laughed. "A vendor? Is that what he told you? That's rich. No, honey, I was his girlfriend." She threw the used sheet into a basket.

In his initial interview, Blasdel had been vague about the supplies he'd purchased from Gerda Pittman, claiming only that they were "cleaning products." There was nothing in the police reports indicating that Blasdel and Pittman had a personal relationship. Withholding information was just another form of lying. Davie wondered what other facts he'd failed to disclose.

"One of our detectives made several attempts to interview you back then. He could never make contact. Why is that?"

Pittman pulled a clean sheet from a cupboard. "I don't remember. It was a long time ago."

Her dismissive tone made Davie wonder if she was hiding something.

"It wasn't that long ago. What were you talking to Blasdel about that day?"

She spread the clean sheet over the chair. "Jack owed me money. I wanted it back."

"For cleaning products he'd purchased from you?"

"I have no idea what you're talking about. I don't sell cleaning products to gunstores."

Davie chalked that up as another of Jack Blasdel's lies. "How did you meet him?"

She hesitated before answering. "On a cruise to Mexico. I'd just lost my second husband and I was feeling sort of low."

"My condolences."

She rolled her eyes. "Bud didn't die. He cheated on me and I kicked him out. Funny how a guilty conscience can turn into a nice divorce settlement."

"So you were on the cruise ... " Davie prompted.

Pittman picked up a square of cloth sprouting dark hairs from a thick coat of wax—probably from the kid's back. "I was sitting at the bar, feeling sorry for myself, when Jack slid onto the stool next to mine and offered to buy me a drink."

"And what happened then?"

Pittman threw the hairy cloth into a trashcan. "Are you kidding me? Who turns down a free drink from a nice-looking man? Look, I don't want you to think it was some cheesy shipboard romance. He was classy, a real gentleman. The next day he sent me flowers from the ship's gift shop. When we got back to L.A. he took me out to dinner at a nice Mexican place in the Marina. He was charming. The sex was good, too. He took his time, if you know what I mean. I appreciate that in a man. What can I say? I fell hard."

In a personal setting Davie would have considered that TMI, too much information, but professionally this case might turn into a homicide investigation so she needed the woman to keep talking, especially since Blasdel had lied about the reason for Pittman's call that day.

"How long did you know Jack Blasdel before he asked you for money?"

Pittman put her hand over the wax warmer to check the temperature and gestured for Davie to sit on the facial chair. Davie declined. Pittman paused for a moment and then shrugged.

"A couple of months," she said. "He was raising money for a real estate deal. He already had a bunch of investors lined up but he wanted to give me an opportunity to get in on the ground floor."

"What was the deal?"

Pittman dipped a stick into the wax and applied it to her own upper lip with guidance from a wall mirror. "He wanted to buy a condo complex in Palm Springs. He told me he used to work scouting investment opportunities for a Miami billionaire, so he knew this was a good deal."

"What was this billionaire's name?"

"No idea, but he met the guy at a casino in Atlantic City," she said. "Jack told me he could get the Palm Springs building for a song. He already had a buyer who'd take it off his hands for double the price he was going to pay. He promised to return my investment in a couple of months along with a nice profit."

"Did you see the place?"

Pittman pressed a strip of cloth over the wax and ripped it off in one quick gesture. Davie winced at the sound.

"He showed me pictures. It looked nice."

"How much money did you give him?"

She patted her upper lip and applied cream from one of the jars arranged on a white towel on the counter. "Nothing at first. You know what they say—if it sounds too good to be true, it probably is, right? He kept telling me if the market went haywire, my nest egg could be gone in a flash, but real estate is always a good bet. He finally wore me down. I gave him fifty grand. A week later, I called to find out if the condo owner had accepted his bid. Jack told me he was on his way to Palm Springs to sign the papers and he'd let me know as soon as the deal was finalized. I didn't hear from him for a couple of weeks, which was weird. I got worried so I drove to his apartment. He'd moved out."

"Did you ever get your money back?"

"Yeah, I got my money back." Her words chewed the air like a buzz saw. "But I had to hire a private eye. It took a while, but she finally found him and gave me his number. I phoned Jack at the gunstore and told him to pay me back or I'd report his Bunco scam to the cops. He knew I'd do it, too. He begged me to give him a few days. Said he was expecting a payment and also needed to sell some inventory. I didn't trust him, so I told him my PI would be watching. If he tried to split again, he'd be sorry. He finally came through, but I had to keep reminding him, including the call the day that woman died."

Davie wondered why Blasdel didn't just disappear with Pittman's cash plus the money he made from selling the gunstore inventory. She also wondered who had bought his guns on such short notice. After the shooting, he'd closed the store and moved on, probably because repaying Pittman had left him with limited capital. Despite having an angry ex-girlfriend on his case, once he'd returned Pittman's money there was technically no victim and no crime. If Pittman filed a police report, Blasdel could claim he borrowed the cash with her consent and repaid it as promised.

"Did Mr. Blasdel ever get violent with you?"

Pittman pulled a small plastic bag from a drawer. It crackled as she began filling it with skincare samples and tiny vials of oil. "Jack doesn't push women around. He flatters them and tells them tall tales. He told me he made his sister a bundle by managing her investment portfolio and that he'd rescued some guy from drowning in a riptide. Jack even claimed he once helped a woman disappear so nobody would ever find her. I got the impression he was really into her but she wasn't interested. He seemed bitter about that, especially given all he'd done to help her."

Davie knit her brow. She assumed Blasdel was exaggerating his resume. It was difficult for a person to disappear without a trace, short of being poured into the concrete pillar of a freeway overpass or falling into a volcano. It was also Davie's experience that many families never gave up searching for their loved one.

Davie shifted her position away from the wall. "Did Mr. Blasdel mention this woman's name?"

The bag was full. Pittman added her business card from a stack on the counter. "Forget it. Those stories were all a bunch of hooey. Just Jack's lame attempt to impress me."

"Did you know Sara Montaine or did you ever hear Mr. Blasdel mention her name?"

"Nope."

Davie pulled a business card from her notebook and handed it to Pittman. "If you remember anything else, please give me a call."

She accepted the card and held out the bag of cosmetic samples. "Here, take these. They're free."

Davie withdrew her hand. "Sorry, I don't accept gifts from citizens."

"I bet you would if it was a six-pack of donuts. Look, they're just samples. They aren't worth anything. If you're not interested, give them to your girlfriends. I'm always looking for new clients." She paused. "You have girlfriends, right?"

Davie thanked her but declined the samples. "One more thing. When you were on the phone with Mr. Blasdel, did you hear the gunshot?"

"Yeah, but I didn't know what it was. I asked Jack but he'd already hung up on me."

Davie stood for a moment processing the information. "I need the name of your private investigator."

Back in the car, Davie called Pittman's PI, Natalie Salinas. The receptionist at Norton Investigations told her Salinas was "out in the field," possibly a euphemism for "I'm not going to give you details so don't ask." Salinas's office was in downtown L.A. Afternoon traffic would be jammed, and Davie couldn't risk missing her appointment at the station with Alma Velez. The interview with Natalie Salinas would have to wait until tomorrow.

8

DAVIE WALKED INTO THE station through the back door near the Kit Room, eager to tell Giordano about what she'd learned. She found him in Records, searching through a file cabinet. He looked up when she entered.

"Hey, kid, what's up?"

She told him about her interview with Trevor Lofaro of Four Paws, the photo of Sara Montaine, and the Gerda Pittman interview.

"Interesting," he said, his tone noncommittal.

Davie's shoulders slumped. "The gun was found in Montaine's right hand, but she was left-handed. Don't you think that's odd?"

"Even if she was left-handed, that doesn't make her death a homicide. Maybe she was ambidextrous or maybe somebody moved the weapon."

His flippant dismissal caused her voice to rise. "Why would anyone do that?"

He shut the file drawer with more force than necessary. "Any idiot at the scene might, including the store owner. Everybody claims they didn't touch anything, but people forget. They also lie." Giordano grabbed his file and headed toward the hallway. Over his shoulder he said, "Keep digging."

Those were the same words Gerda Pittman had said about Jack Blasdel. Davie returned to her desk. A moment later her thoughts were interrupted when she heard footsteps and looked up to see her partner gritting his teeth as he walked into the squad room.

Jason Vaughn's sandy hair and toffee-colored eyes were inherited from his Northern Italian mother. Davie wasn't sure which gene pool accounted for his tall, slim frame but his build was the perfect clothes hanger for the designer suits he preferred. She'd known Vaughn since their academy days but had worked with him for only six months at Pacific Homicide. He was her age—thirty-one—but his corny jokes and the pet names he called her—like a ghetto gunslinger and green-eyed ninja—were a tad too high school for her taste. That said, he was the best partner she'd ever had.

"How was your interview?" she asked.

He slammed his leather briefcase on the desk. "A big fat zero. Plus, on my way back from Tarzana there was a brush fire on the side of the 101. I had a hard time convincing the fire crew to let me pass through the roadblock."

"Glad you're safe."

"CRO is having a pancake breakfast in the parking lot. Seven bucks. We can talk about it while we wait in line."

Davie glanced at her watch. "It's almost noon. That's lunch."

"Lunch. Brunch. Whatever. Let's go."

The Community Relations Office worked out of a doublewide trailer in the parking lot. Half the space belonged to CRO; Senior

Lead Officers occupied the other half. The SLOs acted as liaisons between the department and the Pacific community. CRO periodically put on fundraisers for events like Pacific's annual holiday party, but Davie knew they were eating fried dough for only one reason: Vaughn had a crush on one of the P-2s in CRO, a leggy brunette with a crop of freckles and a full-throated laugh that Davie's partner found intoxicating. He wanted to impress her and was willing to invest seven bucks just to see her smile.

The garage mechanic was pouring batter onto a sizzling griddle fitted to a rusty metal half-barrel topped with briquettes. A dozen officers and civilian personnel were milling around holding plates. The P-2 emerged from the trailer carrying a tray of diced fruit.

Davie saw immediately that the scene was not conducive for talking. "I'm going back to my desk. I have an interview at five and a ton of work to do before then."

Vaughn leaned over and whispered. "If pancakes aren't your thing, I have an Italian sandwich on homemade bread at my desk. My mom made it but nobody has to know it wasn't my talent with yeast and flour."

"Until I rat you out."

He tapped his finger on her nose. "You'd never do that, but I love the way your green eyes sparkle when you lie."

"Don't try that cheesy line on your P-2. She'll laugh you out of the CRO trailer."

Vaughn chuckled and headed toward the buffet table.

Davie spent the next few minutes looking for information on the Four Paws embezzlement investigation. When she checked the Detective Case Tracking System she found that Burglary/Theft detectives at Wilshire Division had investigated the theft and discovered

Four Paws wasn't the only victim. In four years, the accountant had embezzled over a half-million dollars from various clients.

The case required the services of a forensic accountant to audit bank statements, cancelled checks, and online payments. Divisional detectives didn't have the resources for complex cases, so Wilshire Burglary had transferred the file to the Commercial Crimes Division. CCD detectives put the case together and the District Attorney's office had filed charges. An arrest warrant was issued months ago, but law enforcement hadn't been able to locate the suspect. His whereabouts were still unknown.

Davie wondered if the embezzlement scam was connected to Montaine's death. There was no evidence of that at the moment, but Davie couldn't rule it out, either.

For the next fifteen minutes she reviewed the Montaine file again. Fingerprints had been taken by the coroner's office, but they'd never been run through AFIS. Instead, they'd identified Montaine by comparing the body to the information and photo on the California driver's license in her purse. Her stepson Robert Montaine had confirmed her identity from images taken at the morgue. No further effort was made.

Davie decided to start from scratch and approach the case as if it had just happened and nothing was known. The first step was to run Sara Montaine's prints. The Automated Fingerprint Identification System, or AFIS, was a national database maintained by the FBI. Its master file held fingerprints and criminal histories of 55 million bad guys and millions more civilians. It might be a waste of time, but Davie found it best to be thorough. Maybe the search would turn up something that wasn't known before—records that hadn't been found because a clerk had misspelled Sara Montaine's name or some other mixup.

Davie called Sharonda West, an analyst she knew at the latent print unit of the Scientific Investigation Division to ask what she knew was a big favor—move Davie's AFIS request to the front of the line.

"Send the prints ASAP," Sharonda said, "but just so you know, there's a processing backlog. Nonviolent offenses are low priority. You know what's lower than that? Suicide cases that aren't even open, like yours. I'm just warning you, it might take a while before I can get back to you."

"I understand, Shar. I know it isn't a homicide now, but I have a feeling it will be. Just do what you can. That's all I'm asking."

"I'll do my best, Davie."

Davie cradled the receiver and leaned back in her chair, plotting her next move. She nodded to Vaughn as he arrived at his desk looking glum. Things must not have gone well with the P-2.

He handed Davie a sheet of paper from the fax machine. "This was on my desk, but it belongs to you."

The paperwork was in response to a search warrant for records she'd written ten days ago for another one of the Homicide detectives. At the bottom was a notification that no records had been found. The detective was in training for the next two weeks, but the court required Davie to return the warrant to the clerk's office before then.

She accessed the correct form on her computer and entered the required data. It would take an hour or so to drive to the Airport Court and back, including time spent standing in line at the window. She checked her watch. She could just make it to court and back before Alma Velez arrived for the interview.

9

DAVIE ENTERED THE FRONT door of the Airport Court building, flashed her badge, and waited for security to wave her around the metal detector.

"Richards?"

She turned to see Detective Jon Striker huddled near the elevator with an attractive woman in a business suit. Her badge and gun told Davie she was also in law enforcement.

Striker was assigned to the Homicide Special Section of the elite Robbery Homicide Division headquartered in downtown L.A. They'd worked a case together a month or so ago. She'd found him to be a smart and tenacious investigator. She hoped he felt the same about her.

Davie raised her hand in a quick wave and kept walking. He leaned over and said something to the woman. Davie was too far away to hear his conversation, but the woman turned her head with a loud sigh. A moment later he headed toward Davie.

At six-one, Striker towered over her by a foot, forcing her to look up to meet his gaze. The sun beaming through a nearby window highlighted the premature gray in his dark hair and the deep blue of his eyes.

Davie wasn't sure how to greet him. After what they'd gone through on the case they'd worked together, a handshake seemed too formal. A hug was definitely out of bounds, especially in a Superior Court lobby with attorneys, jurors, and law enforcement looking on. A fist bump? Not her style.

"I'm surprised to see you so far from home base," she said. "What brings you here?"

"A subpoena." He scrutinized her expression. "Haven't seen you for a while. What have you been up to?"

Davie glanced toward the clerk's office and saw there was a long line of people waiting at the window. "Work. You?"

"Are you still running?"

Davie had been preparing for the Baker to Las Vegas relay race, an LAPD team competition that promoted physical fitness among its officers. She hadn't run distances since her academy days, but one of the Pacific Autos detectives had talked her into competing in the event, so she'd hit the road in a new pair of running shoes. The next event wasn't until the following spring, but she figured it would take her that long to get into shape, considering the limited time she had to train.

"I'm up to ten miles," she said.

He whistled. "Impressive. On your way to a marathon."

She glanced at the line in the clerk's office. It was shorter now. "Not sure about that. Baker to Vegas is good for now. What about you? Why not join us? It could be fun."

The creases around his eyes deepened. "I have other ways to stay in shape."

She raised her eyebrows. "I'd love to know what they are."

He grinned. "You might be surprised. So what are you working on?"

She hesitated to mention the Sara Montaine case because Giordano might not want people knowing she was spending time on a year-old undetermined death that was probably a suicide.

"Giordano has everybody on the table reviewing unsolved cases for now. I just stopped by to return a records warrant."

"Those old cases are tough. Maybe we could go out for coffee sometime and bounce ideas around."

Before Davie could respond, she heard Striker's companion call his name. The woman's arms were crossed over her chest and she was shooting daggers at him from across the room. Striker frowned, but Davie couldn't tell if it was from concern or irritation. In high-pressure situations, his face was always an unreadable mask, which made her wonder if the woman was more than a colleague.

Striker glanced at Davie. "Sorry. Gotta discuss a few things with my partner before we testify. Can I call you later?"

Davie turned and walked toward the clerk's office. Over her shoulder she said, "You have my number." She sensed his eyes on her as she walked away.

"Talk to you soon then," he said.

Davie doubted he would call and supposed it didn't matter if he did. She had no skin in the game with Striker. She didn't even know much about him except he had an intriguing tattoo on the inside of his right forearm. Once when he'd rolled up his shirtsleeves, she'd gotten a peek of a word ending in e. She'd asked him what it said, but he only teased that he might tell her when he knew her better. He'd made no attempt to do so, and they hadn't spoken in the weeks since their joint case. That's why she wasn't about to hold her breath waiting for her phone to ring.

Davie returned the records warrant to the clerk's office and headed back to the station. She spent the next couple hours at her desk in the squad room calling witnesses in the Javier Hernandez gang murder. Many of the phone numbers had been disconnected and of the people she reached, none had anything new they were willing to offer. Five o'clock came and went. Alma Velez didn't show for the interview. Davie called the young woman's cell and got a generic voice message. She called her workplace, but it was closed.

Earlier in the day, Davie had confirmed with Velez that she still lived with her mother at the address listed on her driver's license, a unit in a nearby housing project called Mar Vista Gardens. If the mother was still around, she might know where to find her daughter.

"Hey, Jason," she said. "You want to drive with me to Mar Vista Gardens and talk to a gang queen?"

"It's getting dark. Can't it wait till tomorrow?"

"If you're scared, I could take somebody else."

He sniffed and straightened his tie. "Somebody else doesn't have my superpowers."

"I guess that means you're in?"

"Only because you need me, Davie."

She stifled a smile. "I'll check out a car and meet you in the parking lot."

10

Engagement.

He was nearby on another job when he got the call. He'd been following her ever since. She was a small woman, but he wasn't fooled by her size. She had already killed two men and he'd discovered long ago that underestimating an opponent could be fatal. In the light, her red hair reminded him of threads of Spanish saffron in the paella from his favorite café in Zaragoza. But that pantsuit was a turnoff. Too bad, because he was a man who appreciated the female form and he could tell by the way she moved that underneath that polyester was a body worth admiring.

The client hadn't confirmed details of the plan, not yet, but the detective had pushed buttons—big time. If surveillance was all they needed, they could have hired another contractor for less money. He assumed part two of the assignment was going to be more interesting, but for now, his instructions were to follow her and report on the people she talked to.

He'd kept his distance. Cops noticed people tailing them, even when they were driving a lowbrow Toyota rental like he was. Didn't really matter if he lost her. He knew where she worked, where she lived, and the license plate number of her Camaro SS V8. The car used to be a dude-mobile. Lately he was seeing a lot of chicks behind the wheels of muscle cars. At least her Camaro was red, not some bullshit color like purple. Later this evening he'd turn in the Toyota and rent an SUV. They were so common in L.A. he'd be practically invisible.

He sat behind the wheel and fingered the military-issued St. Christopher medal around his neck, its rough edges worn flat from three generations of handling. He wasn't a superstitious man, but it had kept his grandfather, his father, and him safe for all these years. He'd reconciled to himself that no son would wear it after he was gone.

He glanced out the window and thought about Gizmo, hoping he was adjusting to the kennel. He'd adopted the cat after receiving an alert. A kill shelter had him listed as a dead cat walking. He'd stared at Gizmo's ink black fur and droopy eye. A chunk of his right ear had been chewed off in a fight, but the battle scars only made him more attractive. An hour later, Gizmo was sprung and headed for a new life. The little guy was jittery around strangers, but other than that he'd been an excellent companion.

At the courthouse, he'd watched Detective Saffron from a distance. He could easily pick her off from where he was hiding, but that wasn't his assignment. Even if it were, it was dangerous to shoot her in a public place. He had two ironclad rules of engagement: No collateral damage and kill only who he was paid to kill. If the client had wet work in mind, they'd want something subtle and all loose ends tied up. That sort of operation took time to plan, but complex jobs satisfied his creative impulses and this client could afford to pay.

For now, he was content to wait, because the money was good and this piece-of-shit Toyota had great air conditioning.

11

BEFORE LEAVING THE STATION, Davie placed another call to Velez's cell phone but got the same disembodied robotic voice inviting her to leave a message. The housing project was less than a mile from the station, so it took Davie and Vaughn only a few minutes to roll into the complex through the open metal gate. Just past the unmanned guardhouse she backed into a parking space. It would make leaving easier should the need arise.

Mar Vista Gardens was a six-hundred-unit housing project that bordered Culver City and Ballona Creek. The residents were predominantly Hispanic and had once included members of the Culver City Boyz, a Mexican-American street gang that used the complex as their home base. LAPD gang injunctions and sustained police presence in the neighborhood eventually forced them out of Pacific and into neighboring communities.

Davie opened her car door. "Ready to rock and roll?"

Vaughn adjusted the frequency on his handheld radio. "I'm ready for a Paco's Tacos combo plate, but whatever."

"I'll buy you dinner after."

His lips parted in a faux look of yearning. "Marry me?"

She gave Vaughn a deprecating smile to acknowledge his running joke and got out of the car as he radioed a Code Six. They had an hour to notify dispatch that they'd safely returned to the car.

All sixty-plus rectangular buildings in the complex were set on flat ground and painted a color Davie thought of as pinky beige. The fading sun filtered through the leaves of a sycamore, dappling the sidewalk and hard-packed grass with lacy shadows. In the air was a faint smell of urine. Behind one of the units Davie saw clothes hanging on a metal T-bar clothesline similar to those that had dotted the landscape in the Jordan Downs projects in Watts. Years ago, an LAPD patrol officer had suffered serious neck injuries when he ran into clothesline wires during a foot pursuit at night.

Davie felt a tug on the sleeve of her jacket. She turned to see Vaughn pointing to a ground-floor apartment at the end of a building just ahead. "That's the unit over there."

Vaughn followed as Davie walked up to the door. Out of the corner of her eye, she saw her partner scanning the surrounding area for potential threats, his leather holster creaking as he rested a hand on his weapon. By mutual agreement, their usual routine was that she conducted the interview and he watched her back.

Before knocking, Davie put her ear to the door and listened for sounds of life inside. Gunshots blared from a TV—a Western or maybe a cop show.

She knocked. A woman shouted, "Who's there?"

"LAPD," she said, stepping to the side of the door in case someone inside decided to blast a couple of rounds through the wood.

Seconds later the door opened, releasing the smell of mildew and rancid grease. Standing in front of her was a heavyset white female in her forties with stringy blonde hair. Balanced on her hip was a dark-haired boy under two, Davie guessed, with round brown eyes and cupid-bow lips. In his hand, the kid held a soggy cracker.

"Good evening, ma'am." Davie held up her badge. "Are you Alma Velez's mother?"

The woman's lips pressed into a hard line. "Yeah, so what?"

"I'm looking for your daughter. Is she here?"

Her expression turned glacial. "She's not back from work yet."

"When do you expect her?"

She shrugged. "Sometimes she comes home. Sometime she don't. What do you want with her?"

"I'm investigating the murder of Javier Hernandez. Ms. Velez was supposed to meet me for an interview at the station after work. She didn't show up. I'm just worried, that's all."

The woman's smile was forced. "Worried? That's a good one. Like I told you, she ain't here."

Davie stepped back. "I want to ask her about Felix Malo. Do you know him?"

She frowned. "He's in prison, but you already know that, right?"

"Is your daughter still in touch with him?"

"She's a grownup. I don't keep track of who she talks to."

Davie nodded toward the child, who seemed uncommonly stoic for a kid his age. "Cute baby. Yours?"

The woman looked at the child like she'd forgotten about him. "No."

"So, he must be your daughter's kid. Who's the father?"

The baby could have belonged to anybody, but if Velez and Malo had a child together, it increased the likelihood they were still in touch.

"That's none of your business," she said.

"Where does Ms. Velez hang out when she's not at home?"

The toddler tried to force the cracker into the woman's mouth. She batted away his hand, sending crumbs cascading down her shirt.

"I already told you, she's an adult."

Davie noticed Vaughn inching toward the door. "You mind if my partner and I come in and look around?"

"You got a warrant?"

"You got something to hide?"

The kid began squirming to get down. "Manny, be good!" The woman bounced him on her hip and he settled back into silence. "I know what you're thinking," she said, her chin raised in defiance, "that Alma's inside hiding under the bed or something. Well, she ain't. I'm done talking. I got things to do." The woman moved to close the door.

Davie stopped it with her boot and held out a business card. "If Ms. Velez comes home, please ask her to call me." Baby Manny reached out, grabbed the card, and stuck it in his mouth. Strings of drool began falling from his lips. Davie figured it didn't matter. It was unlikely Velez would use the number on the card to call Davie back.

It was dark outside now. Sounds always seemed more sinister at night, especially in the projects. Davie tensed when she heard loud voices arguing.

She didn't speak to Vaughn until they reached the main sidewalk. "That was fun."

"Yeah, it warms my heart when a citizen goes out of her way to support law enforcement."

"You think Velez was inside the apartment?" Davie asked.

"We could hang around for a while and see what happens, but it's probably a waste of time."

They were nearing the parking lot when Davie swept her gaze across the area and saw a young female walking across the lawn.

She grabbed Vaughn's arm and pointed to the woman. "You think that's Alma Velez?"

"Could be, but it's dark and she's too far away for me to be sure."

Davie called out. "Alma Velez?"

The young woman stopped and turned toward Davie. Then she started running.

"What the—?" Davie ran after her. "Alma Velez, it's Detective Richards. I want to talk."

Velez kept running. Davie heard her partner's heavy breathing behind her. With every step she felt the heft of her weapon and the flashlight on her belt, as well as the metal handcuffs inside the pouch at the small of her back. A moment later, Velez disappeared behind a building.

Davie had been running three times a week for the better part of a month, so she was pretty sure Alma Velez couldn't outrun her. She doubted the woman would return to her mother's apartment, but others in the complex might hide her.

"Let's split up," Vaughn said, pointing to the left. "I'll go this way. You circle around back."

Separating from her partner was a bad idea and against protocol, but if it meant cornering Velez it was worth it. Davie ran around the building, but her quarry had melted into the landscape. There was also no sign of Vaughn. Davie stopped to survey the grounds and to collect her thoughts. She did a three-sixty pivot but detected no movement in the shadows nor did she hear any footsteps.

Just ahead was the unit with the clothesline. Nearby was a fetid commercial garbage bin. The back of her neck prickled with tension when she heard a rustling sound. The bin was large enough for someone to hide behind. Davie's hand brushed across the smooth leather of her holster as she drew her .45 and inched closer to the bin, using a tree trunk for cover.

"Police!" she shouted. "Put your hands behind your head and step out in the open."

Nothing moved. She glanced over her shoulder, but Vaughn was nowhere in sight. He must have been too far away to hear her shout. Behind her, Davie heard the swishing sound of a solid object moving through air at a high rate of speed. Without thinking she stepped away from the tree with her hands in a dive position and executed a shoulder roll. Her technique was rusty. Pain seared her body as her right shoulder collided with the concrete sidewalk. Ignoring the ache, she rolled and sprang into a squatting position in time to see a baseball bat slicing through the air where she'd just been standing. Her adrenaline surged when she realized she was no longer holding her weapon. Blades of dried grass prickled her hand as she groped the area around her, desperately searching for her pistol.

A man stood above her. He raised the bat and stepped into the next swing. She skittered away from his reach. In the dim light she saw he was about five-eight and 140 pounds. Young. Brown skin. He had on jeans and a dark hooded sweatshirt. A ballcap was pulled low on his face. Right-handed. She could smell the acrid sweat of fear. He didn't play by the rules because he didn't know them. His clumsy moves signaled he wasn't a trained fighter. He didn't have a gun or he would have killed her already. Same with a knife. The bat seemed like a weapon of convenience. But squatting on the ground was a bad place to be in a fight, especially with somebody looming over her.

Finding her gun would have to wait. She'd come back later with her flashlight—if there was a later. To survive, she needed leverage. She ran for the clothesline. The man was close behind, breathing heavily. She jumped high and grabbed the T-bar. Swung to build momentum. He was close to her now, the bat raised to swing at her again. With a loud bellow she planted her feet on his chest, shoving him backward with all the force she could muster. He was startled by her shout and thrown off kilter by the kick. He staggered a few steps, dropping the bat as he windmilled his arms to regain his balance.

Somewhere in the distance, Vaughn called her name. She shouted *"Here!"* but there was no time for further conversation. The man came at her again, roaring with rage. She swung on the bar, but this time he grabbed her legs and pulled. Her grip slipped. Her back slammed to the ground, whipping her head with a thud. Air whooshed from her diaphragm. The handcuff pouch dug into her skin.

He stood over her and threw a wild punch. She rolled sideways. His fist connected with the metal clothesline bar. He screamed in pain. She pushed herself off the hard lawn and rose to a standing position. He seemed disoriented. She grabbed the front of his sweatshirt with both hands. Pulled him toward her. Snapped her neck forward in one quick strike, slamming the hardest part of her forehead square onto the bridge of his nose. There was a crunching sound. Blood misted onto her cheeks and blouse. He covered his face and groaned. Then he ran.

Davie's pulse raced. *The gun.* Her shoulder and back ached as she limped back to the garbage bin and swept the beam of her flashlight across the grass until she found her weapon.

Her partner ran down the sidewalk toward her. "You okay?"

She blurted out the man's description. "He's headed toward Braddock. I'm going after him."

"Are you out of your freakin' mind? Stay where you are. I'll call it in—"

She ran before he could finish his sentence. Her head and shoulder throbbed, but she jogged through the dimly lit grounds, keeping watch for obstacles on the path. The last thing she needed was to fall and injure something else.

Just ahead she spotted him, running toward a bicycle propped up against a building. He hopped on and pedaled away. Davie heard sirens. Patrol officers were on the way, but she suspected the man had already blended into the neighborhood.

Vaughn's eyes widened as he saw the blood on her face and clothes. "What the hell happened? You said you were okay."

She winced in pain as she placed the gun in its holster. "I broke his nose."

He shook his head in disbelief. "Well, at least you have his DNA."

She paused a moment to consider all the blood-born diseases that might be splattered on her face and clothes. She was visibly shaking. "Let's go find the bat. It's a long shot, but he might have left prints."

"Whatever you say, partner."

Davie retraced her steps, scanning the area as she walked. "We must have rattled some cages. I wonder if Velez's mom called somebody after we left her place."

"Why would she do that? Even if her daughter had information about Hernandez's murder, the girl has kept her mouth shut for all this time. What would spook her now?"

"Not sure, but I'm going to find out."

When they neared the clothesline, Davie pointed the flashlight beam toward the ground. The bat was gone. Her attacker didn't take it with him or she'd have noticed. Somebody might have walked by and picked it up or maybe Alma Velez had taken it.

Assaulting a police officer was a serious offense. Davie wondered whose idea that had been. If Velez was still part of Felix Malo's inner circle, Davie doubted he would approve. He'd be eligible for parole soon and wouldn't be happy if anything jeopardized his release.

Maybe Velez had decided to initiate the attack by herself. Davie didn't know why, but she'd talk to Pacific Gang detectives when she got back to the station. They might provide insight.

"You want to door knock Velez's mom again?" Vaughn said.

"Let's come back after I talk to somebody in the Gang unit."

All Davie wanted to do was go home and nurse her injuries. Instead, she headed back to the car to wait for the blue-suits to take her report. Once patrol officers arrived, Davie spent the better part of thirty minutes while they took photos of her injuries and recorded her statement for their report—Assault with a Deadly Weapon on a Police Officer, California Penal Code ADW/peace officer 245(b) P.C. When they were finished, Vaughn drove her back to the station. Her partner offered to take her to the ER, but she declined. He must have known arguing with her was a waste of time, because he signed out and went home.

Davie called local hospitals, but none of them had treated a man with a broken nose. She limped upstairs to the Gang unit's office, but the door was locked. They were probably out in the field. She found a clean T-shirt in her locker and dropped the bloody blouse into an evidence bag. She brushed the dirt off her pants and jacket and washed the scratches on her forearms and hands with soap and water.

Davie's head hurt like hell. She glanced at the mirror and saw a red lump on her forehead where the skin was abraded. She released her hair from its bun, brushed out the twigs and dirt with her fingers, and hoped the red of her hair camouflaged the similar shade of the broken skin.

Her whole body ached. Her only focus was on home, ice, and pain relievers. She had just hobbled into her Camaro when her cell phone rang. It was Jon Striker.

12

"SORRY WE DIDN'T HAVE more time to talk this afternoon," Striker said.

Davie sat in the Camaro with the cell to her ear, hesitating a moment before responding. So much had happened since this afternoon that a chance run-in with Striker at the courthouse seemed long ago. "We're both busy."

"Right. Look, I'm near the station. Can you to meet me somewhere for a drink? We could talk over those cases of yours."

She released a faint sigh, but if Striker noticed he didn't say so. Under any other circumstances, she would have said yes to his offer, but it was late, she needed a shower, and her body felt like it had been through a woodchipper. She realized she'd hesitated too long when he said, "I know it's late. Maybe another time."

Davie reached to fasten the seatbelt, triggering a stab of pain in her shoulder. "How do you know I'm still at work? Maybe I'm at home watching old *Law and Order* reruns?"

"I know because you're in the middle of an investigation and there are still hours left in the day."

Davie thought of herself as independent and spontaneous and didn't want him to think of her as predictable. It was true she often worked long hours, but only because the job required boots on the ground.

She fumbled to start the car. "What are you doing on the Westside?"

"Just wrapped up an interview with a witness. Thought I'd give you a call before heading to the Valley."

Davie realized until that moment she had no idea he lived in the San Fernando Valley. She'd been born in Sherman Oaks and spent most of her early life as a Valley girl. She hesitated before accepting his invitation because any decision that didn't involve pain relievers and ice was a bad idea, but the truth was she didn't want to be alone right now.

"My dad owns a bar not far from the station—the Lucky Duck. How soon can you be there?"

"I know the place. Fifteen minutes."

Davie arrived at her dad's bar and scored the last space in the parking lot. The Lucky Duck was a dive bar. In the old days it was a cop bar and a favorite place for neighborhood drunks to sit on cracked leather stools nursing drinks until the place closed or the bartender cut them off. In the past few years the clientele had changed. Millennials and aging hipsters had discovered the place while searching for nostalgia and authenticity among the cheesy neon beer signs and the odor of ancient cigarette smoke that had leeched into the wood paneling.

Davie walk in the front door past the handcarved wooden sign that read *Was a woman who led me down the road to drink. I never wrote to thank her.* She heard the low hum of boozy conversation and the click of cue sticks against billiard balls. Her father stood behind the bar, a tall broad-shouldered former high school football player who'd lost the battle against a taut midsection not long after he retired from the LAPD. Bear could be gruff and somewhat paranoid—once a cop, always a cop—but he always spoke the truth and more often than not made her laugh. He nodded when he saw his daughter, but his smile turned into a frown when he noticed her limping.

He set his towel on the counter. "What gives, Ace? You're walking like an old lady. And what happened to your head?"

Her hand touched the bump. "Some knucklehead in Mar Vista Gardens came at me with a baseball bat."

Bear blinked a couple of times and then nodded. "Is he still above ground?"

"Yeah, but I broke his nose."

He picked up the towel and started wiping a glass. "That's my girl."

Davie surveyed the place and saw mostly people she didn't recognize. There were businessmen in suits, millennials in skinny jeans and expensive shoes, and a guy wearing a ballcap low on his forehead, sitting alone at a table near the restrooms bent over the *Wall Street Journal* and an amber-colored drink.

"So, what brings you here?" Bear said.

"I just wanted to see my old man." She paused, ignoring Bear's intense stare. "Okay, I'm meeting a friend." Bear's expression didn't change. "What? You don't think I have friends?"

"I didn't say that."

Davie felt a whoosh of cool air. She turned to see Jon Striker step into the room. His tie was loose but he was still wearing the suit he'd had on at court. He looked tired. Davie lifted her arm to wave but a stab of pain stopped her midway.

Bear squinted as he watched Striker approach the bar. "That your friend?"

"He's the detective from Homicide Special I told you about. Remember? I worked a case with him last month."

"He a good guy?"

Her father knew about the case and Striker's investigative skills. She'd been juiced about arresting a suspect and might have poured on the praise a little too thick, but that's how she felt at the time. She also knew Bear hadn't forgotten the conversation about Striker being a good detective. What her father was asking was if Striker was a good man.

"As far as I can tell."

Bear mumbled under his breath, "Damn well better be."

Her father's protectiveness had embarrassed her more times than she could count, especially when he got a whiff she was interested in somebody. Striker joined them at the bar. He glanced at the abrasion on Davie's forehead but didn't comment. Davie made introductions.

Striker reached out to shake Bear's hand. "I've heard a lot about you, sir. Honored to finally meet you."

Good start, she thought.

Bear accepted the handshake with a noncommittal nod. "You two drinking or just taking up space?"

"Just water for now," he said.

Bear rolled his eyes. "Please tell me you're not one of those my-body-is-my-temple assholes."

Striker laughed. In all of Davie's interactions with him, he'd been pleasant but low-key. He flashed the occasional smile, but she couldn't recall him responding that way.

"Okay," he said. "In that case, give me a scotch to go with that water."

Bear nodded in approval. "That's more like it. What can I get for you, Ace?"

She thought of the possible negative interactions between alcohol and over-the-counter pain medications, but decided to risk it. "Margarita rocks."

Striker waited at the bar while Bear mixed the drinks. Davie found a table near the front door. She lowered herself into the chair with no little effort and glanced at Striker's stoic reaction as Bear leaned toward him. She cringed to think what her father might be saying. She hoped it wasn't some sort of lecture. Bear was an imposing man but having worked with Striker, she knew he didn't intimidate easily. A moment later, he picked up the drinks and joined her at the table.

"Seemed like a lot of sharing going on between you two," Davie said. "What were you talking about?"

He set the drinks on the table. "None of your business."

Davie had a sinking feeling. "Sorry. My dad can be difficult, but he means well. I just don't want you to get the wrong impression about him."

The right impression was important to her because she liked Striker and she wanted Bear to like him, too.

He poured water into the scotch. "We had a good conversation."

She didn't believe him. "Don't worry. I'll drag the truth out of him after you leave."

He took off his tie and slipped it into his jacket pocket. "Tell me about the case you're working on."

"Actually, there are two cases."

She told him about the Hernandez gang homicide first, then moved on to Sara Montaine's death, which she found more puzzling.

"The Montaine case is interesting," he said when she'd finished. "Seems like everybody has something to hide."

She leaned her forearms on the table. "What about the timeline? Is it even possible for somebody to enter the store, load a revolver from the case, shoot Sara Montaine, place the gun near her hand, and escape without being seen?"

"What do you know about Jack Blasdel? Could he have been involved?"

"I haven't found him yet."

He flashed a playful smirk. "I could help you with that."

"You think he's in your Homicide Special spy-versus-spy databases but not in mine?"

He leaned forward and clinked her glass. "There's only one way to find out."

She pushed a lock of hair behind her ear, dislodging a twig from Mar Vista Gardens. "I still have a few places to look. I'll let you know."

Striker filled her in on a high-profile case he was investigating—an L.A. County Superior Court judge who'd been gunned down in his driveway. The victim had made a lot of enemies in his career, so zeroing in on a suspect was daunting. The Homicide Special Section had the resources to investigate complicated cases. Davie was confident they'd make an arrest, but she understood the pressure Striker faced. HSS detectives were always under klieg lights. The murder of a judge elevated the stakes exponentially.

They'd been talking for about an hour when Striker looked at his watch. "I've got to get up early tomorrow. Where's your car?"

"In the parking lot, but you go ahead. I'm going to say goodbye to Bear."

He lingered at the table for a moment longer. "Are you going to tell me what happened to your head?"

"What did Bear say?"

"He didn't have to say anything. I can see the knot on your forehead and the blood spatters on your neck that you missed when you washed up. None of them were there when I saw you this afternoon."

RHD investigated assaults of on-duty police officers that occurred within the Los Angeles city limits. He'd soon be able to read the details if he wanted to. She hadn't been seriously hurt, so she downplayed the attack because she didn't want to discuss it right now. "I had a run-in with a kid in the projects. No big deal."

Striker stared at her for a long time. Then he stood. "It was great seeing you again, Davie."

"Yeah. Great."

After Striker left, Davie walked to the bar where her father was washing glasses. "What did you think of him?"

"He seems decent but I won't know for sure until your grandmother passes judgment. If he survives that, we'll see."

Davie smiled at the thought of her grandmother interrogating Jon Striker. "Who was the guy sitting at the back table with the newspaper?"

"The Talisker rocks? Don't know. Why?"

"No reason. I've never seen him in here before."

"That's good. We need fresh blood. The old-timers are all in rehab."

Davie hugged her father, got in her car, and drove to Bel Air, the wealthy fortress on Los Angeles's Westside where she rented a furnished guesthouse on the grounds of a large estate. As she waited for the security gate to rumble open she noticed an unfamiliar car parked up the street. Not unusual except it was an older model SUV. Might be a pet sitter making evening rounds.

After she drove up the winding driveway and arrived at her cottage, she parked in the carport, grabbed the Montaine file, and made her way to the front door. Outside on the flagstone patio was a round metal table and three chairs where she sometimes had her morning coffee. She opened the wood and wrought iron front door that always reminded her of the entrance to a medieval castle.

The cottage was just 581 square feet. A loft on the upper floor had twin dormer windows that she accessed by a spiral staircase. There was one bathroom off the bedroom, but so far none of her friends had complained. The color scheme on the walls was a restful combination of amethyst, wisteria, and a soft pink that Alexander Camden called nymph.

Alex owned the property. He was an art dealer who scouted the world for paintings and antiques for the homes and offices of wealthy clients. She'd met him while investigating a theft from an antique shop when she was assigned to Southeast Burglary. When he found out she was looking for a place to live, he offered her the cottage at a reduced rent. She got an affordable place to live and he got a cop to look after the expensive art and antiques he kept on the property. It was the perfect tradeoff for both of them.

Davie walked into the living room and inhaled the fragrance of garlic from the sautéed shrimp takeout that was still in the trashcan from a few days ago. She parked the Montaine file on the kitchen counter and her badge and .45 inside a drawer in the bedside table. She opened a window to air out the place and then took the garbage to the outside bin. Instead of going for a swim, she opted for a long hot shower. A couple of over-the-counter painkillers later, she fell into bed with her damp hair cascading over the pillow in soggy red ringlets and began reading the Montaine interview notes.

In order to solve a homicide case she had to know as much about the victim as she did about the suspect, and there was still a lot to learn about Sara Montaine. Nobody seemed to know much about her before she'd married Charles Montaine. Some people didn't share their personal history because they were wounded by the past, but others withheld the information because they had something to hide. It was too early to tell into which category Montaine fell.

Davie stared at the rocking chair at the foot of the bed that had once belonged to her grandmother. She had a photo of Grammy rocking her in that chair as a newborn. Davie had named the chair Celeste because it was upholstered in French silk that dated back to the 1920s. The wooden arms were hand-carved in the shape of swans' necks. One of the swans had been broken and glued back together without much care. She had just shifted her musings from Celeste to Striker when the pain pills kicked in and she fell into a fitful sleep with the Montaine file strewn across the covers of her bed.

13

PUSSY SCRATCHES BACK.

He'd been at the projects, watching from behind the garbage bin as the punk attacked Detective Saffron. He'd briefly considered stepping in to help—Uncle Sam had taught him how to snap a man's neck like a matchstick—but saving her life wasn't his job. As it turned out, she didn't need his help. She'd kicked the guy's ass. The client had warned him not to underestimate her. Now he knew why. The woman knew how to take care of herself.

After the confrontation he expected her to go home. Instead, she'd gone to her old man's bar. He had to hand it to her. Even he might have crashed for the night in his hidey-hole with a bottle of Talisker and some premium Malana Cream hashish. Maybe she just wanted to lick her wounds and cry on her old man's shoulder.

He'd slipped into the bar without her noticing and sat at a table in the back corner, reading the newspaper like any Joe Customer. Going inside was a risky maneuver, but it was also exciting to know she didn't have a clue how much danger she was in.

The last thing he expected was to see the stud walk in and make a beeline for her, invading her personal space just to let everybody know he was taking possession. There was a gat under the guy's jacket. A glint from his badge reflected in the neon lights above the bar. Saffron's boyfriend was a cop. The brothers and sisters of the LAPD were incestuous that way. He hoped the guy's presence didn't complicate matters.

Out of the corner of his eye, he saw Saffron walk to a table. He was too far away to hear the conversation between her and the boyfriend, but he'd been close enough to watch her old man trade spit with the stud—probing and setting boundaries, he guessed. He'd be pissed if some old man lectured him about how to handle his woman, but the stud took it pretty well. He didn't understand the old man's problem. Saffron was no virgin. She knew what to do. If she didn't, maybe somebody needed to school her.

He watched Saffron and the boyfriend huddle at the table with their foreheads almost touching. Their body language didn't indicate she'd done the nasty with him yet—no touching under the table or running her tongue across her lips. He considered himself an expert in human nature, so he knew sex was definitely part of the boyfriend's agenda—hers, too. The stud didn't take his eyes off her the whole time they were talking. When she said something funny the grin lingered way past the joke. Saffron's eyes were practically twinkling and she seemed to smile for no reason at all. At one point their hands almost touched. She pulled back. She was anxious. That was a tell. She'd been dumped before. She wanted him but was scared. Too bad they might not make it to the bedroom. After watching a while, he finished his drink and left. It had been fun, but the last thing he needed was for either of them to notice him.

He was now sitting in his rental outside the Bel Air compound where she lived, smoking a cigarette, listening to a CD of Bach's Goldberg Variations, and on his phone watching Gizmo lick his balls on the kennel's kitty-cam.

He couldn't stay parked in this location much longer. This was Bel Air and some tightassed one-percenter was sure to call private security. He had on the white doctor coat he kept in his duffle bag in case a rent-a-cop knocked on his window. He'd claim he was phoning patients before heading to the hospital. That usually worked.

He grabbed an Oreo from the bag on the seat next to him and broke it in half, scrapping the frosting off with his teeth. She should have been home by now. Maybe she and the stud had moved the party to his place. If so, that created an opportunity. He'd seen her carrying a file. It might be paperwork about his client. Now was as good a time as any to find out if she kept any records in the house. It would only take ten minutes at most—in and out. He slipped his lock picks into his pants pocket next to the St. Christopher medal. He didn't wear the medal around his neck when he worked in case it reflected light or made noise.

The Bel Air estate where the detective lived was secluded and surrounded by trees, but he'd already scoped out the entire property and knew exactly where to go. He climbed the wall and made his way behind the main residence to the guesthouse she rented. There was no back door. Once she was inside, she was trapped. Based on what he'd observed about her routine, he'd already developed some ideas about how to exploit her vulnerabilities.

Reaching the front door, he pulled out the picks. His skills were rusty but he got inside with little effort. He returned the picks to his pocket and went inside. The furniture and artwork weren't hers—too elegant and formal. He guessed she'd be more comfortable with the smooth, clean lines of contemporary design. The walls were painted girly pink and lavender. He was sure Saffron hadn't chosen that color palette, nor had she purchased the Dom Perignon in the refrigerator. He wondered if the property owner fancied himself a Svengali, exposing Saffron to all his finery in hopes of making her into something other than a middle-class woman living in a rich man's vision of the world.

The place was one bedroom, one bath, with a small kitchen and a loft. He made fast work of checking out the living room but didn't find any files. In her bedroom, he picked up an old T-shirt from her unmade bed, pressed it to his nose, and inhaled. His body stirred when he smelled her essence. Something pleasant but not perfume. Lavender soap?

He was about to go upstairs when he heard dogs barking. Not some wimpy-assed Chihuahua, either. These were big dogs. He'd had a bad experience with a Malinois in Niger. Big dogs still freaked him out. He didn't want to kill an animal unless he was attacked. Better to get out while he still could. He made it outside and ran for the wall.

Once he got back to the car, he licked remnants of frosting off the cookie and popped half into his mouth, letting it melt against his hot tongue. The street was quiet except for a car or two speeding down the hill. He put the other half of the Oreo into his mouth and ground it between his teeth. Then he lowered the window and lit another cigarette as the chocolate aftertaste lingered on his tongue.

He felt the nicotine take hold. He wasn't supposed to smoke in the vehicle. They'd even removed the lighter. Good thing he always carried a cheap Bic in his pocket. Let somebody else worry about the smell.

His contact still hadn't made a decision about what to do next. His instructions remained the same—watch and wait—and that made him feel edgy. If his mission wasn't defined soon, he might act on his own—just to keep his skills sharp. A moment later, he saw her car pull up to the gate.

14

THE FOLLOWING MORNING DAVIE could barely roll out of bed. Her back was stiff and her shoulder ached. A sense of foreboding washed over her when she flipped on the news and saw that the wildfire near Santa Paula was now threatening Ojai, one of her favorite places to visit. It was the go-to destination for wine tasters, spa habitués, and people seeking spiritual enlightenment, not to mention booklovers cruising the aisles of Bart's Books. The California Department of Forestry and Fire Protection had moved in fire crews and heavy equipment to stop the rampage, but homes had been lost and nearly thirty horses had perished when fire consumed a barn where they were boarded.

There was no time to mourn. She had to get ready for work. The cottage had no bathtub and a hot shower didn't sound therapeutic. Her only other option was a swim in Alex Camden's pool. Alex hated swimming in cold water, so summer or winter he kept the temperature at an even eighty degrees. Davie put on her swimming suit and flip-flops and wrapped a towel around her shoulders as she headed down the flagstone path with cell phone in hand.

She threw the towel on a chaise lounge and slipped into the shallow end of the pool, feeling the warmth caress her body. After floating on her back for a few minutes, she tested the shoulder with a gentle side-stroke until the movement and the water began to ease the pain.

She heard a door close and looked up to see Alexander Camden walk out of the French doors and onto the patio wearing his Zegna bathrobe and carrying a mug of what Davie assumed was his favorite premium coffee, an exclusive brand he ordered from a client who knew the roaster from his days as the ambassador to Ethiopia. To Davie, Alex epitomized elegance and class. He was in his sixties, slim and of medium height. His hair was gray and he claimed he'd earned every one of them. His chiseled features reminded her of an aging version of Michelangelo's David. He was also kind, which is what she loved most about him.

Alex walked to the deep end of the pool where Davie was treading water. "You're up early, Davina." He always used her given name, a privilege she granted to few people. "How's the water temperature?"

"Warm. I'd guess around eighty."

He chuckled at the shared joke, but his expression turned serious when he noticed the abrasion on her forehead. "What happened to you?"

She reached up and touched the wound. "I was practicing a head-butt and miscalculated."

He tsk-tsked. "Police work is a dangerous game. Why not consider Hollywood instead? A client of mine is president of the International Stunt Association. I could call in a favor and get you in."

Alex was joking but she could tell by the serious look on his face that he was concerned about her. Davie got out of the pool and wrapped the towel around her body. Alex beckoned her toward a blanket on a chaise lounge next to him. Vincent and Leonardo, Alex's two golden retrievers, barreled out of the house and jumped into the pool, splashing and barking. Alex threw a ball into the water and for a couple of minutes the two of them watched the dogs swim.

"If I showed you a photo of a watercolor, could you tell me who painted it and what it's worth?"

He tilted his head. "What brought on this newfound interest in art?"

"I'm investigating an old case. It's not a homicide, but I hope to have it reclassified. The victim donated a watercolor to a charity shortly before she died. I don't know the name of the piece, but I have a photograph."

Davie grabbed her cell phone and held out the picture of Sara Montaine standing next to the watercolor painting of a farmhouse with sheep in a meadow.

He enlarged the photo with his fingers to get a better look. "I'd have to verify, but it might be one of William Trost Richards's Rhode Island scenes. He lived and painted there toward the end of his life."

"What can you tell me about him."

"He was an American landscape watercolorist who lived from the mid-1800s to sometime just after the turn of the last century. His style is so realistic that many of his pieces appear to be photographs. He's displayed in a number of important museums. Who's the owner?"

"Sara Montaine. She inherited the watercolor when her husband Charles died."

He took a sip of his coffee. "That name sounds familiar. I may have met Charles Montaine at a party or a gallery opening. I keep notes on potential clients. I can check if you want."

"That would be great. I'm not sure it has anything to do with the case, but it might be helpful to find out how much the painting is worth."

"That's an assignment for which I am eminently qualified—as long as it doesn't require me to head-butt anyone."

He went inside the house and returned a few minutes later with a laptop. "I found Charles Montaine on an invitation list to a show I organized at a local gallery a few years ago. He didn't buy anything that night, but that doesn't mean he wasn't a serious collector."

"What else did you find?"

"I looked through a few of my databases. It's definitely a Richards. His watercolors range from a thousand dollars up to the high five digits. His oils are worth much more. It's hard to know the value of this piece without verifying if it's signed or even original."

"Thanks, Alex. I'll follow up with the stepson."

"You're most welcome, Davina. You know how much I enjoy being indispensable to you."

Davie walked back to the cottage to get ready for work. Near the front door she spotted a shiny object lying near one of the metal patio chairs. It was a St. Christopher medal embossed with an emblem from each of the four branches of the military. The saint was almost worn flat but the color was uniformly silver. The medal was likely sterling. Davie guessed it might belong to one of the gardeners, but for sure somebody would be looking for it. The landscape company wouldn't be back until the following Wednesday. She would have Alex mention the medal to the head gardener. In the meantime, she took it inside the house and left it on the eighteenth-century Chippendale dressing table by the front door.

15

BEFORE LEAVING THE HOUSE, Davie swallowed two more pain relievers, hoping they would keep her aches and pains at bay. Then she stopped by the station to pick up a city ride. Giordano was away from his desk and the sign-out log indicated Vaughn had driven to the Scientific Investigation Division, probably to drop off evidence to be analyzed for one of the unsolved cases Giordano had assigned him.

There were no messages from Alma Velez—no surprise—so Davie signed out and made her way toward a strip of downtrodden one-story storefronts on Venice Boulevard that were squeezed together like a life-sized Lego village. Black Jack Guns & Ammo was gone, but she hoped one of the neighboring shop owners was still there and might have information about Blasdel or Sara Montaine's death.

The gunstore's windows were blacked out. The place had been closed for a long time, but she could still make out a faded Black Jack logo painted on the front door. The message on the upholstery shop next door stated it had been in business since 1997. She would start there.

Inside were bolts of fabric piled haphazardly on tables and the floor, along with the skeletons of chairs and sofas in various stages of rehabilitation. A pleasant-looking man with a round face and stooped shoulders sliced through a swatch of brocade with a pair of scissors. Arman Nazarian remembered Montaine's death.

"Terrible, just terrible." He shuddered, shaking his head like a dog repelling water. "I was outside watering the flowers and saw her walk toward the gunstore. I remember her because she didn't belong in this neighborhood—Pasadena maybe, but not here. She was young and beautiful, like a movie star. I tried to catch her eye, but she turned away and went into the store."

"How long was she there before you heard the gunshot?"

He finished cutting the piece of cloth and laid down the scissors. "A few minutes. I finished watering and went back inside my store to empty the bucket. The next thing I heard was an explosion. When I realized it was a gunshot I almost had a heart attack. I dropped the bucket on the floor. I remember because the water ruined a bolt of fabric for an antique chair I was recovering. It took forever to order replacement cloth. Cost a fortune, too. Anyway, twenty minutes later, I heard the sirens."

Blasdel's statement on the crime report claimed he phoned 911 immediately after discovering the body. It was possible it took officers twenty minutes to arrive at the location, but that seemed improbable to Davie. The LAPD's average response time for emergency calls was 5.7 minutes.

"Are you sure about the time?"

Nazarian returned the bolt of fabric to a shelf that was lined with dozens of others. "Positive. I was hiding under the sink. I have a clock

79

on the opposite wall. I call it Big Ben. After the gunshot I hid under the counter. All that time, I stared at Ben, so I remember every minute—twenty of them—until I heard the sirens and the officers arrived. I'll never forget that day. Terrible."

"After the shooting, how long was the gunstore closed?"

"About a week, maybe. At first, the police wouldn't let anyone inside. A few days after the yellow tape was down, I came to work one morning and found the place empty. Mr. Blasdel must have come in the middle of the night and hauled everything away."

"Do you still have his contact information?"

He broke eye contact. "I don't know where he is. I don't want to know. Good riddance."

"The store has been empty for a while, I gather. Has anybody leased it since Blasdel left?"

"At first, nobody wanted it. Mr. Blasdel never cleaned the place after that lady died. The store was a mess. Blood. Flies. The smell was awful. The owner begged me to take over the lease. At first I said no, but he kept offering me better and better deals. What could I do? I paid a service to clean up. My son helped me replace a section of the tile floor. Good as new. Now I use the space for storage."

"What can you tell me about Jack Blasdel?"

Nazarian glanced around, checking to make sure nobody was listening. Davie found that odd since they appeared to be alone in the store. She looked up at the ceiling but saw no cameras, at least none that were visible.

"He wasn't a good neighbor," Nazarian said. "We only have a few parking spaces for customers. All the shopkeepers are supposed to park in the alley, but he always left his car out front. When we complained, he told us he had a bad leg. That was a lie. We could all see he walked just fine."

"The police report said Blasdel and Ms. Montaine were the only two people in the store at the time of her death. Did you see anyone else hanging around the area?"

"I told you, I was in the back of the store when it happened. There might have been somebody running down the alley, but I can't be sure."

"Mr. Nazarian, either you saw somebody or you didn't. Which is it?"

"I told you I was hiding under the sink in the back."

Davie persisted, asking him to describe the person he saw—man, woman, height, weight, clothing, or any distinguishing characteristics like a limp.

"It was a man. He was dressed in black."

"Did you see his face? Could you identify him if I showed you a photo?"

"I don't know. Maybe."

"Why didn't you mention this to the police?"

He avoided her gaze. "The officer told me it was a suicide. I just figured the man in the alley was homeless or somebody who'd heard gunshots and ran. I'd have run, too, but I was too scared."

The man's tardy recollection infuriated her. "A woman was dead and you didn't bother to tell the police you saw a man running from the crime scene?"

He seemed taken aback by her harsh tone. "I've known people like Mr. Blasdel—bad people. I didn't want to get involved in his business. I have a family to protect."

"What do you know about Mr. Blasdel that made you think he would harm you and your family?"

"Nothing. Nothing at all." Nazarian pulled another bolt of fabric from the shelf and placed it on the cutting table. "I'm sorry but I have to get back to work."

The man fleeing the scene could have been either a witness to the killing or the shooter himself. It seemed logical the killer would leave by the back door to avoid being seen. But if he'd chosen that path, presumably Jack Blasdel would have seen him, too. If that's the way it went down, she wondered why the shooter hadn't killed Blasdel. Unless he knew that wouldn't be necessary because Blasdel was an accomplice.

Davie returned to the car, but before heading back to the station she reached Sara Montaine's stepson Robert don't-call-me-Bob Montaine on his cell to request an interview. He answered on the first ring. Davie hadn't expected to reach him so easily, but maybe he'd been expecting a call from his talent agent. In a hushed and hurried voice Robert Montaine agreed to meet with her as long as she arrived within fifteen minutes. Normally, L.A. traffic would have made that impossible, but as it turned out, he was close by.

16

Before leaving the parking lot of the former Black Jack Guns & Ammo, Davie searched for Robert Montaine's acting portfolio on IMDb, an online database of information on film, television, and video games, including people who worked in front of the camera and on the production side. She found no credits under his name.

She maneuvered the car along the coast highway and turned right onto Sunset Boulevard, driving past dusty trees that lined the street. A short distance up the road in Pacific Palisades she saw a sign—Self-Realization Fellowship followed by Lake Shrine—that was ironically lodged in a bed of pink impatiens. As she left her parked car, the pungent aroma of incense from the open door of the Visitor Center beat a path to her sinuses, conjuring thoughts of sugar, jasmine, and moist forests.

Robert Montaine had told her to meet him by the Mahatma Gandhi shrine, but she wasn't sure where to find it. A brick staircase led to the lake and a waterfall but she didn't see a shrine or anyone standing on the viewing platform. A flagstone path led her past several small cement monuments honoring various religions—Christianity, Judaism, Islam, Hinduism—until the flagstones branched into a mulch path lined with rose bushes and sheltered by palm, eucalyptus, and magnolia trees.

At the end of the path, she found Robert Montaine sitting in a small clearing in the center of a white stone bench that was just long enough for a man or three toddlers. His legs were crossed in a modified lotus position with his hands clasped together in front of his chest as though he were praying. He was in his late twenties with a slight build and delicate Waspy features. The neo-hippie getup he wore—bellbottoms, sandals with a toe strap, and a headband wrapped around his shoulder-length brown hair—seemed out of place. A tepid breeze ruffled the ferns bordering what appeared to be statues of two women and a giant teapot.

"Mr. Montaine?"

He looked up with a vapid smile and put his finger to his lips. "Shhh. People are meditating."

A quick glance around revealed no one else in the clearing. Just as well. She doubted anybody could reach the highest level of their vibrations with all those ducks quacking in the lake and the traffic noise on Sunset.

"We could go to the station if it's easier for you."

His smile faded. "I can't leave the grounds. I'm on a retreat. Technically, talking is forbidden. I made an exception for you."

His comment seemed ironic, considering he'd been at the retreat when he answered her call and rattled off instructions on how to find him.

"As I mentioned on the phone, I'm here about your stepmother."

"Please," he said, holding up his palm to stop her. "Don't call her that. She wasn't any kind of mother to me. She was my father's wife, okay? She's been dead for a long time. Why are you here? Did you find out something about her past?"

Davie ignored the question. According to the DOB on Montaine's driver's license, he'd been twenty-five when his father remarried. Interesting that Sara Montaine had been dead for almost a year and he still couldn't find it within himself to be magnanimous. "Did you ever question that Ms. Montaine's death was a suicide?"

He shifted on the bench, stretching one leg straight and folding the other across his thigh. "I didn't know her well, so I didn't question anything. Truth is I didn't care how she died, only that she was dead."

Davie raised her eyebrows at his brutal comment. It must have been difficult for Sara Montaine, knowing her stepson hated her. Davie waited a moment until the roar of a small plane flying overhead subsided. "What did you do with her remains?"

He bent over his legs, averting his gaze. "I had her cremated. I kept her ashes in a self-storage unit until a few weeks ago. I finally had the urn buried in a plot near my father's grave. Why are you asking? Did you locate her relatives? Maybe they'll kick in for the cemetery plot."

"I gather you weren't able to locate Sara's family."

He adjusted the headband. "I didn't try. She said she was raised in a series of foster homes after her parents died, but she refused to give details. Claimed it was too painful. I never knew where Sara lived before she latched on to my father, but she had a decent car. Funny thing, though, she never talked about having a job. That made me suspicious. I figured her for a call girl or a gold digger. Maybe both. I told my father to hire a private investigator to look into her background but he refused. Instead, he bought her a new Mercedes."

"You could have hired a PI yourself."

He placed his feet on the ground and elongated his spine. "Maybe I should have, but at the time I didn't have the money."

Davie was getting tired of standing, but Montaine had taken possession of the only bench in the clearing. It didn't appear he planned to interrupt his routine to accommodate her, not that rubbing shoulders with Robert don't-call-me-Bob sounded at all appealing.

"Did Sara have any enemies?"

He glared at her. "Besides me? Isn't that what you're really asking?"

Davie gave him a hard stare but kept her tone neutral. "I didn't say that, Mr. Montaine. Those are your words. *Were* you her enemy?"

"I thought she was an opportunist. That didn't make us enemies. But as I told you before, I didn't have much contact with her, so I don't know how other people felt about her."

Nobody is universally admired, but opinions about Sara Montaine ran the gamut from loving wife to she-devil. Polar opposite opinions were always hard to reconcile.

Davie shifted her weight and changed the subject. "Sara named the Four Paws rescue organization as a beneficiary in her will. You reversed that. Why? Especially since you were in line to inherit the bulk of your father's estate."

Montaine seemed annoyed by the implication. "She signed a prenuptial agreement before she married my father. If he died first, she got to live in the house plus a modest allowance to maintain her lifestyle. After she died, the estate passed to me. They were married for less than a year. Those giveaways were an abuse of that agreement. My father never expected her to spend my money on a bunch of feral cats."

Davie thought of Hooch, her ex-roommate, and felt peeved on behalf of all felines. "You also asked them to return the watercolor."

Anger flashed across his face. "Sara may have thought the watercolor was valuable, but it was only a print. It was also one of my *real* mother's favorites. She gave it away just to spite me."

If true, the print seemed like a distraction. It might prove relevant later on, but for now Davie would put the issue on the proverbial back burner. "Where were you at the time of Sara's death?"

Montaine turned his head toward her and smiled. "I see your game now. You think she was murdered and I'm your scapegoat. I can't believe I have to say this again but here goes. I didn't kill Sara. I was in New York taking in a few Broadway shows with my friends. My accountant probably still has the hotel receipts attached to my tax return."

Detective Sarlos's report confirmed Robert Montaine had been in Manhattan, but Davie wanted to see his reaction when she asked the question. He seemed more arrogant than angry. On the other hand, maybe he was just acting.

"What happened to Sara's possessions?"

Montaine stood up and bent over in a stretch, touching his toes. "After she died, I hired a moving van to haul everything to storage. The coroner's office sent me a few things after the autopsy. I can't remember what exactly was in that box. I took the cash out of her wallet and cut up the credit cards. She wasn't wearing her diamond engagement ring or the Cartier watch the day she died. I found them in her jewelry box a week later."

It was odd that she had removed her valuables before going out that day. It upped the cred of the suicide theory.

"Where are those other items now?"

"Still in storage." Montaine abandoned the stretch and strolled under an arch topped with a gold lotus sculpture, petal closed, until he reached the lake, talking as he walked. "I remember setting the coroner's box just inside the door of the storage unit. I kept thinking I'd go through her stuff one day, but I never got around to it. It's easier to pay the monthly fee than to confront all that."

Davie joined Montaine at the fence. Her clothes and hair felt damp from the humidity. The atmosphere in the clearing was unusually muggy compared to the brittle heat of the outside world, due in part to a combination of the artificial lake, shade, and overwatering.

"What was Ms. Montaine's name prior to her marriage?"

"I never knew. I went through their papers but couldn't find their marriage license. I was going to order a copy, but it just wasn't worth the bother."

"I want to look through her things if you don't mind."

He shrugged. "Be my guest. In fact, do me a favor and haul it all to the nearest landfill."

She pulled a Consent to Search form from her notebook and jotted down the name, address, and unit number of the storage facility, along with a permission statement that allowed her to take any or all items belonging to Sara Montaine. Her stepson signed without reading the document. If Davie ended up taking anything, she would write up a property receipt that listed the items and then get him to sign off on that, too.

He fished in his wallet until he found a key card. "This will get you in the gate. There's a padlock on the door to the unit. The manager has the combination. I'll call and tell him to let you in."

"Where can I return the card?"

"Keep it. I'll pick up another one next time I'm in the neighborhood. And by the way, if you find anything about Sara's background, please let me know."

It was now clear why Robert Montaine had agreed to break the rules of his retreat to talk to her. He was hoping Davie would find dirt on his stepmom and share it with him.

She turned to leave. "Good luck with the retreat. I hope you find what you're looking for."

"What I'm looking for is inspiration for an audition next week. It's the lead in a major motion picture set in the 1960s." He took a deep breath, pressed his hands together with his thumbs on his chest, and bowed his head. "Namaste."

"Same to you, Bob."

With the image of Robert Montaine's middle finger pointed toward the heavens, Davie made her way back to the car, trying to make sense of the man. The guy had issues. He hadn't addressed his feelings toward his stepmother, much less reflected on why he'd avoided his father as he lay dying of cancer. His lack of compassion seemed pathological. Davie hoped he had an epiphany at the retreat and finally found peace and tolerance, but she suspected he had a long way to go before he was granted absolution by any of the major religions, much less a starring role in a major motion picture.

17

WHEN DAVIE RETURNED TO the station, she found her computer booted up and her chair ratcheted down so far it was like sitting in a pothole. Somebody had used her desk while she was away. At least the offender hadn't exchanged her chair for a less agreeable one. Some detectives considered that a sacrilege and chained their chairs to the desk when they left to discourage such transgressions.

Davie adjusted the chair and walked upstairs where she found Vaughn in the employee lunchroom, reading the *Los Angeles Times* and nursing his latte. She was used to brainstorming with him about their investigations, but she'd been working the Montaine case alone and missed the interaction.

He looked up as she approached the table. "Your head looks like hell. I dated a makeup artist who could turn you into a *Vogue* model. Should I see if she's still speaking to me?"

"Thanks, Jason. You make me feel so special."

He gave her the thumbs-up sign. "I checked with the watch commander when I got here. Blue-suits found the kid's bicycle abandoned a half mile from the projects. SID can't check for prints until later this afternoon."

"I'm heading downtown in a few minutes to interview a PI about the Montaine case. You want to come along?"

He folded up the newspaper and grabbed his latte. "I'm good to go, but better not ask too much of me until the caffeine kicks in."

She headed for the door. "I'll consider myself forewarned."

Before talking to Natalie Salinas, Davie had searched for information on the woman. Salinas worked for Norton Investigations as a private investigator licensed by the State of California. The company leased office space in a downtown skyscraper near the Staples Center and the entertainment complex called L.A. Live.

Salinas was just a year older than Davie—thirty-two—and had been a patrol officer for the Beverly Hills Police Department before joining the PI agency. There were a lot of cops Davie knew who did that kind of work on their days off or after they retired, but not many who left the job to work at it full-time. Unless you were lucky, the pay and benefits weren't in your favor. There must be a story behind her decision. There always was.

Norton's website advertised a variety of services, including investigating personal-injury fraud, burglary, and theft, but also process service and catching cheating spouses in compromising positions. All the investigators had a background in law enforcement or the military. None of them were pictured on the site, for privacy and security reasons, she assumed. The company's dozens of Yelp reviews were mostly five stars. Some of those happy clients praised the investigator who'd handled their case. None of them mentioned Salinas.

On the drive downtown, Vaughn confessed that after his recent trip to Italy to visit his mother's family, he'd been inspired to sign up for an Italian cooking class.

"It's going to make me irresistible to women," he said. "If you're extra nice to me, I might even invite you to my graduation dinner."

"I love Italian food."

He did a Groucho Marx eyebrow wiggle. "Marry me?"

Davie laughed. "That would be wrong on so many levels."

He cocked his head and frowned. "You know I'm joking, right?"

"Right."

Davie and Vaughn entered the fifth-floor office suite of Norton Investigations. She identified herself to the receptionist, a young woman with a criminology textbook on the desk in front of her, and asked to see Salinas. Vaughn hovered in the background, observing.

"She's meeting a new client in fifteen minutes," the receptionist said in a gruff tone.

Davie wondered if the woman was an intern studying for her fedora and trench coat degree. If so, she wasn't going to survive training unless she adjusted her attitude.

"Fifteen minutes is all we need," Davie said.

The young woman lowered her voice as she made the call.

A few minutes later, Natalie Salinas strode into the reception area in a business suit with a thigh-high skirt and a silver cross necklace nestled in her cleavage. She moved with the confidence of a woman who knew she was beautiful and had no interest in hiding the fact. Her vise-like handshake was meant to compensate for her petite stature. Davie knew because she'd been guilty of using the technique herself. Out of the corner of her eye, Davie saw Vaughn straightening his posture and tie.

"What can I do for you?" Salinas said, her full lips shimmering with ruby gloss.

"I'm looking into the death of a woman named Sara Montaine," Davie said. "I was hoping you might have information about the case."

Salinas glanced at the receptionist, checking to see if she was listening. "I can give you five minutes."

As Salinas turned toward the agency's inner sanctum, her luminous dark hair swished across her back, settling at the L4-L5 vertebrae. Davie and Vaughn followed her down the hallway to a corporate office that was generic except for the stout California penal code tomes held between bookends on the credenza near the window.

Salinas sank into an oversized leather chair that seemed to swallow her whole. Vaughn leaned against a wall by the door. Without an invitation, Davie took a guest chair across from Salinas. She grabbed a business card from a leather holder on the desk. Under the name of the agency were the words THOROUGH • TRUSTWORTHY • DISCREET. Beneath that line was the name J.D. NORTON, the owner of the company, Davie presumed. This wasn't Salinas's office. Davie wondered why she didn't rate a space of her own. Another story, no doubt.

"So, how can I help you?" Salinas said, glancing at her watch.

"As I mentioned, I'm looking into the death of Sara Montaine. She died at Black Jack Guns & Ammo on Venice Boulevard a year ago. The store owner was a man named Jack Blasdel."

"Blasdel? Doesn't sound familiar."

"What about Gerda Pittman? Have you heard of her?"

She fiddled with a strand of hair before answering. "Why are you asking?"

"Pittman says she hired you to do a skip trace on Mr. Blasdel. Do you remember that job?"

Salinas's tone was guarded. "What did she tell you about me?"

Davie flashed her a hard stare. "If the information isn't accurate, maybe you can tell me what services you *did* provide?"

She fidgeted in the chair. "I vaguely remember her, but that was some time ago. I can't recall the details."

"How did Ms. Pittman find you?"

"From the telephone book. We still advertise there because not all clients are computer savvy."

Davie sensed Vaughn standing behind her but he didn't join in the questioning because he had only a general knowledge of the case. Davie was eager to hear his take on this interview.

"What did she ask you to do?" Davie asked.

"Find Blasdel. He owed her money, but she didn't want the police involved because she was embarrassed. She'd loaned him a lot of cash and she just wanted it back."

For a person who barely remembered the job a moment ago, Salinas suddenly had amazing recall of the details. "Did you locate him?"

"Of course I did. I used to be a cop. The guy wasn't hard to find. I did a fifteen-minute search and gave Gerda his phone number. That's when she told me she couldn't pay until she got her cash back. What I did for her wasn't worth a lot of money, so I figured she was good for it."

Her trust level was unusually high for a former cop. Davie would never have accepted that deal. "Did you do any surveillance of Blasdel or stake out the gunstore?"

"I told you before, I searched through a few databases. I should have had Gerda sign a contract before I started the work, but I was new back then and I didn't think it was a big deal."

"Did she ever pay your fee?"

Salinas studied her red-polished fingernails. "No. She asked if I'd consider bartering—my services for hers. It wasn't worth pursuing."

Davie studied the woman's well-manicured eyebrows. "So you never took her up on the offer?"

Salinas seemed to wrestle with the answer. "Maybe once. A facial. It was a mistake, I know. When my boss found out I'd done work for free, he was furious. I thought he was going to fire me. I'd appreciate it if you didn't mention it to him. He might still give me the boot. That's how mad he was."

She assumed Salinas had used the company's database subscriptions to access Blasdel's information and probably did so on company time. Then she accepted payment for herself in the form of beauty services. Davie doubted one long-ago misstep would jeopardize her job now unless there had been other lapses in judgment since then. For all she knew, Salinas had a thriving side business she ran through her employer's office.

"Ms. Pittman told me after you found Blasdel you followed him and watched his store, possibly for up to a week."

Salinas struggled to swallow. "I may have driven past the store to verify the address, but if you're asking did I sit in my car with a pair of binoculars, the answer is no."

Davie nodded. "Do you have the date of that drive-by?"

She clutched her cross necklace. "I'm not sure I even made a note of it. It didn't seem important."

Davie leaned forward in the chair. "Did you remember seeing anything unusual at the store?"

She frowned as she inspected a chip in one of her fingernails. "What do you mean by unusual?"

"Perhaps a person running away from the location? Police activity?"

"I don't remember anything like that. When my boss told me to back off the case, I did." She checked her watch again and stood. "I'm sorry, but I have to get ready for my client."

In a perfect world Salinas would have witnessed what happened the day Sara Montaine died. Now Davie would have to dig deeper into the minutiae of the case because she was convinced that eventually the evidence would show Montaine had been murdered.

Davie stood, too, and met Salinas's gaze. "By the way, why did you leave the Beverly Hills PD?"

Salinas's expression hardened. "I got a better offer."

Davie doubted it was that simple. She handed Salinas her business card and invoked the standard line that ended most of her interviews. "If you think of anything I forgot to ask you, please give me a call."

On the walk back to the car, Davie asked Vaughn what he thought of Salinas.

"What a babe! Not as hot as you, but a close second. You think she likes homemade Fagiano Col Risotto?"

Davie grabbed his arm and pulled him to a stop. "I'm serious, Jason. What did you think?"

He squinted as he met her gaze. "She was nervous. She knows way more than she told you about Gerda Pittman *and* Jack Blasdel."

On the ride back to the station, Davie thought about Bear's old admonition—you can love the job but the job will never love you. Davie loved her job. It would be difficult to leave it. Every day she put on her badge she thought of Alice Stebbins and how challenging life must have been for the LAPD'S first female police officer. The department hired Alice in 1910, forty-one years after they started patrolling the streets of L.A. Davie was grateful to her for paving the way.

Natalie Salinas had left the Beverly Hills Police Department. A career in law enforcement wasn't for everybody, but to Davie, that still made her a quitter. She had a feeling her partner was right. Salinas was also a liar.

18

As soon as Davie and her partner entered the squad room, Giordano marched toward her, clutching a fistful of papers.

"When one of my peeps is assaulted, I expect a call," he said. "Day or night. So, I'm wondering why I had to hear about what happened last night from the captain."

Davie glanced at her partner just as he ducked his head behind the partition wall to avoid any fallout that might drift his way.

"It was late," she said. "I was fine."

"I read the report. You said you were fine. But now I'm looking at that bump on your head and I'm thinking maybe you aren't so fine after all. You should have called me."

Giordano was her boss, so she swallowed the urge to defend herself. "Got it."

He walked toward his desk. Over his shoulder he said, "Don't let it happen again. *Capisce?*"

"*Capisce.*"

Davie understood Giordano's concern. He felt responsible for every member of his team. What he didn't grasp was that her father had also been an LAPD detective, and Bear had his own set of rules, the first being *Thou shall not whine.* Her father had trained her to rely on her instincts and not to ask for help unless she'd exhausted all options on her own. But Bear was not her D-3, so bringing his philosophy into the mix was counterproductive.

Davie settled into her desk chair. While she waited for the call from prison officials about the Felix Malo interview, she searched for information on Jack Blasdel. Striker had offered to help locate him, but he was busy with his own cases and she couldn't afford to wait. Two more days had passed with no new homicides in Pacific Division. That gave her space to keeping investigating Sara Montaine's death, but a ticking clock hung around her neck like a giant albatross. She was under pressure to make progress or get bounced from the case.

Blasdel was a man who scammed money from gullible divorcees like Gerda Pittman, so he was probably guilty of other capers, too. First Davie checked the Wanted Person System. Blasdel didn't have any outstanding warrants. He also had no restraining orders issued against him, no California driver's license, and no cases pending with the District Attorney's office. He'd once applied for a gaming license from the New Jersey Casino Control Commission to work in Atlantic City, but Davie couldn't tell if he'd ever landed a job. Gerda Pittman mentioned a billionaire he'd met there, but without the man's name Davie wasn't sure how that made finding Blasdel easier.

Blasdel once had a Florida driver's license, but that had expired over a year ago. She studied the old photo—sour expression, sparse hair, and a scar above his thin lips. She wondered what Gerda Pittman had found attractive about him. It must be true what people said—there's someone out there for everybody.

Blasdel didn't have a criminal record, but that could just mean he'd never been caught. Maybe he'd talked his way out of trouble before it became a police matter, as he'd done after scamming Gerda out of her fifty grand. But trouble *had* touched his life. Three of his businesses had failed, all as he'd drifted from state to state. Court records revealed bankruptcies for a used car dealership in Missouri, a carwash in Florida, and Black Jack Guns & Ammo in L.A. She gave Blasdel credit for his entrepreneurial spirit, but his business skills left much to be desired.

Opening a gunstore took money. The inventory alone had to have cost a bundle. After the two previous bankruptcies, he must have struggled to pull together enough cash or credit to close the deal. Then along came Gerda Pittman and that romantic Mexican cruise. The Palm Springs condo purchase had either fallen through or it was a lie from the beginning. Gerda's fifty grand made the gunstore purchase possible. Still unanswered was how he'd raised the capital to buy his other businesses.

Davie had grown stiff from sitting at the computer. She stood and rotated her shoulder in a stretch. It still hurt. She realized the injury could jeopardize her running program. Giordano had just made a fresh pot of coffee, so she joined him at the credenza behind his desk, waiting as he filled her cup.

"What's happening with the Montaine case?" he said.

Davie was relieved he no longer seemed angry with her. She told him about the meeting with Robert Montaine and what he'd said about the watercolor Sara had donated to Four Paws.

"I don't know the value of Montaine's estate," she said, "but I suspect it's substantial. It was a petty thing for him to do."

"You think the stepson killed her?"

Davie took a sip of her coffee and considered his question. "They were estranged and he all but admitted he wanted her dead. He was in New York when she died, so he didn't pull the trigger, but he could have hired somebody to do the job. There was a lot of money at stake. Maybe he wanted his inheritance sooner rather than later."

Giordano returned to his desk. "Good stuff. Work faster."

She returned to her computer to search for Jack Blasdel. After thirty minutes, she finally located him through a fictitious business license he'd registered at the L.A. County Clerk's office a few months before. He was now hawking mani-pedis at Salon de Manucure. She glanced around the squad room and saw her partner walking out the back door with a Deputy City Attorney from the Airport Court. She considered asking somebody else to go with her, but instead she glanced at her ragged cuticles and decided they could use attention. She signed out and headed to the San Fernando Valley.

19

SALON DE MANUCURE OPERATED out of a building on Ventura Boulevard in Sherman Oaks. Despite the fancy French name, the shop wasn't exactly a destination for the *Avenue des Champs-Élysées* crowd.

The place was a small, no-frills rectangular room with four reclining chairs. Each station had a nail dryer connected by extension cords to a socket extender that was plugged into a wall outlet. A customer with her feet submerged in a plastic tub of water occupied one of the stations. At another, a petite Asian woman brushed teal polish on a customer's toenails. Two other manicurists lounged on chairs in the rear of the store. They both smiled and beckoned to Davie, competing for her business.

In the back corner, two chairs were shoved against a round table that displayed items for sale—tarot cards, crystals, and books on Wiccan rituals. A crystal ball lit from below was plugged into the same socket extender. A sign pinned to the back wall announced tarot card readings were available by appointment on Saturdays between ten and two, cost—sixty bucks for forty-five minutes. She doubted Blasdel did double-duty as a psychic or he would have foreseen Gerda Pittman's bulldog pursuit of her stolen money.

One of the manicurists walked up to her and pointed to a carousel filled with nail polishes. "You pick color." She nodded to an empty station. "Sit here."

Davie identified herself and told her she was looking for Jack Blasdel. The woman frowned as she glanced toward a back room closed off by a plastic shower curtain. "He no here. What you want?"

Davie heard glass shattering and moved toward the sound. As she pushed back the curtain, she saw a man standing over a broken bowl. She recognized Jack Blasdel from the photo on his expired Florida driver's license—five-nine with sparse hair and a scar on the left side of his thin lips. His face had aged since the photo but not that much. He looked like a throwback to the 1980s: a paunch straining the seams of his partially buttoned silk shirt, pleated trousers with no back pockets, and a thick gold chain around his neck.

Blasdel's eyes widened as he stared at her. He must have heard her introduction to the manicurist, because a moment later he ran toward the rear door. Davie was taken aback. She shouted for him to stop, but he kept going.

She bolted into the alley behind the store in time to see Blasdel jogging toward a side street perpendicular to Ventura Boulevard. She didn't know where he was headed but doubted he'd turn left and risk having to run through the traffic light.

Her shoulder ached as she vaulted over a waist-high cinderblock wall and crossed the parking lot of a pizza parlor before reaching the street. Her weapon was still holstered, even though she was ready to break leather if needed. Chasing a man on a public street with a gun in her hand was risky. She could accidentally shoot a bystander or herself. Even worse, when she caught up with Blasdel she would have only one free hand to restrain him.

Blasdel ran past an apartment building a half block in front of her. Davie picked up speed until she grew closer. It was easier to push in the direction of his momentum than to grab his coat and pull him backward, so she planted her hands on his back and shoved, reigniting the pain in her shoulder. Blasdel stumbled onto his hands and knees. His face was flushed. His skin looked gray and greasy from sweat. He was clutching his heart and breathing hard. The last thing she needed was for him to flatline on the sidewalk in front of her.

"Stand up," she said. "Put your hands on the side of the building and spread your legs."

Blasdel's voice was high-pitched and whiny. "Okay, okay, I give up. But I could use a break here, Detective. I know I promised my ex-wife I'd pay her as soon as I had the money, but if you arrest me, I can't work and she'll never get a dime from me."

"I'm not here because you're a deadbeat."

He grunted as he struggled to his feet. "Then why are you has-sling me?"

An elderly man with a cane stopped to gawk. Davie gestured for him to move along before returning her focus to Blasdel.

"Hands on the building." She kicked his legs apart and patted him down but found no weapon. "Tell me about Sara Montaine."

He craned his neck to make eye contact. "Sara who?"

Davie could barely hear his breathy response over the traffic noise. "We can talk about it here or I can hook you up and take you to the station. Your choice."

He hesitated before answering. "Okay, maybe the name rings a bell. She's that dead chick, right? The one who killed herself in my store? She ruined me. I never want to hear her name again."

"Memory's a strange thing, isn't it? Coming back so quickly." Davie snapped her fingers to emphasize the point.

"Do I need a lawyer?"

"I don't know. Do you?"

A nerdy-looking teenage boy slowed to watch the action. Davie turned so he could see her holstered gun. "Shouldn't you be in school?" He bolted across the street.

"Can I put my hands down?" Blasdel asked. "People are watching. It's bad for my reputation."

Davie doubted he had much of a reputation to protect. "Turn around slowly. Don't move away from the wall."

Blasdel turned toward her and straightened the collar of his shirt. "I don't have anything to hide. I told the cops everything back then. Nothing's changed."

"Let's head back to your shop and go over the details again. Maybe the exercise will jog loose a few more of those repressed memories."

"No," he said, his tone panicky. "We can't go back there. I don't want my girls to see me with the police. I've got a business to protect. Look, there's a coffee shop down the street. It's a pit. Nobody ever goes there. We can talk in private."

Davie weighed the pros and cons of going to the cafe with him. She didn't have backup but she'd patted Blasdel down and knew he wasn't armed. He seemed harmless. The worst-case scenario was he'd try to run again. The best-case outcome was he'd be in a comfortable location and more apt to give her information that helped the investigation.

20

DAVIE FOLLOWED BLASDEL TO a hole-in-the-wall cafe with rickety wooden tables and chairs. He purchased a cup of coffee from the kid at the counter while Davie avoided touching the sticky tabletop. When he sat down, she glanced at his chipped ceramic mug and imagined mutant strains of germs trapped in its crevices. She'd postpone coffee for some in her own cup at the station.

"Tell me about the day Sara Montaine died," she said.

Davie listened as Blasdel slowly recited details of what had happened. Halfway into the story, she realized it all sounded very familiar. He was using almost the exact language from the statement he'd given to Ralph Sarlos a year ago. Maybe the trauma of Montaine's death was indelibly imprinted on his brain or else Blasdel had rehearsed the story so often it was committed to memory.

Davie already knew the answer to her next question but asked it anyway, just to see what he'd say. "You said you were talking on the phone to a vendor that day. Who was it?"

He seemed taken aback by her question. "You expect me to remember that? It's been a year. What the hell difference does it make now?"

"You seem to remember every other detail about that day."

"I don't remember that one."

"Let me jog your memory. Gerda Pittman? You told Detective Sarlos she sold you cleaning products." Davie paused to let that sink in.

"I don't remember her."

"Interesting. She said you two were lovers."

Blasdel's eyes darted left, right, and back to center. "Our relationship was over. I gave the detective her name. Isn't that enough? What happened between us was nobody else's business."

"How long were you on the phone with Gerda before you heard the gunshot?"

He blew on the coffee and slurped up a mouthful. "Five minutes. Maybe less."

A bell above the shop door jingled the arrival of a young female with a backpack. Davie lowered her voice before continuing. "Just so I understand the timeline. Ms. Montaine came into the store to look at guns. The phone rang. You left the keys in the case lock and went into the back room. You spoke to Gerda Pittman for five minutes. During that time your theory is that Montaine opened the case, loaded your gun with her rounds, and shot herself, correct?"

"Yeah … sounds about right."

"I couldn't find any record that Sara Montaine ever owned a gun. Five minutes isn't much time to do all that, especially for a novice."

"So what? She certainly knew what she wanted: a Smith & Wesson .38 snubnose. That's what I showed her."

Davie tilted her head and frowned. "The crime report identified the gun as a Colt .38 Special."

Blasdel began nervously tapping his foot. "Right. It was a Colt. It's been a while. Guess I forgot."

"Were you still on the phone with Gerda when you heard the shot?"

His tone sounded cagey. "I don't know. Maybe. What did Gerda say?"

Davie leaned into his personal space without touching the table. "Where exactly were you when you heard the gunshot?"

He stared into his coffee, looking for an answer, she guessed. "I'm not sure, maybe in the back room. Gerda was screaming at me. I shouted back. Things got heavy, so I stepped outside into the alley— no, wait—it was the bathroom. I remember because I closed the door for privacy."

Davie raised her voice over the sound of milk steaming. "What happened when you heard the shot?"

Blasdel wiped sweat from his brow and brushed it on his pant leg. "I ran to the front and found the chick dead on the floor. Then I called 911."

"You just said you were on the phone with Ms. Pittman. Did you end the call when you heard the shot or did you talk a while before hanging up?"

He ran his hand through his greasy hair. "I don't remember. I probably hung up. Yeah, I think I told her I'd call back later. All I know is I saw that woman on the floor and called the police."

Davie nodded and watched him squirm. "Your neighbor Mr. Nazarian said it took first responders twenty minutes to arrive after he heard the gunshot. You say you called right away, but maybe you didn't. What were you doing all that time? Talking on the phone with Gerda or with someone else? I can get a search warrant for your phone records if it helps jog your memory."

Blasdel clutched the coffee mug with both hands. "I could have called somebody else but I can't imagine who."

Davie fired off another question to keep him off balance. "You closed the store shortly after Sara Montaine died. Why is that?"

"It was a crime scene. I couldn't even go inside the place for days. I had to pay somebody to clean up the blood—Hazmat suits, the whole ball of wax. Cost me a fortune. After that, nobody came to buy guns. A few looky-loos stopped by, searching for blood in the grout. The place was cursed. I cut my losses and closed the doors."

The woman with the backpack sat at the table next to them with her muffin and cappuccino. Except for the three of them, the place was empty. Davie wondered why people did that. It was as incomprehensible as parking next to the only car in an otherwise empty lot.

"Who cleaned the place?" Davie asked.

He looked at the ceiling, maybe hoping the answer was written there. "I don't remember."

Blasdel had a bad case of CRS—can't remember shit. Who had paid to clean the store was an odd thing to lie about, but somebody was lying: either Blasdel or Nazarian. Her bet was on Blasdel.

"Your neighbor told me you abandoned the store after Ms. Montaine's death. He said *he* hired a service to clean up the mess and negotiated to lease your space."

Blasdel thrust his index finger toward her face. "Don't trust anything that assclown says. He's nothing but trouble."

"What did you do with your inventory?"

He leaned over the cup and slurped more coffee. "I broke the lease when I moved out early. The mall owner came after his money, so I gave him a few guns and some ammunition and we called it even."

The young woman finished her muffin and pulled a laptop from her backpack. Davie regretted not moving to another table.

"What did you do with the rest of the weapons?"

"Kept a few. Sold the rest to another store."

"You told Detective Sarlos that Montaine must have brought the ammunition into the store with her. What gave you that idea?"

"I'd heard stories about people who can't afford a gun, but can buy a box of shells. So, they bring in their own ammo and load it into a gun from the store. They either rob the place or pop a cap in their temple."

"Had you ever seen Ms. Montaine before?"

Blasdel glanced at the exit and then cleared his throat. "She looked familiar but only because she was a type—just not the type who shopped at my store. She came in wearing pearls and smelling good, like she'd just stepped out of some rich woman's fashion magazine. All I know is she couldn't have gotten the ammo from me. I told the cops. I kept everything locked up and I had the only key."

"You left your key in the gun case. Maybe you forgot and laid the ammo key on the counter."

Blasdel's shoulders slumped. "I got distracted, but I know the key to the ammo case was in my pocket. I found it there when the cops asked to see it."

"Was there anybody else in the store when Ms. Montaine came in?"

He looked at the barista, avoiding her stare. "People were standing on the sidewalk but none of them came into the store."

"Can you describe any of them?"

His voice rose in frustration. "I can't remember that. Who could? Once you walk out of here, I probably won't be able to describe you, either, except for your hair. I've never liked redheads. They remind me of fire. I hate fire."

"Save the phobias for your shrink."

"See? Exactly the kind of shit a redhead would say."

Davie leaned back in the chair, her tone casual. "When did Gerda Pittman call to tell you we'd spoken?"

She was only guessing, but people like her didn't show up at a place of business to collect past-due alimony payments. Blasdel had run when he heard her name, which suggested to Davie that somebody tipped him off that a *homicide* detective was asking questions about an old suicide case.

A slight hand tremor rocked the cup. "Gerda? I don't know what you're talking about. I haven't seen Gerda in a while. How's she doing, by the way?"

Verbal diarrhea. He was nervous, probably lying.

"You know," she said, "I can just call her to find out."

"Okay, whatever," he said, bouncing his knee. "We stay in touch sometimes. What's the big deal?"

Everybody lies, she thought.

"Did either you or Gerda tell anybody else I was looking into Sara Montaine's death?"

"Why would I do that?"

"Answer my question."

His eyes kept darting back and forth, searching for another lie. "No."

"What's your cell number in case I need to reach you?"

He stalled for a moment before rattling off a number. The young woman at the next table watched Davie jot it into her notebook.

"Give me a call if you remember anything else," she said, handing him a business card.

"Don't hold your breath," he mumbled.

Davie walked toward the door, punching in a number on her cell. A moment later, Blasdel's cell rang.

He put the phone to his ear. "Yo."

"Just checking," she said.

Blasdel's lips pressed into a hard line. "Effing redheads."

21

ON THE WAY BACK to the car, Davie wondered why Blasdel couldn't explain the delay between the gunshot and the time the police arrived. Twenty minutes was a long time. She suspected he was covering up the real reason—that he hadn't called 911 right away as he claimed. She wondered if a judge would sign a search warrant for Blasdel's phone records so she could see for herself how long his call with Pittman had lasted and if he'd spoken to anyone else. Getting a warrant was a long shot. This was still a closed case. She would have to establish probable cause that Blasdel had committed a felony. Otherwise, her request would be considered a fishing expedition.

Davie hoped the peace in the division held so she could continue looking deeper into the Montaine case, but she worried every time her cell rang, fearing she'd be called out to a fresh homicide.

Every victim was important to her. She reminded herself that Javi Hernandez's family was also waiting for their measure of justice. She hadn't forgotten about him, but the mystery surrounding Sara

Montaine's life and death intrigued her. Montaine's stepson hated her. The neighbors gossiped behind her back. There was nothing Davie had discovered so far to explain why she deserved the animosity heaped on her. The woman seemed isolated, lonely, and, toward the end of her life, afraid.

Robert Montaine's storage unit was on the way back to the station, so she would stop by and search through Sara's personal property in hopes of finding a new lead. As she approached the overpass near the entrance of the 405 South she could see that traffic heading toward Los Angeles was bumper to bumper. There was no alert on the radio about an accident ahead, but she did learn that the wildfire in the hills above Malibu had grown.

The normal May winds were predominantly from the west, but for the last several days they'd been abnormally high at 15 to 20 miles per hour. It was possible the fast-moving blaze might be forcing drivers on the 101 to take alternate routes. She opted for Sepulveda Boulevard instead, a twisty two-lane road that connected L.A. and the San Fernando Valley. Once she left the residential area and drove into the hills, she could smell the odor of burning wood combined with sage baking in the afternoon sun.

The storage rental where Robert Montaine kept his stepmother's remaining possessions was a sprawling two-story building on Olympic Boulevard about three miles inland from the border of Santa Monica. It consumed a chunk of pricy Westside real estate on a lot where one of Davie's favorite Italian restaurants used to be, a family-owned place that had served the best cannolis this side of Sicily. The Bellini family held on to the place for years, but as high-rise office buildings and big box stores rose from the ground on all sides, it had been only a matter of time before they sold the land to developers.

At the self-storage entrance, Davie pressed Robert Montaine's key card to the sensor and the gate rumbled open. The lot was empty except for her car and one other that she assumed belonged to the manager. The same card opened the door to the building, where she found him in his office.

His manner was brusque. "Mr. Montaine asked me to let you into his unit, but I may have to leave early. Please lock the door when you're finished."

He led her into a freight elevator and pushed the up button. The car creaked and jerked, stopping with a jolt on the second floor. The dim hallway lights paved the way to a metal roll-up door painted orange. The manager aimed the beam of his flashlight at the numbers on the combination lock, rotating the dials until it opened. The door clanked as it rolled onto its spool. He laid the lock just inside the unit and reminded Davie to secure the door when she left. His footsteps echoed in the cavernous building as he strolled toward the elevator.

Davie stepped into Montaine's unit, inhaling a mix of smells—plywood and something flowery. Before beginning her search, she slipped on a pair of powderless latex gloves from her pocket. A string hung from a light fixture on the ceiling. She pulled it, illuminating an aisle carved in the middle of stacks of boxes and items covered by tarps. She lifted one tarp and found an exercise bicycle and a gym bag.

Montaine said he'd dropped the coroner's box just inside the door, but it wasn't there, so she continued searching. Since Sara Montaine's death was officially listed as "undetermined," Davie doubted the coroner would release anything of evidentiary value. The clothes she had worn the day she died would have been stained with blood in any event. Those items would be wrapped in paper, tied with string, labeled with her name and the case number, and stored in the coroner's evidence room. Davie wondered about the pearls Montaine had on that day. She assumed her stepson had taken those, too, since there was nothing in the reports to indicate they were missing. Still, they must have been contaminated with blood.

Davie swept the flashlight beam along the floor where she found a box, but it wasn't an official coroner's evidence box. The contents appeared to be a few nonessential items they'd returned to Montaine as a courtesy. Davie picked it up and moved it under the light. Montaine's wallet was inside but contained only discount cards for a car wash, a grocery store, and a stationary shop. There was also a business card for Four Paws and a receipt from the post office for a hundred first-class stamps she'd purchased the day before she died. If Montaine planned to kill herself the next day, it was curious that she'd bought a hundred stamps she would never use. Davie slipped the receipt in an evidence envelope, just in case it was important.

She sorted through a garbage bag full of clothes until she found a cream-colored silk blouse infused with a light, flowery fragrance. The blouse wasn't Davie's style, but its soft femininity seemed fitting for the Sara Montaine she had come to know. In the bottom of the sack was a bottle of Chanel Bois Des Iles perfume.

This was the moment in the movie where a grieving family member smothered his face in the dead woman's blouse to conjure her essence one last time. Davie's limbs felt heavy as she realized only June Nakamura and a handful of people at Four Paws had ever grieved for Sara Montaine. She sat quietly for a moment before spritzing perfume on her wrists. It was a small gesture to let the universe know that Davie also cared about Montaine and would search until the person responsible for her death was brought to justice, however long it took.

Inside a box marked BOOKS, she found several photographs, a snapshot of what appeared to be the rescued kittens placed with Four Paws, and a close-up photo of three men standing on a street corner.

One wore a Hawaiian shirt, the other a business suit. The third man was in profile but Davie noted his appearance: military-style haircut, a black leather jacket stretched across his broad back, well-defined jaw, medium complexion, and a dark spot on his upper lip, which could have been a mole. His ears looked unusually small. They reminded her of a sliced mushroom glued to the side of his head. It looked like he had a hoop earring in his right earlobe.

Davie set the photographs aside and kept searching. Deep inside the box she found a coffee mug that read *Seaglass Cafe* and a day planner stuffed with old bills and a deposit slip, the generic kind a bank gives you when you open a new account. A list of grocery items had been scrawled across the paper. She thumbed through the pages of the notebook and found a section of lined paper filled with doodles that reminded her of Greek or Arabic handwriting.

Davie had lost track of how long she'd been in the storage unit. She wanted to take the photos and the planner back to the station for a closer look. Robert Montaine had signed a consent form giving her permission, so she tucked the planner and photos under her belt at the small of her back and retrieved the lock from the floor by the metal door. She glanced at the numbers. The manager hadn't reshuffled them after he'd lined up the digits, which meant the sequence on the dial was the code he'd used to open the lock. She jotted the numbers in her notebook. With the gate keycard and now the lock combination, Davie could come back for another look even if the manager wasn't on the premises.

She was about to leave when she heard footsteps in the hallway. It was public storage, so it could be another customer or maybe it was the manager checking to make sure she'd secured the unit.

"Who's there?" she shouted.

The footsteps immediately halted. There was no response.

She drew her weapon and listened. Fear prickled her jawline. She was alone in a small room in a cavernous building and still spooked by the assault at Mar Vista Gardens. She quietly inched toward the unit's roll-up door. With her back to the wall, she peeked around the corner. In the dim light she saw a shadow. Somebody was standing out of sight where the hallway made a turn. Whoever it was must have heard her call out.

Her muscles felt hard as granite. Her pulse raced as she called out again, louder this time, "Who's there?"

In the distance, she heard the sound of a door creak and footsteps clanking down a metal stairway. Davie inched down the hallway with her gun drawn until she reached the place where she'd seen the shadow. She craned her head to look around the corner. The hallway was empty. Her pulse hammered in her ears as she sprinted down the stairs, exiting the building in time to see a white van race out of the gate and barrel into traffic on Olympic Boulevard.

22

DAVIE RAN TOWARD THE van to jot down the license plate number, but by the time she got to the street, the vehicle had disappeared into the scrum of L.A. traffic. She considered the possibility she was overreacting, but her life had been threatened enough times in her career to embrace paranoia.

She glanced around the parking lot and noticed hers was the only car remaining. The manager was gone. She returned to Montaine's storage unit, locked it, and headed for the station. On the way, her cell phone rang. Still feeling unnerved, she flinched. She steered to the side of the street to answer the call, checking the time on the display. It read 3:30 p.m.

"Hey, Davie. Got a minute?" It was SID latent print analyst Sharonda West.

"Only if you have good news."

"Let's call it a mixed bag," she said. "I caught a break in my schedule so I ran Sara Montaine's prints through AFIS."

Back in the day when prints were on cards and had to be transmitted and analyzed by hand, results could take a couple of months. Now everything was electronic and could be returned within a couple of hours. But the department was always backlogged, so fingerprint submissions were prioritized with the most urgent cases processed first. She was lucky Shar had been able to shoehorn Montaine's prints into the queue.

"I was going to fax you the report," Shar said, "but I thought I should call first. Are you sure you sent me the right prints?"

That heavy feeling in Davie's stomach was back. "I think so. They're the same ones the coroner's office lifted at the morgue. Why?"

"Because they came back to a woman named Sabine Ponti and get this—according to DOJ records, she's been dead for over two years. I don't know the details, but I'm sure you can find out. I'll fax the report to the station."

Davie shook her head, as if that might help process the news. There could have been a mix up at the coroner's office, of course, but that seemed unlikely. If the information was accurate, she understood why Sara Montaine spoke little of her past—she was hiding her real identity.

"Were the prints in the criminal database?" Davie asked.

"No, they were in with the civilians. Ponti was probably printed because of her job."

Sara Montaine died a year ago. Sabine Ponti died a year before that. The math raised so many troubling questions it was hard to sort them out.

"Thanks, Shar. I owe you one."

She chuckled. "Just one?"

"You're right. More than one."

Davie sat in the car, still shocked by the news. It must have been difficult for Sara Montaine to manage the lies of her cover story. Her stepson had pushed his father to hire a private investigator because of his suspicions about her, but he was met with resistance. Robert's suspicions may have been justified. Davie wondered what a PI might have found about Sara Montaine's background and whether that information would have changed anything. All along Davie had been searching for a motive for Montaine's death, but the fingerprints opened a whole new line of inquiry. Who was Sabine Ponti and why had she morphed into Sara Montaine?

Davie returned to the station and scanned the photo of the three men on the street corner and also printed a hard copy for the file. She searched for Sabine Ponti's name in law enforcement databases but found no criminal history for the woman. After that, she typed the name into an Internet browser and saw a notice from the *Register* in New Haven, Connecticut.

> The Coast Guard has called off the search for Branford native Sabine Ponti, who left the Bahia Mar Marina in Fort Lauderdale, Florida, in a rented thirty-foot sailboat last week. When she failed to return at the appointed time, marina personnel notified the Coast Guard. The seas were calm that day, but authorities said they couldn't rule out the possibility the boat sank after colliding with another vessel, possibly a container ship.
>
> Ponti is a graduate of North Branford High School and Florida State University in Tallahassee. At the time of her disappearance she was employed as a hostess at the Seaglass Cafe, a Fort Lauderdale eatery.
>
> Roscoe Ponti, the missing woman's father, told reporters his daughter was an experienced sailor who was accustomed to single-handed sailing. "She's also a strong swimmer," he added. "We're all praying she's out there somewhere waiting to be rescued."

The Seaglass Cafe was the name on the coffee mug found among Montaine's possessions. An online search for the Seaglass produced a notice that claimed the cafe had gone out of business.

The newspaper reporter's name and email address were listed at the end of the article, but when Davie called, she was told he'd been laid off during the last downsizing.

The telephone number for Roscoe Ponti was easier to find in a commercial database the department used. Davie punched the numbers onto her desk phone keypad. Three rings and a man with a gravelly voice answered. Davie identified herself and told him she was calling about Sara Montaine.

"You must have dialed wrong. Happens all the time. My wife and I have had this number for forty years. I don't know anybody named Montaine. Is she from around here?"

He didn't seem in any particular hurry to end the call, so Davie kept asking him questions.

"Is your wife at home?"

He hesitated before answering. "Let's see. I haven't seen her in a couple of hours." He paused for a beat or two. "I think she's at her church knitting group."

"Maybe Ms. Montaine was a friend of your wife's?"

He chuckled. "When you've been married as long as we have, you don't have secret friends."

"What about your children? Would they know her?"

"We have a son, Boyd, but he hasn't lived with us for years. He's a graphic artist. Very successful."

Davie noted that Roscoe Ponti made no mention of his daughter, Sabine. She wondered why. "I need to speak with him. Can you give me his number?"

Ponti hesitated. "I suppose so, but it's unlisted so don't spread it around town—unless you need a graphic artist, of course."

Davie jotted the number in her notebook. She didn't recognize the area code, but if it was a cell he could be anywhere.

"Where does your son live?"

"Pasadena. That's in California. Didn't you say that's where you're from? Maybe you've heard of him? Boyd Ponti? The wife and I are so proud of our boy. He's a graphic artist. Did I tell you that?"

They chatted for a couple more minutes but he again assured her he had never heard of Sara Montaine, so she thanked him and hung up.

Davie didn't know the state of the Pontis' physical or mental health and was unsure how they'd take the news that their daughter had survived that boat accident only to be dead again a year later, this time for real. Before telling them anything, she wanted to talk to the brother in Pasadena. Davie picked up the phone once again.

A man answered her call. Davie identified herself. "Are you Boyd Ponti?"

"Yeah. How can I help you?"

"I'm calling about your sister, Sabine."

He didn't respond right away and when he did his tone was neutral. "Why? Did you find her?"

Davie didn't want to tell him Sabine Ponti had become Sara Montaine and died a year ago of a gunshot wound to the head. Not yet. One of the worst parts of her job was informing a grieving family that their loved one had turned up dead, and in this case, twice. She wanted to tread softly.

"I think your sister may be connected to a case I'm working on. Can you describe her?"

"Okay, I'll play your game. Blonde hair, blue eyes, five-three. She called herself fat but I'd call her chubby."

Sara Montaine's hair was brown and she had a thin build, but she could have lost weight and colored her hair. Davie remembered the cosmetic surgery scars from the autopsy report. This might even have been an attempt to change her appearance.

"Did she have any distinguishing marks, a tattoo or scars?"

"Why are you asking? Connect the dots for me."

"I'm investigating the death of a woman named Sara Montaine. I ran her prints through a national database and they came back registered to your sister. I need to make sure it's not some sort of mix-up."

"Is this a scam? You say you're a detective but I don't know that. If you want information about my sister, you can come over and show me your ID."

"Happy to. Give me your address."

"You're the detective. Find it yourself."

The line went dead.

23

Davie had expected Boyd Ponti to pepper her with questions about his sister's whereabouts for the past couple of years or at least display some sort of emotion or concern that she may have been alive and using an alias. Normal people with missing relatives usually wanted all the details, especially after not knowing if the loved one was dead or alive. But Ponti didn't seem all that interested in news about his sister. She wondered why but supposed she'd find out soon enough.

Ponti was correct about one thing: finding his address was easy. He lived at the base of the San Gabriel Mountains in a single family home in Pasadena about ten miles east of downtown Los Angeles. Traffic would suck this late in the day, but she was too close to a breakthrough in the case to worry about that. She grabbed a set of car keys from Giordano's desk and headed east.

Davie had always loved Pasadena's tree-lined streets and stately old homes on Millionaire's Row, not to mention the Rose Parade and

Cal Tech's *Athenaeum*. But as appealing as the city was, she couldn't imagine living that far away from the ocean.

Ponti's house was a vintage Craftsman, painted pale olive green. Davie parked the department vehicle and noted the time as 4:56 p.m. She climbed five wide steps to a wraparound porch. To the left were two cushy chairs and a small round table perfect for cocktails at five. Planter boxes rested on the ledge to the right. Someone must have been watching her walk up the sidewalk because the door opened before she could knock.

An attractive woman with dark hair and a thin build beckoned her inside. She was in her late thirties and wore a tasteful gray silk shirt and matching trousers. Her ears were accented with large diamond studs. In her hand was a glass of white wine. It was barely cocktail hour, but Davie wasn't an expert on the drinking habits of the upper middle class.

"Come in, Detective," she said, sweeping her hand in a grand gesture. "Boyd said you might drop by. I'm his wife, Darleen."

Davie stepped into a living room with large windows, dark wood ceiling beams, and matching built-in bookcases. The fireplace was a charming feature, but the addition of more dark wood on the mantel made the room feel gloomy.

"Please sit down," she said, pointing to a couch with a raised back at one end, a fainting couch if Davie remembered her Victorian furniture history. "My husband is in his office designing a corporate logo." She walked to the base of the stairs and shouted, "Boyd. That detective is here." Darleen returned to the living room and lowered herself into a chair across from Davie, sloshing wine on her silk pants. "Boyd told me you have news about Sabine. You know, his parents never gave up hope. Have you told them yet?"

Her tone seemed hushed and gossipy. Davie wanted Boyd Ponti present before laying out the details. "I'd prefer to wait for your husband."

"Boyd said you identified Sabine—something about fingerprints. I always wondered if she survived that boat accident but didn't reach out to the family because she had amnesia. Is that what happened? Have you spoken to her? Does she remember us?"

Davie heard footsteps and turned toward the sound. A doughy man in his early forties with a beard and an air of annoyance ambled down the stairs. Boyd Ponti acknowledged Davie with a nod but distanced himself by the fireplace with his arms crossed.

"Show me your ID," he said.

Darleen leaned forward, sloshing wine on the area rug. "Boyd—"

He held up his hand to silence her. "I have the right to know who I'm talking to."

Davie had already identified herself during their earlier telephone conversation. Nevertheless, she opened her jacket to reveal her badge and gun and pulled a business card from her notebook. She held out her hand toward him. Apparently he considered the long-distance stretch too taxing because he made no attempt to take the card. Instead, he slumped into a nearby chair so the three of them formed a triangle.

Darleen snagged the card and began reading. "Homicide. How intriguing. Who's dead?"

"Shut up, Darleen."

She flashed her husband a tight smile. "Whatever you say, dear."

"Let's cut to the chase," he said. "On the phone you mentioned a woman named Sara Montaine. Who is she?"

Ponti's curt response didn't make Davie inclined to sugarcoat the truth. "Your sister may have been living in L.A. under that name, possibly for up to a year after she went missing in Florida. Sara Montaine died a year ago of a gunshot wound to the head. I need to know if she was your sister."

"Continue," he said with a flip of his hand.

"I have photographs." Davie pulled out the picture of Sara Montaine at Four Paws.

"Please ignore the hair color. And it's possible this shot shows her heavier or thinner than she was when you last saw her. Just concentrate on her facial features."

Ponti took the photo, studying it for a long time. Darleen got up and wandered to the bar to refill her wineglass. Then she strolled to her husband's side and leaned over to study the photo.

"She's thin," Darleen said. "Not at all like our sweet chunky little Sabine. And look at her face. She had some work."

Ponti frowned and handed the photo back to Davie.

"Is that your sister?" Davie asked.

His expression was somber. "So, Sabine lived under our noses for a year as this Sara person? Just so you know, I'm not responsible for her debts."

Davie was taken aback by his lack of compassion. His reaction was almost as bad as Robert Montaine's. "She didn't owe any money, but thanks for asking."

"How sad," Darleen said. "This is the second goodbye for our dear Sabine. That must be some sort of record."

Davie had to stop thinking of the woman as Sara Montaine. That name was a phantom creation from a forger's tool bag. Sara Montaine had never existed. Her name was Sabine Ponti and from now on, that's what Davie would call her.

From the beginning of the investigation, Davie had felt compassion for Sabine Ponti. Her life couldn't have been easy with her husband dying so soon after the marriage and a hostile stepson intent on making her life difficult. She didn't know what Ponti had done to earn all the distain, but her father hadn't even mentioned his daughter when Davie spoke to him on the telephone, and now her brother and his wife seemed detached and uncaring about her life or her death. Darleen might be excited about the drama factor, but Davie sensed no other personal feeling. Davie hoped Sabine Ponti had enjoyed some measure of happiness in her short life. It saddened her to think otherwise.

Boyd Ponti stared out the window. "You want me to tell my parents?"

"You can if that would be easier on them."

"I suppose it would."

Davie handed him the picture she'd found in the storage unit of the three people standing on the street corner. "Can you identify these men?"

Boyd glanced at the photo and then looked away. "Never seen any of them before."

"I found a newspaper article about your sister's disappearance," Davie said. "She worked for a restaurant in Florida before she went missing. Can you tell me about her job?"

"She was hired as a hostess," he said. "Sabine had a business degree with an emphasis in accounting. Working in a restaurant was a big step down for her."

Davie jotted the information in her chrono notes. "What's the restaurant owner's name?"

He leaned forward and rested his forearms on his knees, staring at the floor. "Nate something."

Darleen took another sip of her wine. "His last name was Gillen, honey, but he's dead, the poor man."

Davie poised her pen over the page. "When did he die?"

Boyd continued staring at his feet, appearing disinterested in the conversation. "I'd guess—"

Darleen interrupted again. "A few days before Sabine disappeared. He was killed by a hit-and-run driver. She took it hard." Darleen flashed a sly smile. "No surprise there. We heard a rumor that Nate was more than her boss."

The discovery made Davie's scalp tingle. She didn't want to get ahead of the story, but this information was tripping alarms. "You mean they were involved in a romantic relationship?"

"That's bullshit," Ponti said, his voice bristling with anger. "Nate had a wife. Sabine didn't date married men."

Darleen batted her eyelashes. "I hear you, honey, but I think you mean *anymore*. You know … she'd done it before."

He scowled. "Stop slut-shaming my sister. Sabine made some mistakes, but she was trying to start over."

"Okay, let's just say Sabine specialized in close relationships with coworkers. Is that better?"

Davie attempted to break the tension. "Sabine's fingerprints were found in the civilian database. Did she have a security clearance from her work?"

"Yes," he said, his voice so low Davie strained to hear. "Before the restaurant gig."

Darleen turned toward Davie, still eager to dish out information. "Sabine worked in the accounting department of a defense contractor in Hartford. She loved the people there … one of them she loved a little too much. That's why her boss fired her. Awful man. Remember, Boyd, how he treated her like his personal secretary? Even made her learn shorthand. Anyway, her parents were appalled and embarrassed by the affair, so Sabine moved away from Connecticut. Memories, you know how that is. It took her a long time to find even the hostess job. References do matter, I guess."

Ponti sat in his chair fuming, but he didn't contradict Darleen, which told Davie that Sabine's affair with a coworker in Hartford was probably the truth.

"Look," Ponti said, "Sabine was pretty. Men were attracted to her, including Nate Gillen. She told me the guy made inappropriate sexual advances to her, and she wasn't the only one. Lots of girls at the restaurant complained about him. There were other things about working there that bothered her."

"Like what?" Davie asked.

"Sabine told me her boss started throwing a ridiculous amount of money into the restaurant. With her background in accounting, she suspected he was doing something shady, maybe even illegal. I told her to quit, but she wanted to check out a few things first."

"Did she ever follow up with you?"

Ponti pinched the bridge of his nose as he bowed his head. "I never spoke to her again. The next thing I heard she was missing at sea."

Davie waited a beat while he composed himself. "Was the boat ever found? The newspaper said it was a rental."

"The newspaper got that wrong," Darleen said. "We flew to Florida and stayed until the Coast Guard called off the search. That's when we found out Sabine had borrowed the boat from a friend. He stopped by our hotel to offer condolences. Boyd's parents were willing to reimburse him for the loss of his boat, but he'd already filed an insurance claim."

Davie leaned forward. "What was the friend's name?"

"Jack Blasdel," Ponti said.

Darleen held up her glass, as if toasting. "Yes, that's it. Charming man."

Davie felt a chill along her spine. June Nakamura claimed Sara Montaine had become reclusive and fearful in the days before her visit to the gunstore, looking to buy a weapon. The store had been out of her neighborhood and undoubtedly out of her comfort zone. Maybe Sabine picked that particular place because she knew the owner. Gerda Pittman had told her Blasdel bragged about helping a woman disappear. Had that been Sabine? If Blasdel helped Sabine disappear once, perhaps she came to him again for another favor.

Whatever had happened, Jack Blasdel knew more than he'd let on when they'd spoken earlier. Davie would talk to him again, this time in an interview room in the Pacific squad room.

24

DAVIE BEAT A PATH through rush hour traffic to the station and found Giordano cleaning his coffeemaker. She told him everything she'd learned about Nazarian, Robert Montaine, Blasdel, and finally that Sara Montaine was Sabine Ponti.

"Interesting, kid." Giordano scooped fresh coffee grounds into a paper filter. "So, what do you think happened?"

"It's possible the sailboat boom hit Sabine in the head and knocked her overboard. Then somehow she made it to shore and started her life over. But it's more likely that Blasdel picked her up in a dinghy. If he helped her once, she may have asked for his help again, either to sell her a gun or to help her disappear a second time."

He slid the filter basket into the slot. "Okay, you've got me intrigued. I'm not going to make this a homicide just yet, but keep working on it. Blasdel told you he didn't recognize Sabine Ponti when she came into his store that day. I'm guessing that's a lie. From now on, I don't want you going anywhere alone. Take Vaughn. If he's too busy, find somebody else to go with you. You're going to interview Blasdel again, right?"

"Of course," she said. "I'm also going to call his yacht-insurance broker. Darleen Ponti was under the impression Blasdel had filed a claim, but I'm interested in what, if anything, they discovered in their investigation."

"You need to find out why Sabine Ponti faked her death in the first place. What was she running from? Who killed her boss and was his death related to her disappearance? Once you answer those questions, you'll have a suspect. Then I'll reclassify the case as a homicide and you can put all the evidence in a neat little package and drive it to the DA's office."

Davie could smell the aroma of strong coffee as it trickled into the pot. She glanced at her boss. "Boyd Ponti said his sister thought Nate Gillen might be involved in financial shenanigans. Gillen's widow may have information about her husband's death and Sabine's disappearance. If nothing else, she might be able to confirm the affair. The spouse always knows."

Giordano filled his cup under the spigot before it was finished brewing. "I can't get you an air ticket to Florida. Not until the case is official."

"Don't worry. There's always Plan B." Davie didn't yet know what Plan B was, but she'd figure it out.

Every day she'd been holding her breath, hoping there were no new homicides in Pacific to pull her away from either case, but the complexity of the Montaine investigation made her feel as if she were squinting at an eye chart, straining to read that elusive bottom line.

"Here's Plan B," he said. "Bring Blasdel into the station. Squeeze him until he talks. By the way, what's going on with the Hernandez gang murder? The lieutenant is still pressuring me to file some of these old cases with the DA's office."

"I'm working on it," she said, walking back to her desk.

And she was, she told herself, but a feeling of guilt surged through her as she set aside the Hernandez to-do list and instead pulled out Sabine's notebook and studied its doodles. She stuck the pages on the computer screen with tape, comparing them to samples she'd found online of Greek and Arabic handwriting. Neither was a match.

Jason Vaughn breezed through the door of the squad room and sniffed the air. "You smell good." She'd forgotten about Sabine's perfume on her wrists. Her partner glanced at her computer screen. "What's that? You planning a move to Counterterrorism?"

Davie sensed Giordano leaning over her shoulder, studying the screen. "More like the secretarial pool," he said. "That's shorthand."

25

"SHORTHAND?" DAVIE ASKED. "How do you know that?"

"My sister worked as an executive secretary for thirty years. Back when she started, shorthand was a job requirement."

"Darleen Ponti just told me Sabine was forced to learn it for a job. You think your sister can translate?"

"I'm betting it's like riding a bicycle. Once you learn, you never forget. She's retired, but I'm sure she still remembers. Give the pages to me. I'll run copies and drop them by her house tonight on my way home."

Giordano took the doodles and headed to the copy machine. A few minutes later, Davie got a call from the prison. Felix Malo had refused the interview. She wasn't surprised, just disappointed.

"By the way," the prison official said, "I checked Malo's approved visitor list. Alma Velez isn't on it and I couldn't find any record they ever spoke by telephone. Just so you know, that doesn't mean they aren't communicating. Inmates, especially gang members, send messages through official visitors to hide their contacts."

"Any chance he'll change his mind about the interview?"

"Doubt it, but I'll let you know if it happens."

Davie still hadn't been able to reach Alma Velez, so as soon as she ended the call with the prison official, she punched in the number for Velez's mother. No answer. No message option.

Davie walked upstairs to the Gang unit and found one of the detectives glaring at his computer screen. Reggie Banker was a black semi-truck in camo with an encyclopedic memory for gang members and their affiliations. He'd been working the unit for years, so she hoped he remembered Alma Velez.

His intimidating glare turned into a smile when he saw Davie. "Hey, Richards. What's cookin'?"

"I'm hoping you have some intel on an Alma Velez."

"Yeah. Heard you had a little trouble in the projects last night." He pointed to the abrasion on her forehead. "Did she put that bump on your head?"

"Not her, but it may have been one of her homies."

"Hope you gave as good as you got."

"I tried," she said. "Velez wasn't at home when I stopped by and I haven't been able to reach her since then. Any idea where she hangs out when she's not at her mom's place?"

"Haven't seen her around for a while. Malo still runs his drug operation from prison and for a while she was his personal assistant and chief financial officer all rolled into one. But I think she stopped rollin' with the gang once she had that kid of hers."

"You think she's freaked out that I'm looking into the Javi Hernandez case?"

"Alma's not the brightest bulb on the Christmas tree, but I doubt she'd order her peeps to attack a cop. Felix would be pissed if he found out. It just throws negative attention his way."

"Any idea where she might be?"

"I'll ask around."

"Is Felix the father of Velez's kid?"

"Hard to say. Even if it weren't his kid, he wouldn't admit it. That would mean his girlfriend cheated on him. If he believed that, he'd aim a nine at her temple. End of problem."

"If Malo isn't the father, who is?" Davie asked.

He shrugged. "I know a lot, but I don't know everything. It's probably a gangster, though. Those girls put up with a lot, but they still date within the community because they know their homie will kill for them if need be."

Maybe Giordano was right. Behind every homicide was a woman. Davie had no evidence to prove Felix Malo was the baby's father. For now, it was just a working theory.

"Have you heard any talk on the street about Javi Hernandez's murder?"

"Nah. Old news. Too many gangsters popped since then."

"If you hear anything, will you let me know?"

"Absolutely."

Davie walked downstairs to her desk and scoured through the Hernandez Murder Book again, looking through the reports and witness statements. The murder had taken place during the day, so many of the residents were away at work. Those who were at the apartment building claimed they hadn't seen or heard anything. Detectives had interviewed the on-site apartment manager. He was at the dentist's office the afternoon the murder went down but said there was a group of gangbangers who frequently hung out in Hernandez's apartment and sometimes lounged on a mattress in the carport where they drank booze and smoked dope. He claimed it wasn't unusual for fights to break out. Friends and the victim's family members were questioned but provided minimal information. Hernandez's fellow gang members all claimed ignorance of the murder, which wasn't unusual. Nobody wanted to be a rat.

Davie leaned back in her chair and thought about who *hadn't* been interviewed. Hernandez's mother and siblings had given statements, except for his brother Daniel, who was in the military at the time, serving in Afghanistan. He hadn't been around but he might have heard rumors.

Davie called Javi Hernandez's mother, who seemed surprised to get the call but also eager to coorperate. She confirmed that Javi's brother had been discharged from the service and was now working at a food distribution center. It was almost 7:00 p.m. The center was closed. When she pressed in Daniel Hernandez's cell number, the call went straight to message. Tomorrow she would drive to the center and interview him. Until then, she had a stop to make before she headed home.

26

TWENTY MINUTES LATER DAVIE pulled into the parking garage of Garden Vista Assisted Living Apartments, the Westside facility where her grandmother lived. After Grammy moved in, Davie had made it a habit to call or visit her every day. Sometimes the workload at Pacific Homicide had altered her routine, but her grandmother understood.

Every time she visited Grammy, she thought of her mother. She was almost as petite as Davie but with blonde hair not red, blue eyes not green. Davie admired her mother's beauty, her flawless makeup, and her closet full of expensive clothes. Not that she would break any mirrors, but Davie didn't consider herself by any means beautiful.

Her mother and Grammy were opposite in so many ways. Her grandparents' house had always been full of warmth and laughter. Grammy never got ruffled if the Thanksgiving turkey was dry or the piecrusts were hard as brass doorknobs. The family was together and that's all that mattered to her. There were never imperfect piecrusts at her mother's holiday dinners, because dessert always came from an upscale bakery in Brentwood.

In the early years, her mother treated Davie like a doll. Childhood photos showed a tiny red-haired girl with a sweet face dressed in velvet in front of the Christmas tree and in school outfits coordinated with the flair of a Hollywood stylist. When Davie became a teen, her failure to appreciate the finer points of layered skincare products, contouring with makeup, and highlighter that made cheekbones glimmer like dawn on a mountain lake made her mother throw up her hands in despair.

During those times when her mother was angry, Grammy was a tree line protecting Davie from an oncoming gale. That had created an unbreakable bond between the two. When Davie was fifteen her mother had an affair and the family split up. Davie went to live with Bear while her brother stayed with their mother and the real estate agent who'd ended her parents' marriage. The one good thing about living with her own family's dysfunction was that it helped her understand people like Boyd Ponti and Robert Montaine.

She signed in with the Garden Vista receptionist and took the creaky elevator to the second floor. The door to Grammy's apartment was unlocked but Davie knocked before entering. Her grandmother had poor eyesight from macular degeneration and she didn't want to startle her.

"It's me."

Grammy's expression brightened. "Davie, what a surprise. Come in. Can you stay a while?"

"Yup. I'm finished working for the day."

Despite her visual impairment, Grammy immediately spotted the lump on Davie's forehead. "What happened to you?"

She'd hoped her grandmother wouldn't see it. The abrasion was healing but still noticeable. "Just a bruise. Nothing major."

Grammy's cloud of snowy hair tickled Davie's nose as she kissed the soft skin of her forehead, inhaling the fragrance of her freshly laundered cotton housedress and the Jergens lotion. Davie sat on the loveseat in front of a sliding glass door that led to a patio. Her grandmother never opened it because she had trouble judging elevations and was afraid of tripping on the ledge.

"How was dinner?" she asked.

Grammy let out a heavy sigh. "You've eaten here before. I'll leave it to your imagination. The good news is Mrs. Di Vito snuck a hotplate into her room. Tomorrow night is spaghetti—unless the warden smells the sauce and busts her before dinner."

Davie picked up her cell and pretended to make a call. "I can send a couple of patrol officers to guard the door."

"Wouldn't that be a hoot?" Grammy pressed a button and her blue chair reclined. "Tell me what you're working on. Anything special?"

"I have an old unsolved murder case and a suicide that I hope to reclassify as a homicide," Davie said, giving her a brief overview of each.

"That Ponti shooting could be a thriller novel," she said. "Do you think she ran down her boss and then went into hiding?"

Davie had to admit that was a credible theory. "Why would she do that?"

"Maybe it was a love affair gone wrong. Old Nate promised to leave his wife and marry Sabine but of course he didn't. Cads never keep their promises. Some women have to learn the hard way."

"How do you know so much about cads?"

She smoothed her dress over her knees, an uncharacteristically prudish gesture. "I may be old but I'm not dead. I've seen a few things in my lifetime."

"Somehow I knew that."

"And don't forget the Russians. They're everywhere in Florida. Sabine could have been a spy. Plus, you said the woman disappeared in the ocean in Fort Lauderdale. What happened to the boat? Poppy and I went there on vacation years ago. The water is shallow. We walked out a long ways from the shore and the water still wasn't over our heads. Not sure how you lose a boat in shallow water like that."

Davie wondered that, too. It was a question that needed answering. She thought about the San Pedro Channel between Los Angeles and Catalina Island. The water was three thousand feet deep in some places. If a vessel sank, it would likely be lost permanently.

"You would make a great detective, Grammy."

"Thank you, sweetheart, but not in Florida. We read the local paper every day while we were there. That place has strange criminals. Some of them aren't very smart, either." Grammy leaned toward her and lowered her voice even though they were alone in the room. "Did I tell you about my new tablemate, Kathleen Newell? She's from Florida. Lauderdale-by-the-Sea. Her husband was involved in a Ponzi scheme. After he went to prison, her daughter moved her here. They're paying for her room because she lost everything."

"I'm sorry to hear that. It must be hard on her."

Grammy nodded. "Very hard."

It didn't seem as if her grandmother would get tired of her company any time soon, so Davie nestled into the cushions of the loveseat and listened. For the next thirty minutes they chatted about a variety of subjects, including favorite audiobooks she got from the

Braille Institute and a tuba concert the administration had arranged for the residents.

When Davie noticed her grandmother stifle a yawn she knew it was her cue to go. She removed Grammy's shoes and compression stockings, and replaced them with a pair of slippers. Then she helped her into her nightgown.

"I don't want to pry," Grammy said, "but have you met any nice young men lately?"

"I know a lot of nice men, Grammy, but I'm not dating anyone special, if that's what you're asking. If I find someone, you know I'll bring him by for your approval."

Her voice became soft and wistful. "I know you're busy with work. No pressure. I just want you to be happy."

"I have you, Grammy. How could I not be happy?"

Davie remembered Bear's comment that Jon Striker would have to pass muster with her grandmother before their relationship could advance. She didn't know if they would ever get to that point, but it was an amusing thought. She resettled her grandmother on her blue recliner and turned the TV to a news program she liked, even though the faces were a blur to her.

Grammy reached out and took her hand. "Before you leave I have something for you. It's in my bedroom on the dresser in a blue velvet box."

"What is it?"

"You'll see. Bring it to me."

Davie found the box and brought it back to the living room.

Grammy looked up at her, smiling. "Open it."

A jaw-like hinge snapped open. Inside, resting in satin was a pair of small silver drop earrings in the shape of an upside down kite and anchored by a tiny diamond. They were vintage but classic enough to look modern.

For a moment Davie was at a loss for words. "Poppy gave you these the day you got engaged."

Grammy glanced at the earrings and sighed. "He didn't have much money so they were a big splurge for him. My mother wasn't pleased because they were for pierced ears. Back in those days only cheap women punched holes through their skin. I thought they were the most beautiful things I'd ever seen. He proposed at a diner in Santa Monica. It's not there anymore. He put a nickel in the jukebox on the table and played 'When I Fall in Love.' I still remember the words of that song because I gave my heart to him completely that day. After lunch, we walked to the old Santa Monica pier and rode the carousel."

Davie ran her fingers over the soft velvet box to avoid thinking about the lump in her throat. "You used to wear them all the time. Why did you stop?"

"It's too hard to put them on anymore. Besides, I want you to have them so you always know how much Poppy and I love you."

The passing-of-the-heirlooms made Davie feel anxious. It seemed so final. Bear and her grandmother were the most important people in her life. The thought of losing either of them was painful to ponder.

She put on the earrings and squeezed Grammy's hand. "Thank you. They're precious."

At the door as she was leaving, she touched the earrings and felt an unbearable weight in her chest. She recited the words that ended all her Grammy visits. "Love you."

Her grandmother threw an air kiss. "Love you much."

On the drive home, Davie turned on the car radio. If her aim was to banish the blues, it didn't work. The wildfire near Santa Paula was still out of control. The Malibu fire continued to blast through parched canyons, destroying hundreds of acres of brush and several outbuildings. Fire crews were working 24/7. So far there had been no casualties, but the forecast looked bleak.

Once at home, Davie parked in the carport and walked around to the front door. Inside the house, she flipped on the Tiffany lamp and dropped her car keys onto Alex's eighteenth-century Chippendale walnut table. She set her purse on the kitchen breakfast bar, thinking about her conversation with Grammy—how a boat could be lost in Fort Lauderdale's shallow water, whether Sabine killed Nate Gillen over a love affair, and the possibility that Sabine was a Russian spy. Except for that last theory, the others seemed credible.

She couldn't remember the last time she'd eaten but her refrigerator held only a wilted head of iceberg lettuce and a block of Jarlsberg cheese—one slice of bread short of a sandwich. Too bad she hadn't made it to her grandmother's place earlier. Despite Grammy's joking about the bad food, the menu was healthy and as a bonus they could have spent more time together.

There was a bottle of champagne in the refrigerator, a housewarming gift from Alex Camden when she'd moved in over a year ago. Davie used to think people who drank alone were losers, but tonight it might be satisfying to unwind. She stared at the bottle chilling on the rack and then closed the door. At least champagne didn't spoil.

She strolled into the bedroom and stored her weapon in the bedside drawer. That's when she detected a faint aroma of smoke. It wasn't from the nearby wildfires. It smelled of cigarettes. She didn't smoke, nor did she allow anybody who visited to smoke for fear of damaging Alex Camden's artwork. It was possible Alex had brought a client inside her house to show a piece of art. Except he knew she had weapons in the house and would have called or texted to let her know he was dropping by.

The place had only one entrance, a fact that made Bear so uncomfortable he'd bought her a portable ladder with metal steps linked together by chain and a curved arm that was meant to hang over a windowsill in case of an emergency. She'd done a mental eye-roll when opening the box, even though she appreciated his concern.

She retrieved her .45 from the drawer and walked from room to room but found nothing out of place. The front door had been locked when she came home and there was nothing to indicate her space had been breached. She was just being paranoid. Alex always had a parade of tradesmen on the property. Possibly one of them had been smoking by her window.

Davie felt restless, so she stripped the comforter and pillows from her bed and dragged them up to the futon in the loft. She'd dubbed it the eagle's nest because the height gave her a vantage point to watch over the property. At the last minute, she dug out Bear's ladder and placed it at the foot of the futon near the window, just in case.

27

DAVIE COULDN'T SHAKE THE feeling of unease as she arrived at work the following morning. This was the third day she hadn't gotten a call-out for a fresh homicide. She mentally crossed her fingers before stopping at her partner's desk.

"Hey, Jason. You want to go for a ride?"

He looked up from his computer. "Where to?"

"Jefferson and the 405."

"Not if it involves sweating. My suit just came back from the cleaners."

"I just need to interview Javi Hernandez's brother. No sweating required."

"That's what you always say."

Davie signed out the keys to a green Crown Vic and drove to the onramp of the 405 South, merging into traffic. As she always did, she periodically checked her rearview mirror, but this time looking for a white van tailing her. There was an older model Nissan SUV in the next lane that kept close to her for a while but eventually fell back and disappeared in traffic.

She glanced at her partner. "What's happening with your cooking class?"

"You want to see a selfie with my teacher?" Vaughn pulled out his cell and thumbed through his album until he found the photo.

Davie glanced at the image on the screen. "Is that a chef's coat you're wearing?"

"Yeah," he said, his tone defensive. "It gets messy in the kitchen. I picked it up at a cooking supply store after my Sauces 101 class."

"Picked it up? It's got your name embroidered on the pocket."

His cheeks flushed. "Okay. So what?"

"So ... interesting. Let me know when you graduate from sauces and move on to pizza."

"Dough is week three, so don't hold your breath."

The food distribution center where Daniel Hernandez worked was in a warehouse with rows of multi-tiered metal shelves stacked with boxed food and canned goods. When they walked inside, a co-worker pointed to a man standing near a stack of reusable shopping bags stamped with the logo of a local grocery chain.

Daniel Hernandez had a headset threaded through his short dark hair, bobbing his head to the music. His body was bulked up from lifting weights or maybe lifting MP5s in Afghanistan. His face and eyes were pleasantly round, the double curve of his upper lip pronounced. He looked vaguely familiar but Davie wasn't sure why. She watched him open one of the bags and drop in a box of cereal from the nearby shelf.

Davie called out to him as she approached. He didn't hear her at first, so she tapped his arm. He turned, startled. He glanced at her badge and smiled as he pulled off the headphones exposing a scar running through his military haircut.

He wrapped the headset around his neck. "You here about the open house?"

Davie tilted her head. "Open house?"

He paused to study her blank expression. "You're from Harbor Division, right? They said they'd send somebody, but I didn't expect you today. We're not done filling the bags, but I can get a couple more people to help if you want to wait."

Vaughn handed him a business card. "We're not from Harbor."

He looked puzzled as he read the card. "Pacific? My mistake. We're donating food for Harbor's annual open house so I just assumed ... so, what brings you here?"

"I want to talk about your brother's murder," Davie said.

"Which brother? Javi or Sparky?"

Vaughn shot him a look. "Sparky?"

"He was lit up in a drive-by a year before Javi died."

Davie wasn't shocked that two members of the Hernandez family had been victims of violence. It was an all-too-familiar story. Still, she couldn't imagine how it felt for parents to lose two sons to murder.

"We're here about Javi," Vaughn said. "He was killed in Pacific Division a couple of years ago."

Daniel Hernandez fixed his brown eyes on her partner. "I know where he was killed, Detective. You don't have to remind me. So, what do you want? Have you reopened the case?"

"Unsolved homicides are never closed," Davie said. "We've just taken over the investigation."

He grabbed another box of cereal from the shelf and stuck it in a bag. "What do you want from me?"

"Maybe you can start by telling us about your brother," she said. "What kind of man was he? Why do you think he was targeted?"

He lifted his chin and glared at her, his voice cracking with emotion. "My dad worked his ass off mowing lawns to support his family. He charged forty bucks a month per client. He never raised his rates—not once—because he couldn't afford to lose even one. My mother cleaned other people's houses. My parents didn't have a lot of money, but they didn't raise us to be gangsters."

"How many kids in your family?" Vaughn asked.

Hernandez blew out a puff of air. "Five. I was the oldest. Javi was in the middle. My dad died when Javi was about twelve. I had to leave school and go to work. Javi took care of the younger kids after school until my mom got home. He was a sweet kid back then."

"Is your mother still alive?" Vaughn asked. Davie knew she was alive but was curious what Daniel would say about their current family dynamic.

He nodded. "She works as a school janitor now. The job is easier. The money is good and she's got benefits. I joined the Marines because I thought everyone was okay. While I was away fighting the Taliban, some homegrown terrorist was killing another brother."

Vaughn's phone chirped. He walked away to answer the call while Davie continued asking questions.

"Who do you think killed him?"

"If I knew, he'd be dead by now."

"Do you know Felix Malo?"

"Yeah. What about him?"

"What was his relationship to your brother?"

"Felix is a drug dealer. Javi was his loyal soldier. They were also friends."

"What can you tell me about Alma Velez?"

149

Hernandez resumed filling grocery bags. "I know her. I went to school with her cousin."

"Can you describe her relationship with Malo?"

"He wasn't true to her. Felix screwed anybody who wasn't in a coma."

"Did Ms. Velez know that?"

He looked away, hiding his frown from her view. "Even if she did, there was nothing she could do about it."

"Did you know she has a baby?"

The ex-soldier tossed a few more items in the grocery bags. "A lot of girls do."

"You think the baby was your brother's?"

He pivoted toward her, angry. "That's crazy. Javi had more sense than that. Look, I have work to do. I have nothing more to tell you."

She handed him her business card. "Give me a call if you want to talk."

"Talk? That's all you people do. How about finding out who killed my brother."

Davie chose her words carefully because she knew Daniel Hernandez was in pain. "I will."

28

PLAN THE DIVE AND DIVE THE PLAN.

That scuba safety mantra was worth remembering. He'd followed Saffron and her partner to the food bank, but the interview didn't interest him, so he went back to the motel room and crashed with a bottle of Scotch and fantasies of Saffron in his bed, her eyes flickering with pleasure.

He'd been camped out at a no-tell motel on Sepulveda for a couple of days because it offered nightly rates and was close to the police station where she worked. That suited his needs because he didn't know how long this job would last. The place looked clean but only a black light could confirm, and he didn't have one.

He'd slept in worse places while on assignment. He could get used to anything if there was a payday at the end of the mission, but he was growing restless as this dull job wore on. It would end soon, he guessed. In a way, he was disappointed. Following Saffron was entertaining, but she was asking questions of the wrong people and that would eventually lead her to trouble.

If the client decided to eliminate another threat, he'd suggest one of several plans he'd developed. The death would have to pass as an accident, so no freak heart attack or hit-and-run. He'd done that before. A drive-by might be plausible—this was L.A. after all, but that almost seemed like a cliché.

He was stretched out on the bed, listening through the paper-thin walls to the man next door screwing a hooker when his client called, wanting to discuss the surveillance notes he'd sent by encrypted email earlier that morning. His mouth was dry as he waited for new instructions. After he got the go-ahead his body relaxed.

As soon as he ended the call, he felt the energy escape from his gut and pulse through his arms and hands. The hooker was getting loud. He threw his cell against the wall to shut her up. He could tell by the sound of shattering plastic that the phone was toast. Didn't matter. It was just one of many he used and he wouldn't need that one again. He couldn't leave the carcass for somebody to find, though, for fear they'd raise the phone from the dead. He picked up the broken parts and tossed them into his backpack.

He was smart enough to know that eliminating one person wouldn't stop the LAPD from uncovering the truth about his client, but it might slow them down. He would make it seem like an accident. By the time they figured out the truth, if ever, he'd be on an extended vacation, basking in the sun on a beach in Turks and Caicos. He went to his bag and reached into the pocket of the jeans he'd worn the day he'd started this job. His lock picks were there. His St. Christopher medal wasn't. His pulse spiked as he tore through his bag and then took the room apart looking for it.

It was gone.

29

DAVIE LEFT THE FOOD distribution center and found Vaughn standing outside near the car, still talking on his cell. She hoped the conversation was something routine and not a new homicide. Her partner held up his index finger, indicating he'd just be a minute. A moment later, he ended the call.

"What was that all about?" Davie asked.

"An anonymous tip about my case. Could be nothing. Could be everything."

She got into the car and started the engine. "What did you think of Daniel Hernandez?"

Vaughn joined her in the passenger's seat. "The guy has a Sequoia-sized chip on his shoulder. At least, he must have heard rumors about his brother's murder, so why not tell us?"

"Maybe it's in his best interests to keep quiet."

As soon as they got back to the station, Davie returned her attention to the death of Sabine Ponti. She called the insurance investigator who'd processed Jack Blasdel's boat claim to ask if she found anything suspicious about the case.

"Most of my cases are suspicious," she said, "especially when there's loss of life. In this instance, the missing person was said to be an accomplished sailor who borrowed the boat from our insured. We first look for what's called hard fraud. That's when the claimant simply manufactures the loss. That wasn't what happened here. The boat was lost. Next we determine if the claimant added fraudulent information to an otherwise legitimate claim. That's called soft fraud. For example, saying the boat was in Bristol condition or that expensive valuables were inside when the vessel went missing. Mr. Blasdel didn't hide the fact the boat was old and never even claimed it was seaworthy. Nor did he say there was anything of value inside. Risk Management didn't want to invite any lawsuits, so they told me to get the claim off the books. The boat wasn't worth much and we couldn't prove the loss involved fraud, so we sent Mr. Blasdel a check."

"Did Ms. Ponti's family ever sue?"

"Not yet. The statute of limitations in Florida is two years. If they don't file soon, it'll be too late. We're betting they've moved on."

"Do you know if Ms. Ponti had life insurance?"

"We always check in case the amount of life insurance was unusually high, which could indicate some broader crime like suicide or even murder. Ms. Ponti was covered through her work, but the policy wasn't worth much, twenty-five hundred dollars as I recall. Three months after her disappearance, her parents declared her dead and filed a claim."

"How is that possible? In California the waiting period is five years."

"It's the same in Florida. It's unusual but the family can file a petition with the court, claiming the missing person was in 'peril of death' at sea and in fact died. If there's no evidence she used her credit cards

154

or bank accounts after the disappearance and she hasn't been seen alive, the courts can declare her dead."

Ending the call, Davie sat for a few minutes processing the information. It was interesting the Pontis declared their daughter dead so soon after the Coast Guard had suspended their search. In Davie's experience, families generally waited longer because they didn't want to accept the loss of their loved one. Darleen Ponti had told her Sabine's parents were upset with her over the affair and the firing, but this reaction seemed extreme.

Davie had to speak with the widow of Sabine's employer at the Seaglass Cafe. After a short search, she located Ms. Lacy Gillen still living in Florida in the house she had once shared with her husband, Nate. A housesitter answered the call and explained that Gillen was on vacation on the island of Tortola in the British Virgin Islands without her cell. In the event Gillen called home, she promised to pass along Davie's message. The sitter refused to say where she was staying and warned Davie in the politest terms not to hold her breath waiting for a return call.

Since the widow was out of her reach at the moment, Davie used her desk phone to call the Fort Lauderdale Police Department and was transferred to the Criminal Investigation Division and a female detective named Brooks.

"Nate Gillen's death is classified as Vehicular Homicide," Brooks said. "The case is still open. I was just reviewing the file a few days ago. If it helps, I can give you an overview from my notes."

Davie poised her pen on her notebook tablet. "That would be much appreciated."

She heard Brooks typing on a keyboard and then a pause. "The night Mr. Gillen died, he called for a tow, said he had car trouble. He was standing by the side of the car waiting for the truck to arrive when another vehicle hit him. The tow driver found the body. There were no skidmarks to indicate the other vehicle tried to stop. It was night and there were no witnesses, so no license plate number or descriptions. No suspects."

"Did you inspect the car?"

"The only thing the mechanics found was a faulty fuel gauge. Mr. Gillen simply ran out of gas."

"Are you sure the gauge hadn't been tampered with?"

An edge crept into Brooks's tone. "Are you suggesting we don't know what we're doing?"

"Of course not," Davie said. "I assume you interviewed Lacy Gillen."

"We did. She took it hard. Why are you asking these questions? You have information about the case?"

"Maybe. Have you heard of a woman named Sabine Ponti? She worked at Gillen's restaurant. She disappeared on a sailing trip shortly after her boss was killed."

"Sure, I remember her. That was a Broward County Sheriff's Department investigation, but our two cases dovetailed so we shared information. Her disappearance caught our attention. The owner of a restaurant dies under suspicious circumstances and a few days later his employee turns up missing and presumed dead."

"What do you know about the search for Ms. Ponti?"

"The marina office called the Coast Guard when she didn't return the boat, so they were first on the scene. They did everything possible to find her, even took a specialized cadaver dog on a boat to see if it could pick up a scent from the surface of the water. The dog had a ninety-five percent success rate, but it never alerted to a body. They kept looking but eventually they shifted from rescue to recovery."

"I hear the near-shore water is shallow," Davie said, remembering Grammy's memory of her trip to Fort Lauderdale. "Did they ever find the boat?"

"Not at first. There are three large reefs that parallel the shoreline. In some places you can swim out a hundred yards and the water's still only fifteen feet deep. It's a mile to the second reef line, where the water drops to fifty feet deep. Once you get to the third reef, it's a hundred feet deep and the current can be strong but the moving water makes for better visibility. That's why they expected to find the boat, but even from the air there was no sign of it or of any floating debris."

"Could the boat have floated beyond the reefs and sank in deep water?"

"Possibly, but that's not what happened. The vessel drifted off in the current and eventually ran aground in South Carolina and broke apart. The boat was identified by a documentation number painted on what was left of the hull. Otherwise, there was no evidence to be found. The boat was a total loss.

Davie guessed that would explain why no one notified the insurance company that the boat had been recovered. "How did it get so far without anybody noticing?"

"Good question. The boat had a head start because it took a while for the marina office to report Ponti missing. I'm not making excuses, but the Gulf Stream current flows north at a fast pace through the Straits of Florida. It's a big ocean out there with lots of boats. Fort Lauderdale alone has fifty thousand registered yachts—not that they're all out of the slip at the same time. There's nothing to stop a ghost boat except for land or another vessel."

"Did you ever find a connection between Gillen's death and Ponti's disappearance?"

"Nope. Between the two agencies, we questioned over seventy people, including Ponti's coworkers and Gillen's friends and known associates."

"I heard a rumor that Gillen and Ponti were having an affair. Can you confirm that?"

"A waitress named Karen Nord floated that theory in my interview with her, but there was no corroborating evidence—in fact, just the opposite. A cook leaving the restaurant after his shift told me he saw Gillen and *Nord* making out in his car in the parking lot. And Nord may not have been the only employee he was screwing. Almost everyone who worked there described Gillen as a horndog who went after pretty women, including Ms. Ponti. A couple of people said her attempts to avoid him made them uncomfortable."

"And yet nobody reported him."

"People need to keep their jobs."

"Did you find any witnesses who saw Ms. Ponti's boat leave the marina?"

"We found a dockworker who claimed he saw her with a man the day she disappeared, but his description of the guy was hazy. We thought it might have been the boat owner, but Blasdel denied it and the witness couldn't identify him from a photo lineup. Later, we found out the witness had several citations for disorderly intoxication and driving while under the influence. That neutralized him as a witness. After all was said and done, we found no clear connection."

"What can you tell me about the restaurant?"

"Several employees told me Gillen was having financial problems until he consulted a business advisor. That helped for a while, but I guess it wasn't enough. After he died, his widow closed the place."

"Who was the business advisor?"

"Lacy Gillen had no idea. Seemed weird her husband hadn't told her, and we found no records of the consultations. So what do you know about the case?"

Davie told Brooks that Sabine had survived the boating accident. She had moved to Los Angeles and resurfaced as Sara Montaine, only to die in a gunstore a year later.

Brooks whistled. "Well, that's interesting."

Davie tapped her pen on the desk. "Can you email me a copy of your report and maybe the witness statements so I can compare notes?"

Brooks hesitated. "I'll ask my boss. I don't anticipate a problem as long as you send information our way, too."

Davie felt relieved. "I found a photo in Ponti's property. If I email it to you, can you tell me if you recognize anybody?"

"Can you send it now?"

Davie emailed the scanned photo and waited on the phone for Brooks to respond. It only took a few moments.

"The man in the Hawaiian shirt is Nate Gillen," she said. "The other two men I don't recognize, but I can run the photo through our facial recognition technology to see if either of them is in our driver's license database."

All law enforcement agencies in L.A. County, including the LAPD, had access to FRT and wireless video cameras that did real-time face recognition. Since one of the men in the photo had been murdered and that murder might be linked to Sabine Ponti's death, Davie had a responsibility to identify the other two men. The picture was taken in Florida, so she took Brooks up on her offer.

But Davie adhered to the belt-and-suspenders philosophy of law enforcement, so as soon as she ended the call with Detective Brooks, she arranged for the photo to be analyzed by LAPD facial recognition analysts as well.

30

DAVIE HAD JUST CRADLED the phone when she noticed the blinking message light. She punched in her code and listened to a voicemail from Reggie Banker in the Gang Unit. She walked upstairs and found him checking a Cal-Gangs profile on his computer.

"Got your call," she said. "What's up?"

Banker glanced up from the screen. "I might have a lead on the whereabouts of Alma Velez. Thought you'd want to know. I got a tip last night about a drug dealer I've been tracking—street name Loco. My snitch tells me when Loco isn't selling drugs in Venice he crashes at his cousin's house in Inglewood. Loco hangs with Velez. He might know where she's staying. A few of us are going to the boardwalk tomorrow afternoon to make a buy. You ever work undercover?"

"I've bent the rules in a few interrogations. Does that count?"

He chuckled. "In that case, I won't ask you to come along. Too dangerous."

"Dangerous for me or for you?"

"You're all kind of dangerous, Davie. For one thing you look too much like—"

Davie held up her hand to stop him. "If you say Raggedy Ann, Howdy Doody, a fire hydrant, or a member of the Irish Mafia, our friendship is over."

He tilted back his head and laughed. "You know me better than that, but I don't see you passing as a gangsta queen."

Davie put her hands on her hips so he wouldn't miss the point. "I can look 'street' if that's your worry."

"That would be something to see. You'll need a couple of tats and a hoochie-mama dress."

She didn't have anything in her closet that qualified, but there was a thrift store on Venice Boulevard. She'd carve out some time to drop by and look through the gang-queen couture. There must be a few pieces that would suit her purpose. Of course, she'd have to sterilize them before they touched her body.

She gave him the thumbs-up sign. "I can manage that."

Davie returned to her desk and opened the Hernandez Murder Book to Section 14, the witness statements. Everybody in the Palms apartment building where Javi Hernandez had lived and died had been interviewed. At the time, all claimed they hadn't seen anything. Davie intended to interview all of them again. First, she needed to find out how many of those tenants still lived in the building. After two years, somebody might have had a crisis of conscience and be willing to talk.

The place was under new ownership. Over the phone, the current manager told her the rent had been raised after the building underwent a major upgrade. A lot of the old-timers had moved out. Davie read the list of occupants from the time of the murder while the manager gave her the dates they'd moved and a forwarding address, if the tenant had left one. Her interest spiked when he got to Emma Wainford, who had moved out the day after the murder.

"Do you have Wainford's address?" Davie asked.

"Nope. She didn't give notice, so she forfeited her first and last month's rent and the security deposit. Didn't even take all her stuff, just her cat."

"What did you do with her possessions?"

"We paid a service to haul everything to the dump."

After Davie ended the call, she searched through the witness statements for the interview with Wainford. It wasn't there. There was a printout of her driver's license photo and a criminal records search, showing she had no arrests. The detective's notes stated he'd found her at her parents' home in Oregon but was told her doctor had left instructions that the young woman was "too traumatized to speak to anyone." It didn't appear there had been any further follow up. That was about to change.

31

Before Davie had a chance to search for Emma Wainford, she saw Giordano walk into the squad room carrying several sheets of paper clenched in his fist.

"My sis came through," he said, grinning. "I hope you can decipher this. Doesn't mean shit to me." He handed her the documents and headed for his desk. "Let me know when you figure it out."

"Thank her for me."

"Already did."

Davie placed the Hernandez Murder Book back on the shelf above her desk between the 187 bookends. She fanned the doodle pages across the desktop. Giordano's sister had done a good job. There were two sets of documents—a simple translation of the doodles and another with the numbers organized into a pro forma monthly cash flow statement, four pages in total. The top of each page read RECEIPTS, which included cash sales and loans. The bottom was reserved for disbursements. Each page represented a month of income and expenses for the Seaglass Cafe, Nate Gillen's Florida restaurant. The increase in sales over the four months before Gillen's death was dramatic.

Davie used the calculator on her cell to work the numbers. In November, Seaglass's sales averaged around $1,200 per day for a monthly total of $36,000 for the month. Over the next four months, the gross receipts doubled every day until the income reached a plateau of $9,600 per day, over a quarter million dollars for the last month recorded in Sabine's doodles.

Under DISBURSEMENTS was a list of payments to various vendors, including liquor and food suppliers, linen service, and personnel. Davie had never run a restaurant, but the costs seemed normal until she came to several exorbitant expenditures for advertising and public relations to companies called Advantage, Hydra, and Pomme. All of them had LLCs after their names, which she'd learned from a previous case stood for limited liability company. Some payments didn't reference invoice numbers or even services rendered. It was possible those exorbitant payments were legitimate expenses. Overcharging wasn't a crime as far as she knew, but she was suspicious.

Davie searched online for the companies but found no websites identifying who they were or what they did. She knew from that previous case that an LLC's ownership was hidden from the public. That wasn't illegal, but many of those organizations had little or no physical presence except for a post office box. Some were shell companies used for tax evasion or other illicit transactions.

On the final sheet was a list of banks, some in Florida, but many outside the US, including Panama, the Cayman Islands, and one account in the British Virgin Islands. Davie didn't need to be a forensic accountant to peg those places as safe havens where rich people parked their money to avoid government scrutiny. Next to each bank was a list of dates and wire transfers for large amounts of money. She knew there was a way to search for the history of wire transfers, but she didn't know how.

Gillen's windfall profits at the Seaglass Cafe looked too good to be true. Boyd Ponti had told Davie his sister suspected something shady was going on at the restaurant and wanted to check it out, but how did she get access to its financial records and why hadn't she photocopied the actual documents or at least taken shots with her cell camera?

Written at the bottom of the final sheet was a ten-digit number with a question mark behind it. A short search confirmed it was the telephone number of the Miami, Florida, field office of the FBI.

If Sabine had discovered evidence of a crime at the restaurant, the question mark might indicate she was planning to blow the whistle. Before doing that, she may have conveyed her fears to somebody she shouldn't have trusted. When her boss ended up dead, she had reason to believe she was next. She staged her death with the help of Jack Blasdel and resurfaced in Los Angeles as cat-loving Sara Montaine. A year later somebody silenced her permanently. The question was, how did they find her?

One of the offshore accounts listed in the doodles was in the British Virgin Islands. Lacy Gillen was at this moment somewhere in Tortola. Davie wondered if she was visiting her money.

Davie left a message for an FBI special agent she knew, asking if the bureau had been investigating Nate Gillen. After that, she tapped another number on her cell display and waited.

"Homicide Special, Detective Striker speaking. How can I help you?"

"You can tell me everything you know about money laundering."

32

STRIKER WAS DUE IN a meeting but promised to call her as soon as he was free. Until then, she would search for Lacy Gillen, because the wife might be the connection between her husband's death and Sabine's disappearance.

Davie had never been to Tortola and had no idea where Lacy Gillen might be staying, but she'd searched for obscure information before, so she found an online list of resorts on the island, created a pretext, and began calling each of them. It took over an hour, but she finally found Gillen booked at the Apple Bay Resort & Spa, not far from the Beef Island airport. Davie asked to speak to her but was told Gillen did not wish to be disturbed during her stay.

Frustrated, she turned her attention back to the Hernandez case. Emma Wainford had moved out of the apartment the day after the murder without giving notice. The young woman had left behind food, personal items, and a boatload of forfeited money. Her parents and an attending physician claimed she was traumatized. Not surprising; her neighbor had been stabbed fifteen times and left to die. Davie had to speak with her.

Emma Wainford had no criminal record, so she searched through a non–law enforcement database and found the woman living in North University Park, a historic neighborhood near the University of Southern California in Southwest Division.

Vaughn was out in the field investigating the anonymous tip he'd received. Normally she would have asked one of the other detectives to go with her to the interview, but everybody was busy working their own cases. She felt no threat from Emma Wainford and decided to go alone.

The decorative trim adorning the three-story Victorian house was cracked and faded. Its dowdy towers and turrets needed the level of restoration only a rich preservationist could afford. Judging from the bicycles chained to the railing of the wraparound porch and the thrift-store beanbag chairs, the place was operating as a boarding house, most likely for students.

Davie walked up the sloping lawn to the front entrance but before she could knock, the door burst open and a young man bolted out, nearly knocking her over.

"Sorry," he said, looking stricken.

"I'm here to see Emma Wainford."

"She's upstairs, studying."

"Can you get her down here?"

"Nope," he said, unchaining one of the bikes. "Gotta run. I'm late to class." He rolled the bike down the steps. "She's on the second floor, first room on the right." Then he mounted the bike and rode off, leaving the front door wide open.

Davie heard a door slam as she stepped into the foyer. Cooking odors baked into the wallpaper and the smell of ancient dust slammed her olfactory receptors. There were no curtains on the bay window but at least the grimy glass provided some privacy. The living room was empty except for thrift store furniture that served as a dumpsite for everything from textbooks to empty potato chip bags. A pair of tighty-whities hung from a chandelier above a slouching sofa.

The wooden stairs creaked as Davie climbed toward the second floor. In the distance she heard the ear-splitting thrum of a percussion instrument. When she reached Emma's room, she put her ear to the door, listening for sounds of life inside but heard nothing.

Davie knocked on the door. "Ms. Wainford? I'm with the LAPD. I need to speak to you."

Emma Wainford did not answer the second, louder knock. Davie turned the knob. Meeting no resistance, the door swung open, revealing a monk's cell of a room with a mattress on the floor and clothes hanging from a department store dressing-room rack.

She found Wainford crouched in a corner of the closet among duffle bags and boxes. She was a willowy young woman with pasty skin and a trembling chin who looked stricken with a bad case of Blue Light Fever, that jittery feeling when a patrol car's flashing blue lights are bearing down on you. You don't know what you did, but you're sure you're good for something. Davie had no idea why this girl was hiding but hoped her nerves had something to do with Javi Hernandez's murder.

"Ms. Wainford?"

Wainford wiped away a tear. "How did you find me?"

Davie held out her badge. "I'm a detective. It's what I do for a living. We need to talk."

Wainford shook her head. "My roommates can't see us together."

Davie closed the door to the hallway and waited for Wainford to crawl out of the closet. There were no chairs in the room, so Davie leaned against the peeling paint of the windowsill. Wainford slouched on the mattress, staring at her hands.

Davie took the pen from her notebook and prepared to write. "How long have you lived here?"

Wainford dabbed at the moisture in her eyes with her finger. "About three months. I'm in the film school at USC. This place is all I can afford right now."

"You moved out of the apartment in Palms the day after Javi Hernandez's murder. The police never interviewed you. Why?"

She wiped her nose on the sleeve of her shirt. "They came to the door that day, but I was afraid they'd kill me if I talked to the police."

"They?"

"Thugs, gangbangers, whatever you call them. I hid in the bathroom for hours until the police left. The next morning, I packed some clothes, grabbed my cat, and went to stay with a friend. I was a mess. I didn't want to leave the house. I had to drop out of school and move back in with my parents. They saved my life."

"Tell me everything you know about the day of the murder. Start from the beginning."

Wainford grabbed a pillow and hugged it to her chest. "Like I said, I was going to USC. Rent in a decent part of town was crazy expensive and I barely had enough money to pay for tuition. I found the Palms apartment on craigslist. The place looked skuzzy but it was cheap and the manager seemed nice so I moved in."

"Where were you when the murder went down?"

She let out a heavy sigh. "I didn't go to class that day because I had a paper due and I wasn't finished. Around two o'clock I heard loud music and people laughing. It was hard to concentrate. I was afraid to say anything because I'd seen scary-looking guys hanging out in the carport. I think they were doing drugs."

"How long did the noise go on?"

"At least an hour. Finally, I couldn't take it anymore. I put on my earphones and turned the music up as high as I could stand it. At around three o'clock I glanced out the window and saw a man running down the street. I wasn't getting anything done, so I decided to go study at the library. I grabbed my computer and walked down the steps toward the carport. When I got there I saw that man lying on a mattress covered in blood. It was horrible."

"Can you describe the man who ran away?"

"Twenties. Hispanic."

"Did you recognize him?"

She shook her head. "He was nice-looking, though. He had on a sweatshirt with one of the seven dwarfs on the back—Grumpy, I think. That seemed weird. That's all I remember."

"Will you come to the station and look at some photos? See if you can identify the man?"

Wainford rested her head on the pillow. Her voice was barely audible. "I don't have a car."

"I can drive you there and bring you back. It won't take long, thirty minutes to put together some mug shots to see if you can ID the guy."

She looked up and wiped at her eyes. "Do I have to go?"

"No, you don't."

Davie remembered an Edmund Burke quote her high school history teacher had posted on the wall of his classroom. *All that is required for evil to triumph is for good men to do nothing.*

She considered mentioning that to Emma Wainford but in the end, it wasn't necessary.

33

Twenty minutes later Wainford waited in an interview room in the detective squad room while Davie sat at her computer selecting pictures. Her photo show-up would be arranged in a folder behind six cutout frames. She remembered her first six-pack. Her sergeant laughed when he saw it. "Jeez, Richards. I said pick people who resemble the suspect, not the Gosselin sextuplets. Do it over."

Even though he had since died, the gang member who'd been in possession of Hernandez's car the day after the murder was the original suspect, so she included his photo and used his physical characteristics as a template for the others. If he were the person Emma Wainford had seen running from the crime scene, it would help her close the case.

There was no shortage of mug shots for the other five photos. There were over 450 active gangs in the City of Los Angeles with 45,000-plus members. In the past three years there had been about

190 gang homicides. The men in the photos just had to share some physical characteristics with the suspect.

Davie chose three booking photos of known Westside gang members with violent crimes on their rap sheets, including Felix Malo. The last two photos were selected from Department of Motor Vehicle files. They were people she *knew* weren't involved in Javi Hernandez's murder, including a patrol officer she'd worked with in Southeast Division. To finish the process, she stripped all identifying information from the photos, assorted them randomly, and made two copies. Under each photo, she wrote a number from one to six.

As Davie headed for the interview room, she thought about stories she'd heard from the bad-old days when a detective would hold up a six-pack with his finger tapping the photo he wanted the witness to choose. Those days were history, but it didn't hurt to remind herself how crucial it was to remain neutral when presenting the show-up to Wainford. Not all witnesses were good at picking a suspect from a two-dimensional photo, but if she felt any undue pressure or influence in the selection process, her testimony could fall apart in court.

Through the window of the interview room, Davie saw Wainford's head resting on the battered wood table. She looked up when Davie laid the copy in front of her. The wording of the admonition was on the back of the photo display folder, but Davie had done this so many times she had almost committed the script to memory.

"Just so you know," Davie said. "The photo of the person you saw leaving the apartment that day may or may not be included here. You are under no obligation to select any of the pictures. When you're considering the photos, remember that people change their hair. They gain and lose weight. They sometimes alter their appearance. But if you recognize the man you saw, please circle the photo and initial below it."

Wainford nodded and then stared at the pictures. Her focus shifted from one man to another. After about thirty seconds, she said. "I don't know."

Davie kept her voice low and calm, hoping her tone didn't convey disappointment. "It's okay if you don't know. Take your time."

"You don't understand," she said. "I just don't know if I want to get involved."

Wainford's words were a punch to Davie's gut. "Are you saying you recognize one of the photos but you don't want to tell me?"

Her voice was barely audible. "I wish I could be brave like you, but I'm not."

Reluctant or fearful witnesses were always a challenge for law enforcement. Davie decided against guilt-tripping Wainford. Instead, she let the young woman's words bounce against the walls of the interview room until the echoes faded.

Wainford focused on her folded hands. "You're mad at me, aren't you?"

Davie released the breath she'd been holding. "No. I'm not mad."

"Yes, you are. I can tell. Look, I've been a mess for two years. I'm finally getting my life back together. I can't go back to that place."

"We have witness assistance programs—"

She interrupted Davie mid-sentence. "No. I'm sorry. Can I go now?"

Davie slowly stood and picked up the photos. "Sure. I'll ask somebody to take you home."

The reserve officer who worked in Autos agreed to drive Wainford back to North University Park. Davie returned to her desk where Detective Giordano was waiting for her.

"She ID anybody?" he asked.

Davie shook her head. "She didn't want to get involved."

"You can't win 'em all, kid," he said. "At least you turned up a new witness. Maybe you'll find someone else with more guts." He grabbed a stack of reports and headed toward Records.

Vaughn popped his head over the partition wall. He pointed to his eye, formed a heart with his fingers, and pointed to Davie. She raised her index finger toward her temple and made a circular motion, the universal gesture for *you're crazy*. Vaughn was clearly joking, but she wasn't in the mood for his corny humor. He must have noticed her frown because he sank back down out of sight.

Davie's notebook tablet was almost empty. She strolled toward Records, intending to pick up a new one in the supply room. In the hallway, she was startled to see an ashen Emma Wainford coming through the back door followed by the reserve officer. Davie glanced at him and frowned. He shrugged.

"Did you forget something?" Davie asked.

Wainford shook her head. "Number four. That's the man I saw."

Davie's breath caught in her throat. Photo number four was Daniel Hernandez, Javi's brother.

34

DAVIE HAD INCLUDED DANIEL Hernandez's DMV photo in the six-pack for the same reason she'd added her friend from Southeast Division. They both looked somewhat like the man who took Javi Hernandez's car and neither were suspects in his murder. Her friend was a cop. Daniel had an alibi: he'd been in Afghanistan, fighting in a war. She didn't understand why Wainford had placed him at the scene of the murder.

A few minutes later, Davie watched as Emma Wainford poised her pen over the six-pack, circled, and then initialed the photo of Daniel Hernandez. Davie gave no hint about the correctness of her selection, nor did she reveal Daniel Hernandez's name.

Davie ticked off the remaining items on her show-up checklist, asking Wainford to note any differences between the man in the photo and the person she'd seen leaving the scene of the murder. Afterward, Davie cautioned her not to discuss the photos or her selection with anyone. She didn't want the results tainted should Wainford talk with other witnesses. When the interview was over, Davie asked the reserve officer to drive the young woman home.

After she left the squad room, Jason Vaughn walked around the corner to Davie's workstation and folded his lanky body into the chair next to hers. He'd obviously been following the drama.

"You trust her memory?" he asked. "It's been two years since the shooting and you know how unreliable eyewitnesses can be."

"She seemed confident Daniel was the guy, but I agree it doesn't make sense. His mother swore her son was in Afghanistan at the time of the murder. Either she believed he was or she knew he wasn't and wanted to protect him."

"What motive would Daniel have to kill his little brother? He told us the family was close."

"People lie, Jason, sometimes even Marines."

"Daniel said another brother was killed in a drive-by. Maybe he freaked when he found out Javi was selling drugs for Felix Malo. He wanted to school the kid before he left town but things got tense and—*kapow!* Bro ends up dead."

"Maybe."

"Look," Vaughn said. "My investigation just hit a wall. That anonymous tip I told you about was a hoax. I have time if you need help."

Davie was up her to chest in quicksand, juggling both the Hernandez and Ponti cases. She *could* use a hand. "Daniel's mother said he was stationed at the Marine Corp Base at Camp Pendleton before deploying to Afghanistan. Oceanside can't be more than ninety miles from the murder scene. If Daniel Hernandez was on the base and not in Afghanistan, he could have made the trip to his brother's apartment in a couple of hours, killed him, and returned before anybody knew he was missing. Can you call Pendleton and confirm the date he was shipped out?"

Vaughn gave her the thumbs-up sign. "I'm on it."

35

DAVIE HAD NO PLANS to contact Daniel Hernandez until the base commander confirmed his whereabouts on the day of the murder, but in preparation for the interview she called the community food bank to get his work schedule. It was only 4:45 p.m. but a recorded message informed her the center was already closed for the day.

Before leaving the station, she slipped the transcribed shorthand doodles and the pro forma cash flow statements into an envelope, planning to study them in depth at home. Before driving to Bel Air, she detoured by the thrift store to buy clothes for the undercover gig with Reggie Banker the following day. She'd just thrown the getup in the trunk of her Camaro when her cell phone buzzed with an incoming call. It was Jon Striker.

"Where are you?" he said.

"On my way home."

"Sorry I couldn't get back to you sooner on your money laundering question," he said. "Things got complicated at work. I'm available now if you want to talk."

"I have some financial documents I want you to look at, so we should meet. But the Lucky Duck is too noisy."

There was a short silence and then, "I can stop by your place. It's on my way home."

Davie felt a knot forming in her stomach as she tried to remember the last time she'd cleaned the guesthouse. There were probably crumbs on the kitchen counter and dust bunnies collecting in the corners of the living room, not to mention the mess she'd left in the bathroom that morning before leaving for work—toothpaste she'd accidentally squirted all over the sink. Worse yet, Striker would have to walk through the bedroom to get there. He'd see the unmade bed and the ratty oversized T-shirt she slept in. She favored it because it was stretchy and didn't bind her in knots when she tossed and turned.

"Okay." Davie stretched out the word, hoping her tone didn't sound too tepid as she gave him the address. "Thirty minutes?"

The tires of the Camaro screeched as she tore out of the thrift store parking lot, ignoring the speed limit. She arrived at the cottage in twenty minutes—ten minutes to spare. Once inside, she bolted into the bathroom and used her fingernail to scrape the petrified toothpaste from the sink and swept a pile of assorted cosmetics from the countertop into a drawer of the vanity. She didn't have time to empty the wastebasket, so she placed two tissues on top to camouflage whatever was in there.

Her hair fell from the bun as she ripped out the band that held it in place. A few precious seconds in front of the mirror was all it took to fluff the red curls into a cloud around her shoulders and down her back. At the last minute, she swiped a layer of gloss on her lips and tossed the comforter over the bed. It wouldn't pass military inspection but if she kept the lights dimmed, Striker might not notice the chaos.

She was jogging to the kitchen to tidy up when she heard the doorbell ring. Her breath caught in her throat. No time to clean the sink or dispose of the crumbs.

Striker stood at her front door with the overhead porch light casting shadows on his angular face. Davie inhaled the faint odor of menthol as she gestured him inside with a grand sweep of her arm, wondering if he'd recently been at a crime scene.

His gaze moved across the room. "Nice setup."

"Yeah, I was lucky to find the place," she said, walking toward the kitchen. "Can I get you something to drink?"

His fingers loosened the knot of his tie. "If you're talking alcohol, then scotch. Neat."

Davie held up her hand to cut him off. "Let me rephrase the question. How about a glass of champagne? That's all I have."

He tilted his head and smiled. "Let me rephrase the answer. Champagne sounds good."

She pulled the Dom Perignon from the refrigerator where it had been chilling since Alex Camden had given it to her a year ago. "Stand back. I'm not good with corks."

He reached for the bottle. "I worked as a waiter in college. Shall I open it?"

"Marry me?"

Striker's forehead creased in a frown. "Pardon?"

Her cheeks burned with embarrassment as she handed him the bottle. "Sorry. It's a joke. My partner and I … never mind."

He raised his eyebrows when he read the label. The foil crackled as he pulled it off and unwound the wire. Davie's eyes widened as

Striker grabbed a dishtowel from the counter near the sink, disturbing the leftover crumbs from her morning toast. Or were they from the day before? Striker didn't comment, but he was a detective. He must have noticed.

He looked at her with a steady gaze. "Here's the only waiter advice you'll ever hear from me. Tilt the bottle. Cover the cork with a towel. Turn the bottom of the bottle with your hand."

While Striker focused on opening the champagne, Davie brushed the crumbs into her hand and stuffed them in her pocket.

The cork slid off with a hiss.

"Impressive." She pulled a couple of juice glasses from the cupboard. "These are lame, but they're all I have."

"They're perfect." He filled the glasses and handed her one.

"Thanks for coming over on such short notice," she said.

Striker removed his suit jacket and draped it over the back of a chair at the breakfast bar, exposing his crisp white shirt. He made no attempt to roll up his sleeves, and that left Davie wishing for X-ray vision to read the mysterious tattoo inked on the inside of his right forearm with that word ending in the letter *e*.

"I was curious when you mentioned money laundering," he said, sliding onto the chair. "I'm not an expert, but I worked a case at Metro Forgery before I transferred to Robbery Homicide."

Metro Forgery was a unit within the Commercial Crimes Division that investigated white-collar crimes. Both CCD and Robbery Homicide were high-profile divisions. The fact that he'd worked both was no mediocre accomplishment.

Davie sat across from him and removed the financial statements from the envelope, spreading them across the counter. "This has to do with that year-old suicide case I told you about. I've turned up enough evidence to convince my boss there was something suspicious about the victim's death. He's not ready to reclassify it yet, but I'm sure he will. If I can't persuade him with new evidence, he'll make me stop."

What Davie didn't tell Striker was that she wouldn't stop, even if it meant investigating on her own time and with her own money.

"Tough situation, but you'll figure it out."

Davie took a sip of the champagne and summarized in great detail the events surrounding Sabine Ponti's disappearance and eventual death. She kept talking until she unspooled everything she'd learned in the past few days.

"Look at this," she said, pointing to the cash flow statements. "Sabine started working at the Seaglass Cafe in July three years ago, but she didn't begin keeping this ledger until the following November, which tells me that's when she noticed something suspicious. That November, the cafe's monthly income was around thirty-six grand. But look how the numbers doubled starting in December and continued doubling for the next three months. By February, the monthly income had grown to over a quarter-million dollars. There were no entries in March, because that's when her boss Nate Gillen was killed and Sabine disappeared."

She studied Striker's dark eyelashes as he pored over the documents. His face was motionless except for the movement of his eyes under the lids as he read. His expression seemed placid, almost as if he were sleeping. Davie couldn't take her eyes off him.

"It's possible sales legitimately increased," he said, looking up, "but more likely Gillen was mixing dirty money with legitimate income."

Davie knew banks were required by law to tell the Feds about cash deposits of more than ten grand in a single day. Gillen seemed to have followed those rules to avoid detection.

The champagne bubbles tickled her nose as she took still another sip from the glass. "I understand the basics of money laundering. You have illegal cash. You don't want the police to confiscate it or the IRS to tax it. And for sure you don't want anyone tracing it back to its criminal origins. So, what do you do?"

"If the money wasn't legitimate income from the restaurant, then somebody probably gave it to Gillen to launder. Those bank deposits he made are called placement—moving dirty money one degree away from its illegal source."

"Once the money is deposited in a bank account, it's clean, right?"

Striker shook his head. "Not clean enough. That's where step two comes in—layering. The goal is to hide those initial bank deposits under layers of paperwork by moving the money multiple times to multiple banks until tracking it becomes difficult, if not impossible."

"What about all those payments to LLCs? I couldn't find information on any of them. They appear to be shell companies. And those wire transfers to offshore banks? They don't seem like normal business practices for a restaurant."

"Those payments and transfers are the final stage—integration. By moving the funds out of the country, Gillen hoped to obscure the source of the money so nobody would ever question it."

The champagne was making Davie feel a bit lightheaded. "Wouldn't the government notice all those foreign transfers?"

"Not necessarily. The Treasury department has a division called Financial Crimes Enforcement Network. It collects data on all wire transactions, but there are so many that FinCEN can't possibly monitor all of them. They count on banks to flag suspicious transactions."

"What happens if Gillen had too much money to launder through the restaurant?"

"There may be additional accounts. If he washed more money than we know about now, he'd have lots of options. Gambling for one. Anybody can walk into a casino, trade dirty money for chips. Shoot craps for a while, maybe even lose a few bucks. Take the leftover chips and ask for a check. Now the money is clean enough to deposit in a bank."

Jack Blasdel had applied for a license to work in a casino in Atlantic City. Plus, his ex-girlfriend Gerda Pittman claimed he'd scouted business opportunities for a billionaire he'd met there. He also helped Sabine disappear, and later bought the gunstore where she was shot and killed. Davie wondered if he'd been involved in the money-laundering scheme at the Seaglass Cafe, as well.

Davie's gaze caught Striker's. "The big question is, where did the money come from?"

He shrugged. "Criminals are always looking for ways to wash money through legitimate businesses. Somebody might have made Gillen an offer he couldn't refuse."

"A detective from Florida told me Gillen got business tips from some mysterious advisor, but nobody knows who he is or what kind of miracle advice he gave Gillen to turn the restaurant around so spectacularly. Maybe that person was the source of the money." Davie pulled out the photo of the three men. "I emailed this photo to Detective Brooks. I also sent it to our facial recognition unit. Gillen is the man in the Hawaiian shirt. I haven't identified the others. Sabine kept the picture, so it must have meant something to her."

Striker studied the photo and then refilled both glasses. The bottle was now empty and Davie was buzzed.

"There's still a lot of this story to unpack," he said. "Are you even sure those are Sabine's doodles?"

"I think so. Her sister-in-law told me Sabine had to learn short-hand for a job. I'm guessing not many people use it these days. "

"We still don't know if she was a whistle blower or a coconspirator."

"There's a ten-digit number at the bottom of the last page of Sa-bine's notes with a question mark behind it. The number belongs to the FBI's Miami field office. Looks like she was considering calling them about what she'd discovered. Not sure if she did, but I left a mes-sage for someone I know in the Bureau to see if Sabine made contact with them."

"Looks like you'll need forensic accountants and other resources you don't have at the division. Why don't you ask the captain to send the case to Homicide Special? The unit can bring you back on loan and maybe borrow a detective from CCD. Lieutenant Repetto would sign off on that in a hot minute."

Davie managed a mock frown and wagged her index finger at him. "You trying to steal another case from me?"

His eyes were alive and receptive. "You do good work, Davie. I thought you might stay at RHD after the Woodrow case. The lieuten-ant would have made it happen."

Davie thought about how to respond. She'd been upset when the captain transferred her case to Homicide Special, even though that brought her closer to Striker. But she loved her job at Pacific and was happy working with Giordano and Vaughn. She also knew her boss was retiring and sensed her partner was restless. It was possible Vaughn wouldn't stay at Pacific much longer. Truth was, few detec-tives spent their entire careers at the same division.

Davie didn't want to get ahead of the situation, but she knew being in the same unit with Striker could get complicated, especially if their relationship turned personal. Striker outranked her. Techni-cally that gave him power over her. The LAPD considered that troubling. If she and Striker started dating, the department would require them to notify their supervisor. Once that happened, people would be watching for a messy breakup that might jeopardize a high-profile homicide case.

Davie hesitated but plunged ahead. "How would Lieutenant Repetto feel about you sitting in my kitchen drinking champagne if we worked together?" Asking the question had made her feel vulnerable, and self-doubt crept in when Striker didn't answer right away.

He leaned forward with his elbows on the table, his vivid blue eyes within a foot of hers. "You know the lieutenant isn't one to hold back. I guess we'd find out soon enough."

The lip gloss had been a mistake. Davie wanted to say something witty and clever but the gloss seemed to have glued her lips shut. She glanced at her watch and was surprised to see they'd been talking for two hours.

Striker waited without a word for her next move. The problem was she didn't have one. A moment later, he took his jacket from the back of the chair and slung it over his shoulder. "I guess I should go."

Davie's body became taut from toe to temple. Her throat felt dry. She followed him to the door while the words *don't go* ping-ponged in her brain.

Striker paused by the door, resting his hand lightly on her arm a little longer than expected. "Thanks for the champagne, Detective. Most enjoyable. Let me know if there's anything I can do to help. I met a guy from the Florida Department of Law Enforcement at a conference a few weeks ago. I can call him if you need information."

Davie hovered by the open door, obsessing about what Striker had meant by that touch. She hoped she wasn't jeopardizing the Montaine case by brushing off his offer to help, but for now she'd continue pulling threads until she'd unraveled all the leads.

The taillights of his car turned onto the main road and disappeared. The cottage seemed deadly silent as she cleaned up the kitchen, mentally kicking herself for not asking Striker to stay. But she knew if he'd said no, it would have cut a hole in her self-esteem that no ER doc could repair.

She emptied the crumbs from her pocket and then washed and dried the thrift store clothes. As she got ready for bed she replayed in her mind Bear's warning: Don't date cops. She'd had a toxic relationship with another detective that had nearly ended her career and she didn't want to repeat that error.

Before falling asleep, she mentally scheduled a workday that included a high-priority second interview with Jack Blasdel. He was at the center of everything. Sabine had been in Fort Lauderdale for less than a year when she borrowed his sailboat and disappeared into the abyss. Davie had to know whether she'd met him at the marina, at the restaurant where she worked, or somewhere else. Why had they both ended up in L.A.? Was Blasdel lying when he denied recognizing her at the gunstore or were the changes she'd made to her appearance enough to fool him? The biggest question of all: Did Blasdel have a hand in her murder?

36

THE FOLLOWING MORNING DAVIE awoke with a start and reached for her cell on the nightstand. It was five a.m. and for the fourth day in a row there were no messages calling her out to a new homicide. Relieved, she showered and dressed for work.

As she steered the Camaro south on the 405, she thought about probable cause—her strong suspicion that a felony had been committed and evidence of that felony was contained in the records she wanted to search. That's what she needed in order to get a warrant for the Seaglass Cafe's bank statements. So far, all she had were hunches; strong ones to be sure, but no judge would grant a warrant for intuition alone.

As soon as Davie arrived at work, she walked upstairs and put the clean thrift store clothes in her locker. Returning to her desk in the squad room, she saw a message from the FBI special agent she'd contacted the night before. The agent confirmed they had no open case on Nate Gillen for money laundering or any other crime and there was no record that Sabine Ponti had contacted the Bureau.

Davie stood and waved to her partner across the gray partition wall. "Hey, Jason. You want to ride with me to the Valley?"

He looked up from an email he'd been reading. "Is that a serious question? It's hot over there and smoky as hell from the fires."

"I have to interview a witness in Sherman Oaks and I may need backup. Good news? He owns a nail salon. He might give you a free manicure."

Vaughn opened his arms wide. "In that case. Take me, I'm yours."

On the drive to the San Fernando Valley, Davie filled Vaughn in on the progress she'd made in the Ponti investigation. "It's an adrenaline rush every time I discover some new piece of evidence."

"Does Giordano know all the time you're spending on this? It's not even an open case."

"He's totally on board," she said. "Besides, I'm not giving it preference over other homicides. I'm still looking for Javi Hernandez's killer."

She prided herself on caring about all her victims, but she felt Sabine's death hadn't been given the attention it deserved. The pressure was mounting to find answers before the file was forced back into Giordano's bottom drawer. Still, her partner's question reminded her to make sure Javi Hernandez got equal attention. Vaughn was busy checking his Twitter feed. They didn't speak again until she neared the exit.

Ahead, the sky was dusky from smoke. The wildfire was still devouring dry brush on the hills above Malibu and was showing no sign of containment. Even before she left the freeway, she could see a billow of black smoke, but it wasn't coming from Malibu. This fire was closer. Her anxiety spiked when she realized it came from the vicinity of the nail salon. She stomped her foot hard on the accelerator, exited the freeway, and headed for Blasdel's shop. The sudden jolt caught Vaughn off guard.

"What's going on?"

Davie nodded toward the smoke.

Her partner slid his phone into his jacket pocket. "That doesn't look good."

Behind her, a siren blared. Davie swerved to the curb to let a fire department emergency-medical vehicle pass before continuing toward the smoke, passing a group of citizens watching the fire from the sidewalk. Even from a distance, Davie could see the looks of horror on their faces.

The tires of the detective car squealed as Davie braked a short distance from a hook and ladder truck. Firefighters and EMTs were already on the scene as flames licked at the Salon de Manucure sign above Blasdel's shop door. Van Nuys patrol officers kept bystanders away from the area.

She stepped out of the car into a river of water cascading down the gutter. The intense heat of the blaze sucked the oxygen from her lungs and burned her eyes. Ashes rained down around her, casting a gray pallor on the surrounding landscape. She covered her nose and mouth with her hand as she and Vaughn walked toward a makeshift command post that included an LAFD arson team and homicide detectives from the LAPD's Van Nuys Division.

Davie presented her badge to one of the Van Nuys detectives, a man named Harper. "Any idea how the fire started?"

"Not yet. The FD just sent in a crew, so I assume the flames are at least partly contained."

Davie pointed to the EMT vehicle. "Was anybody inside the building?"

He eyed her with suspicion. "What's your interest?"

"My partner and I are from Pacific Homicide. We're here to talk to the owner of that shop about a case we're working on," she said, pointing toward the blaze. "His name is Jack Blasdel. He also had several manicurists working for him."

He nodded, apparently satisfied with her explanation. "Let me talk to the hose monkeys."

Davie and Vaughn waited on the sidewalk as the detective walked around the hook and ladder truck and disappeared from view.

Vaughn tied his pocket-handkerchief around his face like a bandit. The cloth fluttered as he spoke. "Maybe Blasdel torched the shop to collect the insurance. Isn't that what he did with his boat?"

"That's one theory."

Davie's skin prickled with apprehension as she considered another explanation. Blasdel was a grifter, a failed businessman, and possibly a lot worse. With that kind of history there could be any number of explanations for the fire, payback being one. What she didn't know was if the blaze was connected to Sabine Ponti's death.

Vaughn began coughing. "My lungs are on fire. I'm going back to the car. Call if you need anything." He untied the handkerchief and handed it to her. "Better put this on."

Davie waited for the detective to return, shielding her lungs from the smoke with Vaughn's handkerchief. Ten minutes later Detective Harper rounded the corner and walked toward her.

"Patrol officers spoke to the woman who manages the store next door. She said the salon's employees showed up for work this morning but the doors were locked. They hung around for a while and then left. No official word on what started the blaze, but there was a flashpoint near an overloaded outlet, so it could be faulty wiring."

Davie remembered the multiple appliances inside the shop—everything from nail dryers to foot massagers all plugged into that single wall socket.

"They also found a white male inside, deceased. Can you identify Blasdel?"

Davie nodded.

"Come with me."

Her expression remained stone cold, but her stomach churned with dread as she followed Detective Harper. She'd once taken a training class on fire-related homicides. All she remembered were the grotesque photos of charred remains and the instructor's description of what happens when you're trapped in a building fire: blinded by smoke, the crackling sounds of walls and ceilings burning, the pop, pop, pop of light bulbs bursting, and the taste of smoke on your tongue.

When she got to the gurney, the coroner's assistant unzipped the body bag. He wasn't wearing the gold chain, but his hair and face were singed and his silk shirt had melted into his skin. Smoke stains around his nostrils suggested he might have been alive and breathing when the fire started. Smoke inhalation could have caused his death, but Davie knew toxic fumes from building materials or other substances often killed victims before the smoke did. What she didn't see were burns on the hands or scuff marks on the knees of the clothing that might indicate he'd tried to crawl to safety.

"It's Blasdel," she said.

As deaths go his must have been a horrible one and for that she felt a measure of sorrow. She thought back to her first conversation with Blasdel at the cafe down the street. He'd told her he didn't like redheads because they reminded him of fire and he hated fire. Given his attitude, it seemed unlikely he would have set the blaze.

Davie willed her gaze to leave the body and focus on Detective Harper. "Any idea how he died?"

"It's hard to speculate. The medical examiner will look at the body. If there are no obvious signs of trauma or gunshot wounds, they'll check other things, like elevated levels of carbon monoxide in his blood and determine the cause of death."

Davie's gaze turned toward the salon's charred facade. The shop was such a small space. Even if Blasdel had been blinded by smoke, she wondered why he hadn't been able to find his way out, unless something or someone had rendered him unconscious before the fire started.

She waited until the body was loaded into the coroner's van before heading back to the car. Her shoes were saturated with water and every step was accompanied by a squish and ooze. She slid into the driver's seat next to her partner.

"What happened?" Vaughn said.

The horror of seeing Blasdel's burned body washed over her and she almost lashed out at him for not staying with her. Instead, she rested her head on the steering wheel, rhythmically inhaling and exhaling as she'd been taught—three deep breaths, hold each for four seconds, count to four while exhaling—until her anger faded and she gathered her thoughts.

"Blasdel is dead. He was my last best hope to solve Sabine Ponti's death."

"What about Gillen's widow?"

Davie blew out a puff of air and lifted her head. "She's in Tortola on vacation and won't be home for a couple of weeks."

"She doesn't have a cell phone?"

"The housesitter told me she didn't take it with her."

"Can't you call her hotel?"

"I tried. She's not answering any calls." Davie paused for a moment to think. "Maybe I need a tan. You think there's sun in the BVIs?"

Vaughn smirked. "Yeah, plenty of it, but forget about going there. The powers that be will never send you to Tortola for a case that's not even a case. Besides, redheads don't tan. They burn."

Davie shot him a stink eye.

He held up his hands in surrender. "Sorry. Bad timing."

37

THREAT ASSESSMENT.

He was crouched on the rooftop of a building down the street, watching the flames. He wasn't an arsonist. Didn't fit the profile. He felt no sense of power, no thrill. He wasn't going to take photos or videos to relive the excitement later on over a beer and a TV dinner. Setting the fire had been a job, a way to vary his routine so nobody detected a pattern.

Blasdel had become a liability. His client couldn't allow Detective Saffron to score a second interview with him, so he had to be eliminated. Before the decision was made, he'd already developed a list of alternatives for the client to choose from. Careful planning allowed for a rapid response. Torching the salon was the best option given Blasdel's history. His business was tanking. He'd checked. His death would seem like a scam gone wrong.

To prepare, yesterday afternoon he'd walked into the shop to ask for directions. One thing he noticed was there were multiple pillows on the chairs, on the floor, and on the table near a sign advertising psychic readings. On his way back to the no-tell motel he'd stopped by a craft store and bought several highly flammable polyurethane cushions that would add fuel to the flames. Investigators weren't going to search through the rubble to conduct a pillow count.

When he'd arrived at the salon early that morning, he picked the back door lock and waited inside. Old Jack showed up at eight to open the store at nine. He slapped the cloth over his nose and mouth before he had time to pocket his keys. It took a minute or so of struggling before the ether rendered Blasdel unconscious. The guy was flabby and no match for his superior strength. Ether was highly flammable, which was perfect for his purposes. It was legal to buy in the States, but to avoid attention he purchased his supply from a doctor in Malawi.

He waited until the employees gave up knocking on the door and left, then kept silent for a while longer to make sure they didn't come back. After that he took his time igniting the blaze with a simple incendiary timing-device he'd learned years ago from a TV show about the arson investigator/serial arsonist John Orr. He'd been fascinated by the simplicity of the gadget and had sketched a diagram of the items Orr used—matches wrapped in yellow-ruled writing paper and held together by a rubber band, and ignited by a lit cigarette. He hadn't planned to set any fires, but in his business it was wise to have a full toolkit ready.

For this job, he'd modified Orr's device—the cigarette and matches were wrapped with plain white paper and tied with silk thread he'd purchased at the craft store—but the principal was the same. He'd taken a gallon of highly flammable acetone he'd found in the back room and set it near the electrical outlet. He dragged Blasdel's unconscious body to a nearby chair, propped up by the polyurethane pillows.

He set the device near the acetone and the outlet and lit the cigarette. He'd used gloves, of course. That's what tripped up Orr. A partial fingerprint on a piece of yellow paper had survived one of his arson fires. Bad luck, but he wasn't Orr. Arson fires were difficult to detect and prosecute, and this would likely be his last and only fire.

It was unfortunate the blaze had been reported before the shop was fully engulfed, but at least the building was still smoldering. He was about to leave his hiding place on the roof when he saw Detective Saffron and her partner arrive at the scene. He hadn't expected that. At least she wouldn't be handling Blasdel's death investigation. It was outside her jurisdiction, but she would certainly share whatever information she had with the other investigators. That troubled him.

Following the detective had been useful, but that usefulness was over now. If she kept sticking her nose where it didn't belong, she'd soon become part of the problem. He would assess the threat and advise his client of the options.

Meanwhile, he would continue retracing his movements in search of the St. Christopher medal. He *had* to find it, feared for his safety without it. The medal was more than a family heirloom. It was a talisman that made him invincible.

38

THE SMELL OF CHARRED wood and chemicals had seeped into the fabric of Davie's pantsuit and now permeated the air in the car. She lowered her window as she drove back to the station, unable to shake the image of Blasdel's silk shirt melted into his skin.

"I know you're bummed, Davie," Vaughn said, "but Blasdel isn't the only one who knows what happened to Sabine Ponti. What about that hottie PI, Natalie Salinas? Maybe she did more on that surveillance job for Gerda Pittman than she let on. I think we should call on her again. If you're too busy, I can go and take another detective with me." His cell pinged an incoming message. He paused to read it. "I just got an email from Pendleton. Daniel Hernandez had a weekend leave before he shipped out. He left the base on Friday afternoon and didn't come back until Sunday morning. That means he was still in the area the day of his brother's murder, which means Emma Wainford could have seen him at the crime scene."

"Call the food bank," she said. "See if he's there now."

Vaughn pressed the number into his cell display and waited while Hernandez's supervisor confirmed he was expected at work within the hour. When they arrived at the station, Davie opened the rear door near the Kit Room and nearly collided with Detective Giordano as he read a notice on the hallway bulletin board.

Her boss glanced at his watch and then at Davie and Vaughn. "Where have you two been? You didn't sign out."

"We were at a fire," Vaughn said.

Giordano pointed to the stairway. "Roll-call room. Now."

Davie and her partner led the way upstairs. The roll-call room was empty. Giordano didn't bother to sit. He crossed his arms and glared at Davie. "What's up?"

She glanced at her partner and then at her boss. "It's a long story. You may want to sit."

"I don't need to sit. What I need is to know what's going on."

Davie told him about Blasdel and the fire, about her suspicion that Sabine Ponti may have uncovered a money-laundering scheme at the restaurant where she worked.

"We have to interview Nate Gillen's widow, but I also need access to the books and records of the Seaglass Cafe," she concluded. "I can't do that unless the case is reclassified."

Giordano's muscles stiffened. "The bodies are piling up, so I'm going to reclassify the case from suicide to homicide. First, I've got to make a few phone calls."

Davie could barely contain her excitement. "That's great."

"What about the Hernandez case?"

Vaughn jumped into the conversation. "A witness saw the victim's brother running from the scene of the murder. We were just about to head over to Daniel Hernandez's work and question him again."

"Good. From now on I want to know everything you're doing." He took a few steps toward the exit but turned back. "And air yourselves out before you come back or bury those clothes."

As Giordano left the room, Vaughn sniffed the arm of his jacket. "What's his problem? Smells fine to me."

She patted him on the back, not mentioning that he'd been waiting in the car most of the time they were at the fire. "Don't worry. You smell like fresh laundry drying in a spring breeze. Me? Not so much. I'm going upstairs to change."

Once Davie had put on the pantsuit she kept in her locker, she went downstairs, signed out on the log sheet, and picked up the keys to the Jetta. She found Vaughn standing at the Kit Room door, checking out a new battery for his handheld radio. They took the 405 South to Jefferson. She was half a block from the food bank when her partner pointed toward a late-model black Toyota exiting the parking lot and turning onto the street.

"That's Daniel Hernandez's car. You think his supervisor tipped him off we were on our way?"

Davie glanced at her watch. "It's almost noon. Maybe he's just going out for an early lunch."

"You want to pull him over?"

She tapped her fingers on the steering wheel, thinking about the options. "No. Let's see where he's going."

Davie kept the Jetta a couple of car-lengths behind Daniel, guessing he wouldn't notice a junker on his tail. She followed him on the 405 North, inching along in heavy traffic until he exited at Sunset Boulevard and headed toward Beverly Hills. He turned left at Beverly Drive and continued to the intersection of Woodland Drive, where he pulled to the curb near a small park. Davie stopped a short distance away and watched him get out of the car and walk across a lawn shaded by mature trees.

Vaughn opened the door. "Let's see what he's up to."

Davie set her phone to vibrate in case she got a call. Daniel didn't notice their presence because his focus was riveted on a heavy-set white woman sitting on a bench holding a small child.

Vaughn grabbed Davie's arm. "Is that who I think it is?"

It was Alma Velez's mother and Velez's son, Manny.

"Interesting," said Davie.

Daniel must have called out to the woman because she looked up and so did the child. Manny slid off his grandmother's lap and made his way toward Daniel with that unsteady toddler's gait. The kid was wearing a black sweatshirt with a Snow White dwarf printed on the front—Grumpy. Manny giggled as Daniel scooped him into his arms. In Davie's limited experience, toddlers were squirrely. She doubted this one would run to greet a stranger. The kid not only seemed to know Daniel Hernandez, but Davie guessed Manny had also spent a fair amount of time with him.

"What's the deal?" Vaughn said. "I got the impression Daniel Hernandez hardly knew Alma Velez. So why's he meeting her son and her mom in Beverly Hills?"

"Because it's about as far away from Mar Vista Gardens as you can get and still be in the same universe." She pulled her partner behind the trunk of a tree out of Daniel's line of sight. "I thought he looked familiar when I met him. Now I know why. Those big round eyes and cupid-bow lips. Manny has the same features."

Vaughn looked surprised by her conclusion. "You think the kid is his?"

"Does anything else make sense?"

"That means Daniel and Alma were screwing behind Felix Malo's back." Vaughn opened the calculator app on his cell. "Let me do the math. Let's say she was maybe two months pregnant when Javi was killed in February. The baby was born seven months later in September. That would make Manny about twenty months old."

"That sounds about right."

"I wonder if Daniel knew she was pregnant with his kid."

"Hard to know," Davie said. "If our theory is correct, the baby might have had something to do with Javi's death."

"Daniel said his brother was Malo's loyal soldier. If Javi found out his brother was screwing his homie's girlfriend, where would his loyalty be—with Daniel or Felix Malo?"

She watched Daniel on a swing with Manny in his lap. "What would Velez do to protect her secret?"

"Should we go over and confront him?"

"Let's wait. I don't want a scene with the kid there."

They returned to the car and watched as Daniel supervised Manny, petting a woman's French bulldog and splashing his feet in the shallow water of a pond surrounded by boulders and spiky plants.

Thirty minutes later, Velez's mom motioned for Daniel to join her. They spoke for a couple of minutes. Daniel held Manny until he squirmed to get down. Velez's mother took the child in her arms and walked out of the park as Manny screamed in alarm. Daniel Hernandez lingered behind, sitting on the bench with his head resting in his hands. He was so absorbed in his thoughts he didn't notice Davie and Vaughn approach.

"Mr. Hernandez," Davie said.

He bolted upright and squared off in front of them. His expression was a mix of surprise and alarm. "What the hell are you doing here? Are you following me?"

Davie's hand hovered near her weapon. "We need to clear up a few things you told us the last time we spoke, because I think you lied to us about your brother's death. We know you weren't in Afghanistan the day Javi was murdered. You were in L.A."

Daniel looked caged and ready to bolt. "I don't know what you're talking about. I didn't lie."

"You withheld the truth," Vaughn said. "That's as close to a lie as it gets."

"We have a witness who saw you running away from Javi's apartment around the time he was murdered. You want to tell us what happened?"

The man looked down and jammed his hands into the pockets of his jeans. "It's not what you think."

Davie's voice remained steady but firm. "What I think is you killed your brother. What I don't know is why you did it."

Raw emotion played across Daniel's face. "I didn't kill Javi. I swear. I'd never hurt my mom like that."

Vaughn's tone was sharp and unsympathetic. "Then what were you doing there?"

Daniel collapsed on the bench. "A friend called and told me Alma was there. I needed to talk to her."

"About what?"

"We had a misunderstanding. I needed to clear things up before I was deployed."

Davie moved closer. "What kind of misunderstanding?"

He raised his head and stared at her. "We slept together. I wanted to keep seeing her and I wanted her to write to me while I was away, but she was afraid of Felix. She said if I told anyone about what we did, he'd kill both of us. At first I said okay, but later I wanted to tell her I was going to fight for her. That's why I showed up at Javi's place."

Vaughn moved to the side of the bench to cover him from a different angle. "And was she there?"

"Yeah, with Javi. They were smoking weed and drinking beer."

Davie took a step toward him and lowered her voice. "Did you know Ms. Velez was pregnant with your child?"

He leaned his head back and stared at the treetops. "No. I just wanted to talk to her."

Davie softened her tone. "What happened, Daniel? How did Javi die? You've been carrying this burden for a long time. Let it out."

"I didn't kill Javi," he said, his anger building. "My brother was high, lying on a filthy mattress like a pig. I was pissed and I told him so. He just laughed."

"What did Alma say?" Vaughn asked.

"Nothing." His voice sounded raw and bitter. "I could tell all she wanted was for me to leave. Javi kept asking me why I was there. I told him I came to say goodbye, but I could tell he didn't believe me. So, I left."

Davie felt her phone vibrate with an incoming call, but she didn't dare look for fear it would interrupt Daniel's train of thought. "Your brother was stabbed fifteen times. You must have heard the screams. Why didn't you go back and help him?"

"I was listening to music on my headset. I didn't hear anything. Then I left for Afghanistan. I didn't even know Javi was dead until two weeks later."

"When did Alma tell you the baby was yours?" Davie asked.

"She didn't. I figured it out myself. She hadn't even seen Felix for a couple of months. He was in Texas and didn't come back until after Javi was dead. Manny couldn't have been his kid."

Davie shifted from one foot to another but didn't take her eyes off Daniel. "Does Alma even know?"

"Look at my son and tell me you're not sure. She knows but she doesn't want to be with me. She's afraid."

"Do you think Alma killed your brother?" Vaughn asked.

"Why would she do that?"

"That's what I'm asking you," he said.

He hesitated before responding. "Maybe she did, but I don't know why."

39

DAVIE AND VAUGHN LEFT Daniel Hernandez on the park bench and were heading back to the car when she remembered the phone call. She pulled the cell from her pocket and found a message from her grandmother.

"You think he's telling the truth?" Vaughn said.

"I'll reserve judgment for now but I'm inclined to think so. We'll know more after we talk to Alma Velez—if we can find her."

Vaughn slid into the passenger seat. Standing behind the car, Davie tensed when she read the voice message transcript: DAVIE, THIS IS GRAMMY. COME OVER RIGHT AWAY.

"You getting in?" Vaughn said.

"I have to make a call first." Davie's hands felt clammy as she pressed in Grammy's number. As soon as she answered, Davie said, "What's wrong?"

"It's about that case of yours, the girl who disappeared on the sailboat."

Her stomach clenched. This was about a case? "What about her?"

"I have somebody here who might have information. Can you come over?"

Maintaining a calm she didn't feel, Davie said, "Who's in your apartment, Grammy? Are you okay?"

"I'm fine. Just come as quick as you can."

The line went dead.

Davie had encouraged her grandmother's amateur detective skills. Now she questioned whether that had been a good idea. It seemed unlikely Grammy had anything of substance to offer, but she *had* told her about Fort Lauderdale's shallow water and she seemed genuinely alarmed by whatever this new information was. Davie needed to make sure she was okay.

She opened the car door and slid behind the wheel. "I have to stop by my grandmother's place for a few minutes. Something's going on. She won't tell me what."

"A few minutes? I doubt that. Your grandma's a talker. Drop me by the station. I want to check out Natalie Salinas."

She couldn't help the eye roll. "Thanks, Jason. The entire law enforcement community will be grateful for your sacrifice."

He smirked. "Good to know *somebody* recognizes my superpowers."

Davie dropped Vaughn off in front of the station before heading to her grandmother's assisted living apartment. She arrived, signed in at the front desk, and took the ancient elevator to the second floor. She tapped lightly on the apartment door before entering. Grammy stood in the middle of the living room, leaning on her walker.

Sitting on the loveseat in front of the sliding glass door was a thin woman in her seventies wearing a chic red dress that matched the polish on her long fingernails. Her hair had been molded and sprayed into a blonde helmet.

Grammy rolled her walker toward the woman. "This is Kathleen Newell. She lives down the hall."

Davie stepped closer and offered her hand. "I'm the granddaughter, Davie Richards. Good to meet you."

"You don't look much like a detective," Newell said. "I thought you'd be bigger."

"My life's goal is to defy expectations. Keeps people off guard."

"We think alike," she said. "Me, too."

Davie helped her grandmother into her blue recliner and then sat at the other end of the loveseat with Newell's oversized purse wedged between them.

Grammy pulled her housedress over her knees. "Kathleen is my new tablemate. I told you about her the other day, remember? She moved here from Florida to be closer to her daughter."

"What your nana is trying to say is my daughter forced me to sell my condo on the water and leave all my friends behind after my husband went to prison. He was a good provider but he was also a gambler. He tried to stop but couldn't. Once he left for Club Fed, my daughter told me I was broke, so bye bye Florida. I hate this place— except for your nana, of course. The food sucks."

Most of her grandmother's friends felt the same way about the cuisine, but Davie figured it had more to do with a loss of control than it did with leathery pot roast. She'd eaten in the dining room many times with her grandmother. The food was low salt and low fat: palatable but boring.

"I'm sorry you had to leave your home," Davie said.

Newell flipped her hand as if she were batting away a fly. "I doubt that. You don't even know me."

So much for the sympathy cliché, Davie thought. "My grandmother says you might have information about a case I'm working on."

"I told you," Grammy said. "Kathleen is from Lauderdale-by-the-Sea. It's close to Fort Lauderdale."

"But a hundred times better," Newell added.

"Anyway, she knew Nate Gillen, the man who was killed in the hit-and-run accident."

Davie turned to Newell. "Is that right?"

"Well, I didn't exactly *know* Mr. Gillen. I met him at my going-away party. A few of my girlfriends took me to lunch at his restaurant."

"Had you ever been there before?"

"Nope. Just that one time. My friend Ruthie made the reservation. Mr. Gillen himself showed us to our table on account of the hostess was sick that day."

"How did the place look?" Davie asked. "Did anything strike you as unusual?"

Newell wrinkled her nose. "The menus were greasy. I hate that. Makes me wonder what's going on in the kitchen, if you know what I mean."

Davie hated greasy menus, too. Just imagining the germ count made her cringe. "Did you notice anything else?"

"They gave a discount if you paid in cash. That was odd. I've never heard of a restaurant doing that. We paid by credit card. Split the bill four ways."

Davie didn't know if a cash discount at a restaurant was odd or not. It could be a way to hide income from the IRS. Whatever the case, it didn't appear Newell had valuable information to offer.

Davie felt let down as she rose to leave. "I have to get back to work. Great to meet you, Ms. Newell, and thanks for the information."

"She has a picture, Davie," Grammy said, "if that helps."

That stopped Davie in her tracks. "Really? Can I see it?"

Newell reached inside her purse and extracted a crumpled photo of her and three other women around Newell's age, sitting in a booth. Leaning over the table with his arm around Kathleen Newell in that same Hawaiian shirt he'd been wearing in Sabine Ponti's photo was a smiling Nate Gillen. The dimples in his chin and cheeks gave him a cherubic look, but his squinty, calculating eyes told another story.

Newell pointed with a long red fingernail. "That's the owner, Mr. Gillen. When he found out it was my going-away party he kicked in free dessert for everybody. I had the flourless chocolate cake. Not bad, but I've had better."

Davie studied the photo. Several wrapped gifts were stacked on the table, forming a centerpiece. The desserts were in the photo so it must have been near the end of the lunch. The photographer had captured a woman in profile walking past the table just inside the frame. She had spiky bleached-blonde hair, a prominent nose, and a daisy tattoo on her neck. It wasn't Sabine Ponti, so it might have been a customer looking for the restroom, except she had a laptop computer tucked under her arm.

Davie pointed to the blonde. "Who's the woman walking by your table?"

"She wasn't our waitress, but I think she worked there. Mr. Gillen told her not to charge for the desserts, so she must have been a cashier or something."

Davie pulled out the photo of the three men she'd found at the storage locker. "Do you recognize these men?"

Newell wrinkled her brow and squinted at the photo. "The man in the Hawaiian shirt is Mr. Gillen. Can't say about the others."

"Can I take a photo of your party picture with my cell?"

"Sure, but it might be easier to download it from my Facebook page."

40

As soon as she got back to the station, Davie noticed the faxed copies of Detective Brooks's witness statements sitting on her desk. She put them aside to review later and logged on to Facebook, downloading Newell's photo at the Seaglass Cafe. Unfortunately, the photo of the woman with the spiky blonde hair was only a side view and probably not enough for the LAPD's facial recognition analysts to identify her.

Davie had just printed out a hard copy of the picture when her desk phone rang. It was Reggie Banker in the Gang unit. "You ready? We're starting our briefing in thirty minutes."

Davie glanced at her watch. It was almost noon. She'd lost track of the time. She was scheduled to go with Reg on the undercover drug buy and wasn't ready. The clean thrift store clothes were in her locker, so she told Giordano where she was going and raced upstairs to change once again.

The transformation took fifteen minutes and when she finished, Davie had on a thigh-high mini skirt and a tank top with a plunging neckline. Underneath was a push-up bra that transformed her breasts from a size B to a B-plus. She'd applied heavy black liner above and below her eyes with cat-eye extensions. Her lips were lined with black pencil and filled in with dark maroon lipstick. She'd teased her red hair into a do that resembled a nuclear cloud over the Nevada desert—if you had red hair, you either camouflaged it or you owned it. As a final touch, she pasted a fake diamond stud on the right side of her nose. Davie estimated the weight as just shy of half a carat. She thought about applying a temporary tattoo to disguise her snow-white arms, but there wasn't enough fake ink in the world to cover that territory. Instead, she put on a black hoodie bought at the thrift store.

When she arrived at the Gang unit upstairs, the people in the room greeted her with a chorus of hoots and groans. Reggie Banker sat on the edge of his desk, bare-chested except for a sleeveless denim jean jacket covered with patches from a local motorcycle gang. With him was another Gang detective and four officers—two uniformed and two from the undercover Narco unit.

Reggie's eyebrows shot upward when he saw her. "Huh-uh. That hair has got to go. I want you to blend in, not blow our cover." He reached into his desk drawer and handed her a Dodger ballcap. "Hide that red under Dodger blue."

"Everybody's a critic," Davie said, twisting her hair into a knot and shoving it under the cap.

Reggie laughed when he noticed the fake diamond in her nose. "Wicked cool. Loco will look at that rock and think it's cloudy and the cut is too shallow, but I guess he isn't going to inspect it with a loupe. If he notices it's a cheap paste-on, he'll just think his coke is better than your stone. Where's your piece?"

Davie patted her lower back where her gun was concealed in a hidden pocket under her tank top.

"Good. Here's what's going to happen." Reggie went through the tactical plan and assigned each person a position. He warned that Loco should be considered armed and dangerous. "Davie, you'll come with me but I'll do the talking. In case I don't recognize Alma Velez, scratch your nose to let me know if you spot her. We'll take her down, too. If she's not there, you can ask Loco about her but only after we're done interrogating him."

After discussing logistics, Reggie went through what to do in case the operation went sideways. After the briefing ended, Davie and Reggie headed to the parking lot and slid into an unmarked Vice junker parked near the gas pumps. The ten-minute ride was spent in silence. Once they arrived in Venice, Reggie parked the car a couple blocks from the location where Loco was known to hang out. As the two of them headed to the alley behind a row of shops just off the boardwalk, the rest of the team took their assigned places out of sight. They found Loco pacing near a Dumpster, twitching and snapping his fingers.

He was Latino, early twenties, five-eight, 140 pounds. His right hand was wrapped in a bandage. His dark sunglasses failed to hide black and blue bruises beneath his eyes and a swollen nose—evidence it had been recently broken. It had been dark in Mar Vista Gardens that night, but Loco was definitely the man who had attacked her. Davie wanted to alert Reggie, but he'd warned her to stay invisible unless she spotted Alma Velez, so she pulled the ballcap down lower to hide her face. The last thing she needed was for the drug dealer to recognize her.

Loco pivoted as he saw Reggie heading his way. "What's going on?"

"Just out looking for some blow." Reggie sounded casual but Davie suspected he was anything but.

Loco smacked his lips in search of saliva. "Where you from?"

Davie didn't know why he was asking that question. If Loco thought they were gangbangers, he might want to find out what neighborhood Reggie was from to avoid a territorial war with a rival gang. More often than not, survival meant giving the right answer. But they were a little old for that.

Reggie flashed a wide grin. "I'm from Detroit, but I live here now. You do business with my cousin. He told me you were solid."

Loco's jaw muscles pulsed as he gritted his teeth, looking directly at Davie. "You a cop?"

Her body froze to stone. She hoped Loco was being paranoid rather than psychic. She studied his face but didn't see recognition reflected in his expression. She guessed he was paranoid or high, or both.

"Come on, man," Reggie said. "Why you do me like that?"

The dealer turned again to Reggie, staring at him as if considering what to do next. A moment later, Loco nodded, signaling they had passed some sort of test.

"Let's walk." Loco swiveled and jerked forward. "You got the scratch?"

"Three Jacksons."

Loco stopped and threw up his hands. "Three? I can't walk no two blocks for less than four."

Reggie frowned. "You're not in New York, man. Three. And you didn't say nothing about no walk, either."

"Four, or I walk and you stay."

Reggie's frown deepened. "Shit, man. Okay."

"Show me."

Reggie dug into his pocket and pulled out four twenty-dollar bills. Loco held out his hand. "I want the cheese before we do the walk."

Reggie withdrew the money. "The dust first. Then the scratch. That's the deal, or *we* walk and you stay."

Loco's gaze darted from Reggie to Davie, evaluating his options. Davie didn't like the idea of a drug dealer luring them to another location. It could be a set-up. She could tell by Reggie's rigid posture that he was thinking the same thing. She put her right hand on her hip, slow enough not to make Loco any twitchier than he already was but strategic enough to position herself in easy reach of her weapon.

Reggie stood unyielding and ready. "If you don't have the bump, dude, just say so. I got other options."

Loco wiped sweat from his upper lip. "I got what I say I got."

Reggie was intimidating. She hoped Loco knew he was in over his head.

"C is in my car," Loco said. "I don't keep it on me. Too many cops cruising the boardwalk. You want snow, you got to do the walk."

Last time Davie had seen Loco he wasn't in a car, he was on a bicycle. She didn't want to call attention to her presence, so she didn't say anything. They weren't going to arrest Loco until he produced the drugs, so Reg agreed to follow him to the location. The dealer hurried along the bike path until Davie saw a woman on the bench on the edge of the sand. Her jaw clenched when she recognized it was Alma Velez. If she was a drug dealer it didn't appear she used the products. Her skin was clear, and she looked healthy.

Velez had only seen Davie once in Mar Vista Gardens and it was dark and from a distance, but it would blow their cover now if Velez recognized her. Davie caught Reggie's gaze and scratched her nose. He saw the gesture but didn't react, so she tilted her head down and watched from under the bill of her ballcap.

Loco pointed to Velez. "My girl's got the blow. In her backpack."

On cue, Velez lifted the bag from the bench and held it out. "Where's the money?" she asked.

Reggie looked menacing with his arms crossed over his chest. Loco couldn't tell but Davie knew Reggie's hand was on the nine hidden inside his vest. "You said it was in a car. I'm tired of this bullshit. You got the goods or not?"

"Give it to him," Loco said to Velez.

"Open that bag wide and slow before you stick your hand in there," Reggie said. "I want to make sure the only thing that comes out is Big C."

Velez opened the bag and Reggie glanced inside. "Hand it to me. I don't want to touch your nasty-ass backpack."

This transaction had gone on too long for Loco. He looked agitated and rabbitty. Reggie took the cocaine Velez offered and tucked it under his belt. He looked at Davie and nodded. Both drew their weapons.

"LAPD!" Reggie shouted. "Down on the ground. Now. Hands behind your head."

Loco scrambled to the ground and assumed the position as the rest of the team moved in.

Velez glared at them in defiance. "You don't know who you're messing with."

"Maybe you'll live long enough to tell me, dipshit," Reggie said. "Then again, maybe not. Don't make me say it again. On the ground."

Velez mumbled an expletive in Spanish and slowly knelt on the sand.

41

DAVIE HAD LEFT VELEZ to stew in a cell in the Pacific jail for thirty minutes, long enough for her anxiety to build. So far she'd refused to speak with Reggie but she hadn't asked for an attorney. It was Davie's turn now.

She walked past the glassed-in holding tanks and secured her weapon in a locker outside the jail before entering through the Officers Only door. Velez was lying on the bench in one of the cells with the hood of her sweatshirt pulled over her head and Venice Beach sand still clinging to her shoes. She looked up and scowled when the jailer unlocked the cell and Davie entered.

Davie loomed over Velez with one shoulder braced against the wall. "You're in a lot of trouble, girl. Running from an interview is one thing, but now it's felony possession with intent to sell. If you're convicted, you could spend three to five years in state prison plus a ten-thousand-dollar fine. Manny will be out of kindergarten by the time you get out."

"I was just along for the ride," Velez said, pulling herself into a sitting position. "I can't stay here. I need to go home to my baby. I want to call my mom. She'll come get me."

Davie crossed her arms over her chest "Let me tell you what's going to happen. A bus will take you to court tomorrow where you'll be arraigned. Maybe the judge will release you on bail, or maybe not. Depends if your mom can come up with the money. If she can't, you'll be remanded to the county and locked up somewhere in their jail system. After that, who knows?"

Velez pulled the hood over her head again and sat for a moment, pouting. "My mom doesn't have no money."

"What about you? You have a job, right?"

"I quit. The people were no good."

"Maybe you could call Daniel Hernandez and let him know you're in jail. He's Manny's father, right?"

Velez lifted her chin in defiance as she held up her middle finger. Davie ignored the gesture.

"Tell me about Felix Malo."

"I told you before. I don't know him anymore."

"Let me guess. He sends you instructions from prison. You and Loco sell drugs for him, right?"

Velez leveraged what she thought was a bargaining chip. "If I tell you, will you let me go home?"

"If you tell me Malo is directing the gang's drug traffic from prison and agree to testify against him in court, I'll tell the DA's office. But that's no guarantee you won't still be charged for selling drugs."

Velez didn't respond.

Davie continued. "What do you know about Javi Hernandez's murder? You were with him the day he died. His brother Daniel was there, too. Did you kill Javi after Daniel left?"

Velez stared silently into mid space. If she was surprised Davie knew about Daniel Hernandez's presence at the crime scene, she gave no indication of it.

"You and Javi were together shortly before he was killed. What did you see?"

Velez's tone was subdued as she withdrew farther into her hoodie. "I liked Javi. Why would I hurt him?"

Davie gave her a hard stare, noting a tiny fracture in her tough-girl façade. "You tell *me* why."

"He'll kill me."

"Who? Daniel Hernandez? Felix Malo? Some other boogieman?"

Velez's lips were pressed together so tight the Jaws of Life couldn't pry them open, so Davie continued asking questions. "Loco's nose looks broken. You know anything about that?"

She turned her head to avoid Davie's stare. "I'm no doctor."

Velez still hadn't invoked her Miranda rights, so Davie kept asking questions. "I was assaulted the night I stopped by your mom's place. I broke the guy's nose. He bled all over my shirt. Once the lab matches that blood with Loco's, I'll charge him with assaulting a police officer. If you were an accessory, that could add another ten years to your sentence."

"I don't owe you nothing."

"Not me, but what about Manny?"

Velez wiped her nose on the sleeve of her sweatshirt. "I'm going to take care of him. Don't worry."

Davie turned to leave, closing the cell door. "Good luck with that."

"Where are you going?"

"Home. See you in court."

"You're just going to leave me here?"

Davie walked toward the exit. Over her shoulder she said, "Enjoy your evening."

In a panic, Velez bolted off the bench. "I can't stay here."

Davie kept walking.

"I didn't kill Javi."

Davie signaled the jailer to buzz her into the hallway.

"It was Felix Malo!" Velez shouted.

Davie stopped, slowly turning toward Velez. She waited, unsure whether the girl was just throwing out Malo's name to placate her or if she was telling the truth.

"How can that be? Felix was in Texas when Javi was killed."

"He came back."

Davie grabbed a tape recorder and waited for the jailer to unlock the door to Velez's cell. She sat next to Velez and pressed the machine's record button. "Tell me what happened. Start from the beginning."

Velez slumped back on the bench in her cell, biting her cuticles. "Daniel stopped by to say goodbye to Javi before he went to Afghanistan, but I knew he was there to see me. I didn't want Javi to find out we'd been together, so I treated Daniel mean. I told him to leave and he did."

"That left you and Javi alone together."

She began rocking her body to a rhythm only she could hear. "A few minutes later, Felix showed up. One of his homies had told him I was screwing around behind his back, so he came home from Texas. I said I'd been true to him but he didn't believe me. He went crazy. Started beating on me. Said he'd kill me if I didn't name the man I'd been with. I didn't want to say it was Daniel because I was afraid Felix would kill him."

"What did Javi do?"

Velez put her hands over her face. "He was high and acting kind of slow. At first he didn't realize Daniel and I had been together. Nobody knew but us."

The silence in the room was palpable. Davie waited for a few beats before asking again. "What happened, Alma?"

Her hands began to tremble. "I think Javi finally figured out why his brother came that day. Not to see him. To see me. He told Felix to stop hitting me. Felix asked him why he was there alone with me. Javi didn't say a word. That's when Felix accused Javi of cheating with me. Javi just sat there. Didn't say anything."

"So Felix took his silence as an admission of guilt and killed him?"

She nodded. "He pulled a knife from under his shirt and stabbed Javi over and over again. There was blood everywhere but Javi never fought back, just let Felix kill him. I knew somebody would call the cops so we both ran. All I could think about was that Daniel was safe—on his way back to the base."

Davie's emotions were mixed as she realized what had happened. Some people might have considered Javi Hernandez a failed human being, but his life mattered as much as anybody's. Considering all the wrong choices he'd made, at the end he'd sacrificed his life to save his brother's. That was about the greatest testament to love a person could make.

She also thought about Sabine Ponti and all the denigration she'd endured from her neighbors, stepson, and even her own family members. But whatever bad choices she'd made, her life mattered, too. Davie didn't yet know what all had led to Sabine's death, but now more than ever she felt driven to find the truth.

Moisture pooled in Velez's eyes. "It was my fault. Everything."

Davie gave her credit for telling the truth even if it had taken her two years to do it. Felix Malo was already in prison. With a 187 hanging over his head, he wouldn't be released for a long time—maybe never.

Davie arranged for Velez to call her mother, picked up her weapon from the lock box, and headed upstairs to her locker to change and wash the gang-queen makeup from her face. Then she returned to her desk, where she found Giordano on the telephone. He looked grim.

42

AFTER GIORDANO ENDED HIS call, Davie told him about Alma Velez's confession.

"Good work, Richards. You'll have to verify her story before filing charges, but that shouldn't be difficult." He seemed subdued considering she was on the brink of closing one of his old unsolved cases.

"Now I can devote all my time to the Ponti case."

He didn't respond. Davie wondered why. She wrote up her interview notes and reviewed the case again. She needed verification of Velez's claims to make an ironclad case against Felix Malo. For starters she'd search Malo's cell phone records on the day of the murder to confirm he was in L.A. and not in Texas. It was possible his phone had pinged on a cell tower near Javi's apartment that day. She would also check with Malo's Texas relatives.

Twenty minutes later she was still at the computer typing a report when Vaughn walked into the squad room looking glum.

"I just presented one of my old cases," he said. "The filing DA kicked it back."

"Is it salvageable?"

"No. It's just too old."

"You need partner therapy?"

"Couldn't hurt."

They walked upstairs to the roof deck outside the employee lunchroom and sat on the parapet overlooking the parking lot. Davie listened as her partner vented his frustrations.

"I feel your pain," she said. "I have a similar problem with the Ponti case. Gillen's wife might have information about her husband's murder and maybe Sabine's, too. Meanwhile she's in Tortola where I can't get to her."

Vaughn glanced at a message that lit up his cell phone display. "Yeah, it's frustrating when things don't go your way."

"I'm still thinking about flying to Tortola on my own to interview her. I have a ton of vacation days piled up. I'm guessing I could get there, interview Gillen, and fly home in three days, four max."

Vaughn grabbed her arm with his free hand. "Look at me, Davie. It's my job to protect you from yourself, so read my lips. I told you before that's one crazy-assed idea. The department won't pay for your trip. It'll cost major bucks and if the brass finds out you went alone, your career is over."

"Sabine Ponti was murdered. I just want to find out who killed her. Come to the BVIs with me."

"In a word: no. First, I can't afford it. Second, I burned all my vacation days on that trip to Italy with my parents. Third ... oh, screw it. It's just a bad idea."

Davie felt so close to finding justice for Sabine Ponti. She thought about the hours she'd spent interviewing people and getting Giordano to reclassify the case as a homicide. Now she could finally write search warrants and use other tools to undercover information. She wanted to escalate the pace of the investigation by jumping on the next flight to Tortola, but she had to admit there was still work to be done from here.

She stood to leave. "Thanks for talking me down, Jason."

He slipped his cell inside his jacket pocket. "It's what I do."

Davie walked down the stairs to the squad room and found Giordano at his desk, hanging up the receiver of his desk phone. He raised his hand and waved her over.

"I just got off the phone with Lieutenant Repetto. The captain is sending the Ponti case downtown to Homicide Special. Someone is driving over to pick up the file. Write up a 3.14 Follow-up, reclassifying and transferring the case. Put it on my desk. I'll sign it."

Davie's mind spun. "What? Why?"

"Look, Richards, people are dying all around you. You got multistate felonies, not to mention an arson homicide in another division and a shitload of financial crimes. We don't have the resources to handle that kind of case."

Davie felt sick that this was happening to her again, but she also knew she was powerless to do anything about it. She stood stunned and mute as Giordano rose from his chair and walked toward the lieutenant's office.

She sat at her desk and pulled up a CCAD Update exemplar, reclassifying the case from a suicide to a homicide. Next, she wrote a 3.14 summary of the case that would soon be signed and hand-stamped with RHD HANDLING. She printed both and laid them on Giordano's desk, along with the file. She hadn't been given the chance to set up a Murder Book for Sabine Ponti. It pained her to realize somebody else would do that now.

She wanted to be alone with her thoughts but there was no place to escape. People would be sitting around in the lunchroom eating, watching TV, and otherwise invading her privacy. The roof deck was quieter, but there was no place to sit and she intended to be out there for a while. The parking lot picnic table was the only option, so she grabbed a cup of Giordano's coffee and walked outside to check for news about the wildfires on her phone.

The Santa Paula blaze was still burning out of control, but fire crews had managed to partially contain the Malibu fire. She'd lost track of how long she'd been sitting in the parking lot—forty minutes, she guessed—but her coffee was cold and the news hadn't distracted her from the frustration she felt about losing her case to Homicide Special.

A car she didn't recognize drove into the Culver Boulevard gate and parked in the detective area. A moment later, Jon Striker rolled out of the driver's seat and walked toward the back door of the station. *He must be the Homicide Special errand boy sent here to pick up the Ponti file*, thought Davie. She lowered her head, hoping he wouldn't notice her, but a moment later he changed direction and headed for the table.

Striker's eyes were fixed on hers as he sat on the bench across from her. "I assume you heard. How do you feel about it?"

"Does it really matter?"

Striker's hands were clasped together prayer-like on the table. "It matters to me."

Davie didn't even try to hide her indignation. "Okay, it matters to me, too—a lot. It's *my* investigation and it's being taken away from me for no reason. Sabine Ponti's death was a closed suicide when I got involved. If I hadn't knocked on doors and talked to people, that's what it would still be. Nobody knows the facts the way I do and nobody cares about Sabine Ponti the way I care."

"I know you don't want to believe it at the moment, but we all care, partner."

225

In the LAPD, *partner* was anybody who was working with you at the moment. She'd been Striker's partner on another case, but she didn't think of him that way now. Jason Vaughn was her partner. She didn't answer.

He tilted his head. "I'm confused. Didn't anybody tell you? Lieutenant Repetto asked your captain to loan you to Homicide Special for the duration of the case."

The news didn't completely assuage her disappointment, but it was a step in the right direction. "Giordano didn't tell me that."

"He may not have known, but I'm sure he does by now."

"I don't know what to say."

He stared wide-eyed. "Start with something simple. Can you handle a red eye to Tortola?"

Davie squeezed her eyes shut, hoping she hadn't misheard. When she opened them again, she said, "How soon do we go?"

"I'll make arrangements and let you know. The lieutenant is getting a letter from the Chief of Police, verifying our credentials so we won't have a problem bringing our weapons into a British territory. You've already told me a lot about the case, but I'll read through the files when I get back to my desk. I'll call if I have questions. While we're away, I'll have members of the team start writing search warrants for records."

"Write one for bank records connected to that deposit slip I found in the storage unit and also for Jack Blasdel's cell phone." Davie paused, realizing she'd forgotten something important. "What about Jason Vaughn? Is he on loan, too?"

Striker hesitated, glancing at his watch. "Just you. My understanding is he wasn't involved in the case."

Davie didn't want to leave Vaughn behind, but she suspected he wouldn't mind. His experience with Homicide Special on their last case wasn't entirely positive.

Striker stood. "I need to get back downtown. Let's head inside so I can get the file."

He followed her into the squad room. Her 3.14s were signed. Copies were already in the file. Davie had updated her notes and organized all the photos. Before Striker left, she went to the Records storeroom and picked out a blue binder and dividers that would make up the Murder Book. Homicide Special had binders, too, but Davie felt strongly that this one had to come from Pacific station. She didn't care if anyone accused her of marking her territory.

After Striker left, Davie updated the Javi Hernandez Murder Book and put it on Detective Giordano's desk. Her boss would reassign the case to another detective, but as always she hated to let it go before it had been filed with the DA's office.

At six p.m. she was still at her desk in the squad room when her cell rang. It was Striker. "I suggest you pack a bag. Our flight leaves at twelve fifty-five."

She leaned back in her chair, ignoring the squeaky hinges. "Tonight?"

"Technically, it's tomorrow morning. You can sleep on the plane. I'll see you at the airport."

Davie locked her desk and raced to Bel Air. At least there was no rush to exchange currency at the airport. Tortola was a British protectorate but due to its proximity to the US Virgin Islands, they used the US dollar. She pulled an overnight duffle bag from the closet. Black pantsuits were too hot for the BVIs, but she'd be there on official business so she had to look professional. She picked out several of her nicer T-shirts and a pair of cotton pants. The last thing she threw into the bag was the ratty T-shirt she slept in.

43

DAVIE WATCHED STRIKER'S EVEN breathing as he dozed peacefully in the airplane seat next to hers. It was her experience that men could bag Zs anywhere, but she had never mastered the art of sleeping at 35,000 feet. Instead, she passed the hours flipping through the book on money laundering she'd brought with her and watching the in-flight movie—a romantic comedy that was neither romantic nor very funny.

After arriving in St. Thomas, a cab took them to Redhook. A short ferry ride later, they arrived on the island of Tortola, where they cleared Customs. Another taxi took them to the Apple Bay Hotel & Spa, where Lacy Gillen was staying and where Striker had booked a room for each of them.

Before she left the station, Davie had printed a copy of Lacy Gillen's Florida driver's license photo. Still, she didn't know how easy it would be to find her. They were in the country with official papers so if it proved too difficult, they could request assistance from local law enforcement. Whether they'd get help remained a question mark. Gillen hadn't committed any crimes on the island, at least as far as Davie knew, and local law enforcement might view outsider meddling in island issues as bad for tourism.

The hotel bordered the sea on property that had once been a Colonial-era sugar plantation. The main lobby was housed in a quaint building across the road from the beach. The area was a verdant paradise, but Davie was almost too exhausted to enjoy it. She hadn't slept for over twenty-four hours—or was it twenty-eight? She couldn't remember. Between changing planes and time zones she'd lost track.

A woman with ebony skin and a welcoming smile walked toward them. "Welcome to our little bit of heaven," she said, with an island patois.

Striker nodded toward Davie. "My sister and I are looking forward to our stay. We love the water, the vibe … " He gave Davie a side-glance. " … the rum."

The woman broadened her smile. "Then you will be very happy here."

It was clear Striker didn't want to tell the hotel staff they were cops stalking a hotel guest to question her about her husband's murder. They followed the woman to a small bar with a panoramic view of Apple Bay where they were instructed to wait until their rooms were ready.

"Is this the only bar?" Davie asked, hoping it wasn't the lone place where guests congregated. If Lacy Gillen spent her days touring the island, she and Striker might have to search a wide swath of territory to find her. Worse yet, she might stay in her room.

"There's a restaurant and bar across the road at our private beach," she said. "We serve lunch and dinner there. You can also snorkel, swim, or relax on the sand."

229

Davie thought of how easily her chalky white skin burned in the sun. She hadn't thought to bring sunscreen. If they had to interview Lacy Gillen on the beach, she hoped it would be under an umbrella.

The woman seemed to read her mind. "We have sunscreen for sale in the gift shop." She poured each of them a glass of champagne and gestured toward a rattan couch. "Please sit and enjoy the view."

Davie waited until the clerk was out of earshot. "Why didn't you tell her who we are?"

"We're in a foreign country. Didn't want to raise any alarms."

"Since you're such a good storyteller, maybe you can pretend we're friends with Lacy Gillen and find out where she is."

"I'm working up to that." Striker smiled as he held up the glass. "Maybe after another one of these."

"Hold that thought," she said. "I'm going to the gift shop for sunscreen."

The store was filled with a small selection of travel necessities— toothpaste, seasick meds, and a rack of gauzy sundresses in colorful flower motifs. Against her better judgment—Davie would never wear it once she got back to L.A.—she bought one of the dresses. The flowers were pink but the pattern also included green leaves. She just hoped the color balance was enough to keep her from looking like a lobster tangled in kelp. Armed with the dress and SPF 50+ sunscreen, she returned to the bar.

Striker was still on the couch in the reception area, gazing out the window toward the view.

Davie sat in a nearby chair. "I've been thinking about how the killer found Sabine in California. It must have been shortly before her death. Prior to that, she seemed to be living a quiet life in L.A."

"Maybe Blasdel tipped somebody off."

"It's possible, but I keep thinking about something the director of Four Paws told me. He said Sara Montaine freaked when she found out her picture went out to people on their mailing list. Maybe somebody on that list saw the newsletter photo and recognized her."

"That's a little farfetched."

She hated to admit it, but he was probably right. "I guess, but if we ever identify a suspect, I have the mailing list. It's searchable."

The champagne glasses were empty by the time Davie spotted a man in a golf cart pulling up to the door and beckoning them. She and Striker had each brought only a small overnight bag. If the driver found that strange, he didn't say so. He drove them to a three-story building that crept up the side of a steep hill. He stopped the cart in front of a wooden staircase, where he unloaded the bags and carried them to the second floor. Once the door was unlocked, he waved them inside the room and explained the air conditioning controls, where to find fresh towels, and how to open the sliding glass door, all things that seemed intuitive to Davie.

Striker handed the porter money from his wallet and waited for him to leave. "You look tired. Why don't you rest? I'm going to drop my bag in the room."

"Maybe I will, but just for a minute."

Between the travel and the champagne, Davie felt both tired and mellow. She kicked off her shoes and flopped on the bed. The last thing she remembered was the sound of the door closing.

Sometime later, she opened her eyes and felt disoriented. She glanced at her watch and grew panicky when she realized she'd slept two hours. There were no messages or texts on her phone from Striker. She was about to slip her foot into her shoe when a gecko scurried out of it. She let out a yelp before shaking both shoes to make sure he wasn't throwing a party in there. She didn't know where Striker was but doubted he'd made any major decisions without notifying her. She showered and had just thrown on the robe hanging in the bathroom when she heard a knock on the door.

"Who is it?" she said.

"Just me." She cracked open the door and saw Striker standing on the landing in Bermuda shorts, flip-flops, and a black Grateful Dead T-shirt. It wasn't exactly the attire she'd expected, but he looked relaxed. The short-sleeved shirt also allowed her to finally see the tattoo on his right forearm. It read *Breathe*.

His gaze swept from her wet hair down her body to a gap in the robe where her thigh was visible. "Pardon me. I knocked earlier but ..."

"Sorry," she said, pulling the robe tight across her body. "I didn't mean to sleep so long."

"Not a problem, but you might want to get dressed. We're having dinner with Lacy Gillen at the beach restaurant in fifteen minutes. I'll wait for you in the lobby."

44

DAVIE DRIED HER HAIR, slapped on some makeup, threw on her new sundress, and hurried to the hotel lobby. She spotted Striker sitting by the window, looking pensive. He stood when she entered. His gaze swept her body again but this time his eyes lingered on the sundress. He blinked a couple of times. "Nice dress."

Davie glanced down to make sure he wasn't making fun of her, but the dress did look nice. "Thanks. Does Lacy know who we are?"

"I didn't have time to tell her. She was waiting for a woman named Valerie, somebody she met on the ferry. Until we get her alone, I'm your brother."

"Anything else I should know?"

"Just that Valerie is joining us for dinner. We'll have to figure out some way to pry Lacy away from her so we can interview her in private."

Davie walked beside Striker across the road to the hotel's outdoor restaurant as the fading sun cast ripples of shimmery light on Apple

Bay. The barbeque was fired up. She smelled meat sizzling on the grill and heard the sound of a band, melding guitar, bongos, and ukulele in an upbeat tune.

An attractive woman in her early forties, wearing an ankle-length dress and a hibiscus flower clipped to her fawn-colored hair, waved from across the room. "Jon. Over here."

Striker smiled and waved back.

Lacy Gillen's cheeks were rosy from the sun. Her look of wide-eyed joy at seeing Striker reminded Davie of a high school wallflower crushing on a football jock.

Striker sat in the chair across the table from her. "How was your swim?"

"Glorious." Gillen fingered a gold apple charm on her necklace as she turned toward Davie. "You must be Jon's sister. I hope you got some rest. Coming to the island from Florida is bad enough, but it must be a bear traveling from L.A."

Davie just nodded because she wasn't sure what Striker had told her.

"Where's Valerie?" Striker asked.

Davie pulled up a chair and sat but nobody noticed.

"I think she had to make a phone call. She'll be here soon." Gillen tore her focus from Striker to address Davie. "Jon tells me you've never been to the islands before. What do you think of Tortola?"

"So far it's wonderful."

"Our uncle left us an old beach house in his will," Striker said. "We came to have a look so we can figure out what to do with it."

Gillen's expression turned somber as she clutched the necklace. "So sorry for your loss. It must be sad to come to his place without him. My husband and I met at Foxy's on Jost Van Dyke. I was with friends, but I saw him dancing on the sand by himself. He looked so handsome and carefree. We started talking and one thing led to another. We spent our honeymoon at this hotel. I hope it doesn't sound morbid, but I had to come back here on the anniversary of his death."

A waiter arrived at the table and set down three rum drinks, compliments of the house. Davie noted with interest the ease with which the subject of her husband's death had come up.

"My condolences," Striker said. "I can't imagine your loss."

Nate Gillen's widow reached across the table and placed her hand on Striker's. "So kind of you, Jon. When my husband died I thought I'd never recover, but this beautiful place helps me heal."

She was clearly putting a move on Striker. He wasn't encouraging her, but Davie worried about the risk of alienation once she found out the truth about who they were and why they were here.

Striker waited a few respectful moments. "You mentioned when we first met that you owned a restaurant. I've always had a fantasy about opening one, something small, of course."

Gillen squeezed his hand and then let it go—reluctantly, it seemed. "Take my advice. Don't do it. Buying that place was my husband's idea. He thought it sounded sexy. He didn't realize how much work it would be or how easy it was to fail. As soon as we bought the place, it started bleeding money. I had to quit my job to help out."

He nodded solemnly. "A lot of restaurants fail in the first year. He was lucky to have you."

"Nate loved interacting with the customers, but neither of us had a financial background. It got so bad Nate met with some business people. I guess they gave him good advice, because after that things improved. Nate was finally able to hire a hostess and a new chef. He upgraded the liquor and food. He also started selling logoed coffee mugs and T-shirts and brought somebody in to manage the books. The customers loved the upgrades. Best of all, I got to go back to my old job."

"This business guy must have had some good ideas," Striker said. "Maybe I could consult with him. Do you remember his name?"

"I don't. A regular customer of ours set up the meeting. His name was Jack Blasdel, but I'm not sure I'd recommend contacting him. Nate thought he was charming. I thought he was sleazy. He was always at the restaurant, hanging around and bothering me. After I went back to work, I'm sure he was happier flirting with the pretty new hostess. He seemed to love impressing her with his tall tales."

Davie felt a jolt of adrenalin at hearing Blasdel's name. At least she knew where Sabine had met him. Again, she wondered if those business people had also provided the money Nate Gillen was laundering through his restaurant.

"What job did you go back to?" asked Striker.

"I love children," she said. "Nate and I weren't blessed that way, so I got a job teaching preschool. It was perfect for me."

Davie didn't know what magic Striker had worked on Lacy Gillen for her to bare her soul this way but whatever it was, he deserved kudos.

"Working with children isn't a job," he said. "It's a calling. You must have been relieved when the business improved."

Gillen's expression turned melancholy. "Yes. Things were good ... for a while."

Striker kept his tone light. "Uh-oh. Are you about to crush my dreams of being the next Wolfgang Puck?"

Tears pooled in her eyes. "It might be different for you."

Davie glanced at Striker to warn him the conversation was teetering toward telenovela territory, but he ignored her. This time Striker reached for Gillen's hand and the gesture seemed too genuine to be part of a pretext. "I'm sorry, Lacy. I didn't mean to make you cry. Let's talk about something else."

A woman with spiky blonde hair and a prominent nose walked up to the table and gave Lacy a hug. Her sleeveless silk shirt fluttered in the warm evening breeze, exposing a daisy tattoo on her neck.

"Valerie," Gillen said. "I want you to meet Jon Striker and his sister Davie."

Davie stared in shock as she realized Valerie was the person in Kathleen Newell's going-away party photograph. From the stony expression on Striker's face, he recognized her, too. Nate Gillen had told Valerie not to charge Newell and her friends for their desserts. Davie wondered if she was the new hire who kept the books at the Seaglass Cafe. There was a bigger question—were Valerie and Lacy Gillen only pretending they'd just met on the ferry?

45

DAVIE WAS EAGER TO talk to Striker alone, but she didn't want to interrupt the flow of conversation.

Valerie stared at Davie as the waiter set a rum drink on the table in front of her. "Brother and sister? You don't look anything alike."

"Yeah," Striker said. "Everybody says—"

Davie interrupted. "Don't worry, bro. I'm not sensitive about it anymore." She focused on Valerie. "I'm adopted."

Valerie's face was a hard mask. "Sure." Her tone made it clear she didn't believe a word of it.

"I was telling Davie you two met on the ferry," Striker said.

Lacy Gillen flashed a broad smile. "It was just yesterday, but I feel like I've known Valerie forever. She sat next to me and we just started talking. After about ten minutes we realized we had so much in common. We were both traveling alone and to top it off, we were staying at the same hotel. Isn't that amazing? We were destined to be friends, right, Val?"

"Right," she said in a monotone.

Striker took out his cell and pointed it at them. "Let me take your first bestie picture." The camera flashed before either had time to object. "Give me your number, Valerie. I'll text this to you."

"Oh, send it to me, too," Gillen said, rattling off her number.

Valerie didn't respond, just sat there glaring at Striker.

Davie sipped her rum drink. "What brings you to Tortola, Valerie?"

Before she could answer, Gillen chimed in. "She's a CPA at a big accounting firm. She just broke up with her boyfriend and decided to get away for a while." She slapped one hand over her mouth and grabbed Valerie's arm with the other. "Oh, sorry. Am I talking out of school?"

Valerie shifted uncomfortably in her chair. "It's not exactly a secret."

Gillen's tortured expression eased as she leaned toward Striker. "Sometimes I blab too much. Everybody says so. For a long time after Nate's death I hardly talked at all. At some point I guess the floodgates opened. Sorry. I'll stop now."

Valerie pushed her chair back. "Come on, Lacy. Let's grab a plate and see what's for dinner."

"Sure," she said, glancing at Striker. "Come with us?"

"You go ahead," Davie said. "We'll stay and save the table."

Gillen looked disappointed that her new family was already breaking up. The chairs scraped against the concrete floor as the two women strolled toward a buffet table adjacent to the bar.

As soon as they were out of earshot, Davie leaned toward Striker, keeping her voice low. "Is it even possible Lacy didn't know Valerie worked at her own restaurant?"

"Under different circumstances, I'd say it was unlikely, but she seems naïve and way too trusting. She's telling us a lot of personal information. We have to assume she told Valerie, too. I'm wondering if Valerie followed her here to find out what Gillen knows about her husband's money-laundering scheme."

"You think Lacy is in danger?"

"Possibly. We need more information about Valerie. Right now we don't even know her last name."

"Would the hotel clerk give us her passport number if we tell her who we are?"

Striker shook his head. "I doubt it. We might have more luck asking local law enforcement, but we're in the middle of nowhere. There's no guarantee we can even find a police station close by."

"Let's just ask your new best friend Lacy. Once we know Valerie's full name, you call Detective Quintero and have him run her name through the system."

Striker reached under the table and tapped her knee. Davie looked up and saw Lacy Gillen heading for the table, carrying a plate piled with food.

"What did I miss?" she said. "You two look like you're cooking up trouble."

Striker stood. "Just discussing the age-old question—beef or chicken."

Gillen giggled as she settled into her chair. "I took a little of both. Why do buffets bring out the worst in people? I couldn't fit another thing on my plate. No way I can eat all this. You two better go before they run out of food."

Striker gestured toward the buffet table. "Davie?"

"I'm not that hungry. Could you just get me a salad?"

Striker nodded. "Sure thing."

Gillen called after him. "Get the mango chutney. It's brilliant on the fish."

Davie glanced at the buffet line. Valerie was still loading food onto her plate, so she had Gillen to herself, at least for a minute or two. "What are you doing after dinner?"

She spread the chutney on her fish. "No plans tonight. Tomorrow Valerie and I are going on a boat cruise around the island. Hey, why don't you two come with us? Check with the front desk. I'm sure the boat can hold two more people."

"That sounds great. I'll ask them to add us to the reservation. What's Valerie last name?"

She clapped her hands with enthusiasm. "That would be so much fun. It's Ferrick, but the reservation is under my name."

"Maybe we shouldn't mention it to Valerie until I can confirm. I don't want her to be disappointed if it doesn't work out."

Gillen put her index finger in front of her lips like a shushing librarian. "Our secret."

"Jon and I are going to take a walk on the beach after dinner. Would you come with us?"

"I'd *love* that. I'll tell Valerie."

Davie leaned closer and lowered her voice. "Maybe we should wait. If the boat tour doesn't work out, you'll be with Valerie the whole day tomorrow. Jon and I would love to spend some quality time alone with you. Would that be okay?"

She looked pensive as she considered the idea. "I don't want to hurt her feelings."

"We don't want that, either. I suggest we walk you to your room after dinner, but instead of going inside, you just keep walking with us. Beautiful night. Moon. Warm breeze. Sand between your toes. It'll give us a chance to talk in case the boat trip doesn't work out."

Gillen tilted her head and smiled. "Was this Jon's idea?"

Break her heart now or later? If Davie told her what she wanted to hear, it might crush her spirit when she found out the truth later. Worse, it could make her less likely to cooperate.

"It was my idea, but I know it's what he wants."

She looked disappointed. "Okay. Just the three of us then."

Davie gave her the thumbs-up sign. "Your food is getting cold, so I'll stop talking. I'm going to see what's holding up my bro."

Davie joined Striker at the buffet table where he was juggling two plates, his and one filled with salad.

"Valerie Ferrick," she whispered.

Striker gave her the plates. "Can you handle these? I have to make a phone call."

Valerie was sitting next to Lacy when Davie returned to the table. She seemed sullen and annoyed that her alone time with Lacy had been interrupted.

"So, Valerie," Davie said. "Where are you from?"

She didn't respond. Gillen seemed uncomfortable with the silence so she answered the question herself. "Actually, it turns out Valerie lives not far from me—in Miami. Two Floridians. Just one more thing we have in common."

"Have you heard of Lacy's restaurant?"

"She wouldn't have heard of it, Davie. It's been out of business for a while now." Gillen looked up from her rice and peas. "Where's Jon?"

"Looking for the ... uh, facilities, I think."

That excuse seemed to satisfy Gillen but not Valerie, who kept a watchful eye on the hall leading to the restrooms.

The restaurant was full of people now. Striker returned a few minutes later and the conversation turned to neutral subjects—the best time to snag a beach chair, the nearest shopping opportunities, and the breakfast room hours. Valerie was pleasant but didn't contribute much to the conversation. After the waiter had cleared the dinner plates, Gillen and Valerie went to the dessert table. Davie stayed behind with Striker.

"I talked to Quintero and texted him the photo. He did a quick search and guess what? Valerie has several arrests for check kiting and embezzlement. No convictions. He'll keep looking to see what else he can uncover. We need to talk to Lacy in private before she gets on that boat. We'll tell her who we are and see where the conversation goes."

"It's already arranged," Davie said. "Lacy is going to ditch Valerie after dinner. It's a secret so wait for my cue and be prepared for Valerie to push back."

"Let her try."

46

AFTER THEY'D FINISHED EATING, Valerie stood. "Lacy, let's go to the bar in the lobby and have an after-dinner drink."

Gillen cast a nervous glance at Davie. "I'm sort of tired."

Davie stood and nudged Striker up from his chair. "Me, too. Jon and I will walk you to your room."

Valerie was fuming but didn't seem inclined to start a tug-of-war. "Fine. I'll see you in the morning. The taxi driver is picking us up in the lobby at eight sharp." Then she stomped out of the dining room.

Gillen looked concerned. "She seemed upset."

"Tired from traveling?" Davie said. "I'm sure she'll get over it."

The three of them left the restaurant and stepped onto the beach. Gillen linked her right arm through Davie's and her left through Striker's as if they were middle-school pals at the mall. They chatted amicably for a few minutes while Davie's apprehension grew about Gillen's reaction to the truth.

"I'm *so* glad we met," she said. "I thought coming here would make me sad again, but meeting you and Jon and Valerie changed everything."

Davie was about to break her heart and shatter her sense of safety. She waited for Striker to take the lead, but he didn't. After ten minutes of walking, Gillen stopped and stared at the water, grasping the apple charm in her hand.

"I love your necklace," Davie said. "It must have a history."

"Nate gave it to me when we got engaged. He always told me I was the apple of his eye. Corny, I know, but also sweet. When I came back to the islands this time and looked out at the water, I thought about him. So many unanswered questions."

Davie fingered her own touchstones, her grandmother's earrings. "I'm sorry you're still grieving."

She sighed. "I know people get bored when I go on and on about Nate's death."

"Losing someone we love," Striker said, "leaves an emptiness that's hard to fill.

Gillen turned and put her hands on his chest. "You're such a lovely man, Jon. But the truth is when I stopped working at the restaurant my relationship with Nate deteriorated."

Striker seemed unsure of what to do. "Running a business is a lot of pressure."

Gillen dropped her hands to her sides. "Nate seemed stressed all the time. Whenever I asked him what was going on, he'd shut me down. He became so secretive and distant I began to think he was having an affair. It broke my heart because despite all our ups and downs I thought he and I were forever."

Davie remembered Detective Brooks telling her about Nate Gillen's philandering. "What made you think it was an affair?"

She walked toward the water until the waves lapped at her feet. "He was surrounded by attractive young women—customers, waitresses, and his new hostess. He was constantly telling me how beautiful Sabine was. She even had a beautiful name. Later I realized there was no affair. He just wasn't attracted to me anymore. It's my fault. I'd gained some weight and—"

Davie interrupted, feeling a mixture of anger and sadness that Gillen would carry the blame for a failed relationship over a few extra pounds. "You're a beautiful, vivacious woman, Lacy. Don't ever think otherwise."

She glanced at Striker with a sad little smile, as if wishing those words had come from him. "Thank you."

"How did you learn about your husband's death?" Striker asked.

Lacy stared toward the water, as if she were in a trance. "The night before he died, Nate came home kind of late. He seemed upset, almost afraid. I asked him what was wrong. He told me he caught Sabine snooping through his office and had to fire her. He wouldn't give details. Next thing I knew, he said he had to call his business consultant and disappeared down the hallway. I finally went to sleep and when I woke up the next morning, his side of the bed hadn't been slept in. I was frantic. I called the restaurant and all our friends. Nobody had seen him, so I called the police. Later that day, the sheriff knocked on my door and told me they'd found Nate's body the night before. He'd been killed on the side of the road in a hit-and-run accident."

"That must have been devastating," Striker said.

"Everything was a blur. A few days after Nate died, the police were at my door again, telling me Sabine Ponti had disappeared at sea and was presumed dead."

Davie and Striker exchanged a look. Her frown was meant to say, *Are you going to tell her or shall I?*

"Lacy," Striker said, "I have a confession to make."

She turned toward him and smiled. "I might have one, too, but you go first."

"I didn't tell you the truth. Davie isn't my sister. She's my partner."

Gillen's facial muscles went slack. "Oh, I didn't know. You're in a relationship?"

Striker reached into his pocket and pulled out his department ID. "Yes, but not the kind you're thinking of. We're homicide detectives with the Los Angeles Police Department."

Gillen stared at Striker's ID. She crossed her hands over her chest and struggled to catch her breath. "I don't understand."

"We're investigating the murder of Sabine Ponti. We think it may have something to do with your husband's death."

"But Sabine died in a boating accident in Florida."

Davie caught her gaze. "She died of a gunshot wound in Los Angeles a year ago."

Gillen took a sharp step back. "I want to go back to my room now."

Striker moved closer. "I'm sorry. You have a right to be upset, but we need to ask you a few more questions about Ms. Ponti and your husband."

She stared at the ground, not responding. Davie stood watching but made no effort to comfort her, not knowing how she'd react. She was concerned they'd blown any chance of getting information from her.

Striker spoke in a soft soothing voice. "We suspect Valerie Ferrick isn't who she claims to be. We believe she worked at your husband's restaurant, possibly as the bookkeeper. She may have followed you here."

"Valerie? That can't be true. Why would she do that?"

"We think somebody was laundering money through the Sea-glass. Valerie worked as the bookkeeper, so she had to know about it. She might also know the source of the dirty money. We're not sure what she wants from you, but we're worried you could be in danger."

Lacy Gillen wrapped her arms around herself in a supportive hug. "Nate told me he kept a hundred thousand dollars hidden under a heater vent in the office in case of emergency. I thought it was odd he didn't put it in the bank, but I never questioned his judgment. The day after Sabine disappeared, I went to the restaurant to pick up the money. It was gone. Maybe that's what Valerie is looking for. She thinks I took it."

"Did you report the theft?"

"No. It sounds crazy but I always wondered if Sabine stole it. I guess I should have told somebody, but it seemed wrong to accuse a dead woman when I had no proof. What was I going to tell the police? Maybe Nate changed his mind and deposited the money in the bank and forgot to tell me."

It was hard to believe Lacy Gillen was so clueless, but if she was lying it was an Oscar-worthy performance.

"What happened to the restaurant after Nate died?" Davie asked.

"I hired a commercial real estate broker to sell the place. He told me the restaurant was barely breaking even and no buyer would be interested. I didn't understand. I thought the Seaglass was a success, but there was hardly enough money in the bank to pay our vendors."

"What about the land?"

"We didn't own it. I felt bad about the employees, but I had no choice but to walk away."

Striker put a hand on Gillen's shoulder. "We think you should leave the island tonight. We'll go with you to your room and help you pack. Then we'll take you to the airport and make sure you get on a flight."

"When you get home, stay inside," Davie said. "Don't answer the door unless it's family or close friends. We'll call you when we know more."

Gillen seemed disoriented. "I'm paid through the week."

"I'll tell the hotel you had an emergency," Striker said. "They might give you a refund."

"The airline will charge me for changing my flight."

"Lacy," Davie said. "Now isn't the time to think about that. We're concerned for your safety. I know it's a lot to absorb, but we'll feel better once you're safe at home."

"Okay," she said. "I'll go."

Davie walked with her to her room and stood by as she packed. Striker booked her on a flight to Fort Lauderdale connecting through San Juan, Puerto Rico. When the taxi arrived to pick them up, they rode in silence to the airport on Beef Island. She and Striker waited in the lobby until they saw Lacy Gillen's plane taxi down the runway. Then they caught a cab back to the hotel.

47

DAVIE AND STRIKER WERE booked on a return flight out of the airport on St. Thomas, but there were no ferries leaving Tortola until the next day so they had no choice but to spend the night at the hotel. The sun had long disappeared over the horizon. The bar was closing, so Striker snagged a couple of beach towels and a half-full bottle of champagne from the lobby bar and they headed to the beach.

They were alone on the sand, just she and Striker, watching the twinkling masthead lights of the sailboats anchored offshore. Davie kicked off her flip-flops and moved her shoulders back and forth in the sand until she'd molded herself a cradle to fit her back.

She heard laughter from the cockpit of a catamaran anchored nearby. "Those people sound like they're having a real party out there."

"Do you sail?"

The water lapped at the shore as a breeze lifted the corner of her cotton sundress, exposing one leg. "None of my friends have boats, so I've never been out. You?"

"I grew up in Annapolis. My mom was what you might call a real mariner. She taught me to sail when I was a kid."

Davie propped up her head with her hand, noting that her shoulder was better but still sore. "What about your dad?"

He picked up a shell from the sand and skipped it into the water. "He was a busy man. She gave him an honorable discharge from the Striker Navy early on."

Davie understood family dysfunction but didn't want to read too much into Striker's comments. Maybe his childhood had been normal and happy. If it wasn't, he'd tell her eventually—or not.

"It's interesting that Lacy Gillen came back alone to the place where she and her husband fell in love and spent their honeymoon. I can't imagine how that would feel."

"Which part can't you imagine? Losing a spouse or falling in love?"

Just beyond the shoreline Davie heard splashing in the shallow water, perhaps a school of fish. Speculating about that was a good excuse not to answer right away. "Mostly I can't imagine a man watching me dance on the sand at Foxy's and think I was anything but a hot mess."

He started to respond but held back. "Foxy's is a fun place. You should go sometime."

She dug her toes into the sand. "You've been there?"

"Once," he said. "A long time ago."

"Was dancing involved?" Despite her light tone, Striker didn't respond. Even in profile, she could tell he was frowning. "I see you're taking the Fifth."

He scooped up a handful of sand and let it filter through his fingers. "There may have been dancing."

"Is that where you got your tattoo?"

"You're asking me a lot of deep questions."

Davie sat up. "Just curious. I don't know much about you."

"There are more interesting things to talk about than me."

She hadn't expected Striker's dismissal to cause her pain, but it did. "Isn't that for me to decide?" There was a long silence before Davie changed the subject and the mood. "Did you notice that necklace Lacy was wearing tonight?"

"Yeah, why?"

"It was a gold apple charm. If I remember my high school French, the word for apple is *pomme*."

"And?"

"One of the offshore accounts listed in Sabine's doodles was Pomme, LLC with a post office box in Road Town, Tortola. What if Nate was skimming money from the launderers and stashing it in a bank here? Criminals don't appreciate people stealing from them. They don't forget or forgive. Maybe that's why Nate was killed and why Valerie is tailing Lacy. She's looking for the money."

"You're speculating."

"Maybe, but Lacy claimed a secret stash of money was missing from Nate's office—a hundred thousand dollars. Robert Montaine said his stepmother lived in L.A. for a year with no apparent source of income. How much money would that take? I'd guess the average rent for an apartment is at least two thousand dollars a month, probably more. She'd have other living expenses, too. Before we leave tomorrow, let's stop by the bank in Road Town and see if they'll tell us who owns Pomme, LLC."

48

THE CHAMPAGNE BOTTLE WAS empty. Davie sat next to Striker on the sand, silently admiring the tropical evening tableau—waves lapping against the shore and the glow of a full moon.

Striker was first to break the spell. "We should call it a night. Tomorrow is going to be a long day."

She stood and inched her toes into the flip-flops as a warm breeze brushed against her skin. "It's so beautiful. I hate to leave."

"You can come back, unless your boss has a no-vacation policy."

"I wouldn't know. I haven't taken vacation days since I got to Pacific." That was technically true. She just didn't mention the days she'd been relieved of duty in connection with an officer-involved shooting that was eventually resolved in her favor.

Striker frowned as he shook sand from the beach towels. "Everybody needs some downtime, especially people like us."

She let the subject drop as they crossed the road and made their way up the hill, pausing at the door to her room.

"You need a wake up call?" he asked.

She held up her cell phone. "Alarm app. See you in the morning."

Striker waited on the landing until she went inside. She leaned against the closed door, listening to his footsteps as he walked down the hall to the room next to hers and kept listening until she heard his door close.

She was tired but not sleepy. The room felt hot and muggy, but the noise and artificial coolness of air conditioners didn't appeal to her. Opening the sliding glass door meant fresh air but also an invitation for geckos looking to party in her shoes. She turned on the ceiling fan, undressed, and lay naked on the bed with only a sheet draped over her legs.

The travel magazines and island promotional brochures on the bedside table didn't hold her attention. She opened the book on money laundering but set it aside after a few pages, too distracted by the day's events to concentrate. Finally, she turned off the light and closed her eyes. An hour later, she was still awake, thinking about Sabine Ponti and Lacy Gillen—and about Jon Striker. He had to know her interest in him was more than professional, but he'd never said or done anything to encourage her. Either he thought a relationship with a coworker wasn't in his best interests or the feelings weren't mutual.

After another twenty minutes of wakefulness, she kicked off the sweaty sheet and stepped into the shower, letting the coolness wash over her until she felt guilty about her water usage. In Los Angeles, her showers were limited to five minutes or less, mostly less, because of the years-long drought.

She toweled off and had just switched on the A/C when she heard a knock on the door. It was after 2:00 a.m. It crossed her mind that Valerie Ferrick had discovered Lacy Gillen was no longer at the hotel and had come looking for her. Davie threw on her ratty T-shirt, grabbed her gun, and tiptoed to the door.

"Who is it?" she said.

"Me." It was Striker's voice.

She let go of the breath she was holding and opened the door. He stood under the overhead light wearing warm-up pants and a tight gray T-shirt stretched across his muscular chest. His chronically neat hair was tousled and his eyelids were at half-mast as if he'd just awakened from a deep sleep.

Striker glanced at her gun and raised his hands in a jokey gesture. "Don't shoot." Then his gaze swept over her body. "I just wanted to make sure you were okay."

Her cheeks felt warm, because even though her baggy T-shirt covered her legs to mid thigh, she was naked underneath it. She crossed her arms over her chest, tucking her weapon against her rib cage. "How did you know I was awake?"

"Our rooms share a wall. I heard the shower. Truth is, I couldn't sleep, either. I keep thinking about the case. You have a minute to talk?"

Davie was worried about inviting him into her room. Out of the corner of her eye she saw the red thong underwear abandoned on the floor and remembered the Cinderella toothbrush she'd left on the bathroom counter.

Striker sensed her hesitation. "Never mind. Catch you tomorrow."

"Don't be silly," she said, nudging the thong into the closet with her foot before gesturing him inside.

Striker hesitated and then stepped into the room. "Have you heard from that detective in Fort Lauderdale? Just curious if she identified those two men in the photo with Gillen."

Davie laid her weapon on the nightstand. "She hasn't called back. I'll follow up tomorrow." She sat on the edge of the bed tugging the T-shirt over her knees.

Striker moved to the sliding glass door and draped his muscular body casually onto the chair. "If her people can't ID them, I think our analysts can."

"Have you heard any more from Quintero?"

He rubbed his face as people do when they're tired. "There's a three-hour time difference. He'll get back to us as soon as he knows more."

Davie studied Striker's lean face and the silver highlights in his dark hair. Even with the T-shirt stretched over her knees she felt self-conscious, so she reached for the sheet and pulled it over her legs. "You don't have to babysit me just because I have insomnia."

He leaned forward with his legs spread, forearms on his knees, and head tilted upward with a look that seemed open, almost vulnerable. "I'm aware of that, Detective."

Davie waited a beat, unsure of what to say. Finally, she resumed chatting about the case and jotting down notes. A few moments later she glanced at Striker again and caught him checking his cell phone.

"I'm boring you. Don't worry. It's sort of my specialty."

"You weren't boring me," he said, standing, "but it's late. I should go back to my room."

Davie sat on the bed, listening to the dull hum of the air conditioner and the buzz of the ceiling fan, thinking how much she didn't want Striker to leave, wondering if he felt the same way. Inviting him to stay was a risky move. He might say no or, worse, refuse to work with her anymore. Except, he was still standing there, watching her. Davie glanced around the room and noticed the gecko scampering toward the safety of her overnight bag. The little guy would be okay there tonight. Tomorrow morning when she packed to leave was another story. She took that as a sign. *Tonight is tonight.*

Her chest cramped, her mouth felt dry as she struggled to keep her tone light. "You can stay here. I can bore you to sleep. It'll be better than Ambien."

He smiled as he slipped his cell into his pocket. "Good to know you're keeping me off drugs."

She stood and let the sheet fall in a heap around her legs. Her internal warning bells were sounding, but she no longer cared if Striker saw the outline of her breasts beneath the ratty T-shirt. She moved toward him, taking his hands in hers. "It's such a long way to your room."

He raised his eyebrows in mock surprise. "It's just a few feet down the hall."

She massaged his palms with her thumbs. "But you're here already."

He drew in a deep breath and closed his eyes for a moment. "I don't think this is a good idea."

She let go. "Why?"

He cradled her face in his warm hands and stared into her eyes. "We work together and I outrank you. Some people will see that as a problem."

She was so close to him she could feel the warmth of his body and smell the fragrance of hotel soap from his shower. "It won't be a problem when I go back to Pacific."

He wrapped his arms around her and rested his chin on her head. "Davie …"

His hesitant tone and the slight tension in his muscles were warnings she chose to ignore. She took a step back, as she guided him toward the bed like he was Fred and she was Ginger.

His expression was serious as his eyes probed hers. "Are you sure you know what you're doing?"

She nudged him gently to a sitting position on the bed. "I think I do."

His muscles seemed to relax but his expression remained unreadable for so long she began to wonder if she'd miscalculated. But it was too late to change course.

Davie swept her hand over his smooth cheek. That's when she realized he'd shaved before coming to her door. She smiled. "Are you going to make me do this all by myself?"

Without a sound, he reached toward the lamp and flipped the switch before gathering her into his arms. In the darkness, she felt his warm breath on her neck and the soft brush of his lips against her skin.

His voice was raspy and low as his hands explored her body. "We shouldn't be doing this." But she could tell by his tone that he didn't mean it, not one little bit.

"We can stop any—" A sharp intake of breath cut off the rest of her sentence.

For the next hour or so she floated in and out of an altered state of consciousness. At some point during a brief interlude, Striker fell asleep with his right arm draped over her body. The moon's glow streamed through the glass door as she ran her finger lightly over the tattoo on his forearm—*Breathe*. She felt as she often did when things turned out better than she'd imagined—apprehensive. Maybe the proverbial other shoe wouldn't drop this time, but in case her seduction of Jon Striker was an irredeemable error in judgment, she would enjoy this moment while it lasted.

Tonight is tonight.

Her fingers laced through his. Her cheek rested against the tattoo. She counted her breaths as the department shrink had taught her to do and waited for sunrise.

49

THE SUN STREAMING THROUGH the window awakened Davie the following morning. She glanced around the room, but Striker was gone. She checked the time on her cell and then texted him. WHERE ARE YOU?

A moment later, he responded. RESERVATIONS CONFIRMED FOR FERRY. MEET ME IN THE LOBBY IN 20 MINUTES.

That definitely didn't qualify as postcoital sweet talk.

She showered and dressed, making sure the gecko had moved to safer ground before throwing her clothes and cosmetics into the carry-on bag. She paused over the sundress, wondering if she should leave it in the room. At the last minute, she stuffed it in her bag and applied the sunscreen she'd purchased in the gift shop.

When she arrived in the lobby her gaze swept the room, but Valerie Ferrick was nowhere in sight. Striker was waiting for her, dressed in jeans and a white polo shirt. He seemed remote even as he handed her a croissant wrapped in a paper napkin.

"You missed breakfast," he said.

She kept her response simple. "I overslept. Ambien isn't the best sleeping aid after all."

He didn't take the bait. "The cab is on its way. We have to get to the bank in Road Town as soon as possible or we'll miss the ferry to St. Thomas and our flight back to L.A."

Concern prickled the back of her neck. If she hadn't texted him, would he have left without her? Of course not, but the mere fact the thought had popped into her head was troubling. They would have to talk about what happened last night, but obviously this wasn't the time.

Tense silence in the back of the cab made it impossible to read Striker's thoughts. The cabbie dropped them off at CommerceBank, near Road Town's Wickams Cay. The building was two stories and beige with an unobtrusive sign attached at the second-floor landing. When they arrived at the front entrance, the door was locked.

"It's Saturday," Striker said, pointing to a sign painted on the glass door. "The bank is closed."

Davie knocked on the glass and waved her hand. "There's somebody in the back."

A thin black man in his twenties looked up from his work and walked toward them, pointing to the sign. "Closed."

Davie held up her badge. "We're from Los Angeles. We have a couple of questions. Could you spare a minute or two?"

The man hesitated but pulled a ring of keys from his pocket and opened the door. "What do you want?"

"We're investigating a homicide. We believe the death may be connected to an account at this bank called Pomme, LLC. Could you confirm the name of the owner?"

He shook his head. "Sorry. Privacy regulations and all that."

"Of course," she said. "Maybe you could just tell us if there's been any recent activity on the account?"

"That would be confirming the account exists, which I've just told you I can't do—not without the proper legal request."

"I understand, but if the account isn't relative to our investigation I'd hate to bother you with all that paperwork."

In a carefully controlled voice he said, "Please wait."

He relocked the door and walked to the back room while Davie stood on the sidewalk, peering through the glass door. Striker leaned against the building, watching traffic roll by. Five minutes later the man returned.

"I checked with my manager. I can't give you the information you requested. All I can say is one of our local lawyers specializes in setting up those kinds of accounts. He might be willing to talk to you. His office is a few blocks from here."

It was about a five-minute stroll to the office of Aubrey Purcell, Esquire. The door was open but when Davie walked in, the reception's chair was empty.

Striker called out. "Anybody here?"

A black man, five-eight or so with a slight build, walked into the lobby adjusting wire-rimmed glasses. His expression was placid, his accent British.

"How may I help you?"

"We're with the Los Angeles Police Department," Davie said. "An employee of CommerceBank referred us to you. We understand you may have set up an account for an LLC called Pomme."

His face lit up. "Los Angeles? I've always wanted to visit your city. Tell me, is the Getty Museum as grand as they say?"

Davie struggled to hide her impatience. "It's a sight to behold, all right."

"And the Rose Parade? All those lovely flowers. I understand you can visit the floats up close after the parade."

"All true."

"Come in," Purcell said, waving them into the inner office.

The central focus of the room was a large ornate wooden desk with just enough battle scars to make it look interesting. The two guest chairs were leather, the reddish-brown color of a sorrel horse. A picture of Queen Elizabeth II sat on a credenza behind the desk, along with photos of Purcell with various dignitaries, including Prince Charles and Rihanna.

Purcell sat in his large leather chair. "Can I assume you brought the necessary legal documents?"

Striker leaned forward and with an earnest expression said, "We're a long way from home, Mr. Purcell. We just uncovered this new information. I know it's asking a lot, but maybe you could help a couple of L.A. cops just this one time. The owner of the account has passed away, and we'd like to find out if his death is connected to the murder of a young woman back home."

The lawyer hesitated for a moment and then put his hands on the keyboard of his desktop computer. "Who is the account holder?"

"His name is Nate Gillen." Davie crossed her fingers, hoping her guess was correct.

Purcell leaned back in his chair, shaken. "Oh my. I do remember helping Mr. Gillen set up his account. I never saw him in person, you understand. All our business was done electronically, or over the telephone. There are so many laws these days. He wanted to make sure everything was aboveboard. I'm sorry to learn of his death. What happened?"

"He was killed by a hit-and-run driver a couple of years ago," Davie said.

"How very sad. But he died some time ago. I'm surprised his wife didn't notify me."

"Perhaps she didn't know about the account," Striker said.

"I doubt that's the case." Purcell resumed typing on his keyboard. He pulled his glasses down on his nose and moved his head closer to the screen. "The initial deposit was a million dollars, US, of course. Mr. Gillen made weekly wire transfers after that, but for smaller amounts until the balance reached five million."

"That's a lot of money," Davie said, stating the obvious.

"Actually, it's a modest amount compared to many of my clients, but a good nest egg nonetheless. The bank sends me Pomme's monthly statements. Let me check the current balance." A couple of keystrokes later he stared at the screen. "It appears there've been periodic withdrawals, one as recently as two weeks ago. Nonetheless, I'll contact his wife with instructions about making her the sole owner."

Davie was stunned. If Lacy Gillen was withdrawing cash from the account, it meant she likely knew about the money-laundering scheme.

"We just put Lacy Gillen on a plane back to Florida," she told him.

Purcell looked up from the screen. "Lacy? I don't recognize that name. His wife is a co-owner on the account, but her name is Karen. Karen Nord."

50

It took Davie a moment to remember where she'd heard that name before. Karen Nord was a waitress at the Seaglass Cafe and the person seen making out with Nate Gillen in the backseat of his car. Karen Nord was most definitely not Nate Gillen's wife, but she *was* co-owner of his secret bank account, possibly established for their life together after he divorced his real wife, Lacy.

After she and Striker walked out of Purcell's office, they caught a cab to the ferry terminal. They couldn't debrief in the taxi for fear the driver would overhear the conversation. When they arrived in St. Thomas, they hailed another taxi to Cyril E. King International Airport in the outskirts of Charlotte Amalie.

The airport was teeming with tanned tourists of all ages heading home with their tube-like "noodle" floating devices stuffed into beach bags already overflowing with rumpled towels and soggy swimsuits. She and Striker passed through security and found seats in the small lobby. As they waited to board the flight she noticed Striker staring through the grimy windowpanes onto the tarmac. He waited until two Gen-X parents wrangled three small children into nearby plastic chairs before glancing her way.

He kept his voice low, using the noise level in the room as cover. "I'm sorry about what happened last night. It was unprofessional of me to do anything that might jeopardize this investigation."

For a moment Davie couldn't breathe. The other shoe just dropped. The room felt stuffy. Her mind roiled with confusion. Davie focused on a small bird trapped inside the airport lobby, darting from window to window looking for an exit.

She swallowed hard to clear a path for words. "You said that before—several times. It didn't seem to matter to you last night."

"I got carried away. I should have known better."

Her facial muscles felt slack. "Okay, I get it. It never happened."

He caught her gaze and held it, evaluating the damage. "It happened, Davie, but if our relationship turns personal, Quintero has to know, the lieutenant, too. In that case, I'm guessing they won't let us work this case together."

She straightened her back to make it easier to breathe. He was right, of course. Department regulations were clear on coworker romances. They were taboo if you worked in the same unit, especially if one party outranked the other, and for obvious reasons—breakups, arguments, inappropriate touching while buying Cheez-its at the vending machine.

Their conversation was interrupted when the Gen-X's toddler staggered over to Striker, holding out a plastic sand bucket for inspection. A moment later, the kid's mom grabbed her son's arm and mumbled *sorry*. The distraction gave Davie some time to process her feelings, but not enough time to ease the knot in her stomach. It was painful to think of Striker as a one-night stand, but it wasn't her first and it probably wouldn't be her last. The sad part was she genuinely cared for him; having to pretend last night didn't happen, even temporarily, made her feel empty inside.

"Maybe working together is already too complicated," she said, following the flight path of the little bird. "Maybe I should ask Lieutenant Repetto to drop you from the case and give me a new partner."

Striker's tone was firm, almost paternal. "That's not going to happen."

She wanted to shout *you're not the boss of me* but for obvious reasons—it would be childish and ultimately ineffective—she tempered her tone. "You seem overly confident about how much power you have over me."

He leaned into her personal space to emphasize his point. "I *do* have power over you, Davie. That's the problem. If people find out we're dating, they'll be watching us and judging our work in a different light. Is that what you want?"

"I'm going to stretch my legs," she said, rising from the chair.

The little bird was still looking for a way out. Davie circumnavigated the small lobby, glancing at a gift shop full of cosmetics and booze until she found a ticket agent who was willing to prop open a door. The bird circled the room a half dozen times until it sensed fresh air and flew to freedom. Davie should have felt better but she didn't. Maybe freedom wasn't all it was cracked up to be.

Once she boarded the airplane, she feigned interest in the money-laundering book to avoid engaging with Striker. Her emotions felt raw and she didn't want to say anything to heighten the tension.

It was 5:30 p.m. local time when the plane landed at LAX. Davie mumbled a quick goodbye to Striker before they parted ways. She'd called Vaughn as soon as the plane hit the tarmac. He was waiting at the LAPD's airport substation to take her to Pacific, where she'd left her car.

Her partner accelerated as he maneuvered onto Sepulveda Boulevard. "Your skin is the color of winter in Antarctica. Where's your tan?"

"I wasn't on vacation. I was working." Davie's words sounded harsh even to her.

"Whoa. You sound pissed. What's going on?"

There was no benefit in unloading on Vaughn, so she softened her tone. "I'm just tired."

He slammed his palm on the steering wheel. "It was Striker, right? What did that asshole do to you?"

"Nothing. Let's drop it, okay?"

"Fine, but I'm not buying it." He waited a beat and when she didn't respond, he changed the subject. "I've got something that might perk you up."

"Coffee?"

"Something way better. Remember when I told you I was going to look a little deeper into Gerda Pittman's PI, Natalie Salinas? I did a sweep of social media and she's everywhere, including on one of those employment sites."

Davie leaned her forehead against the cool window as Vaughn veered left onto Lincoln Boulevard. "Is she trolling for clients, or looking for a job?"

"Maybe a little of both. I found something interesting on one of the sites. She's selling photographs online to anybody with a PayPal account, including a couple of tabloids."

"Are private investigators allowed to do that?"

"They have a code of ethics that reads like the Boy Scout pledge, but I doubt Salinas has read it. Anyway, I went to talk to her again."

"That must have made her day."

Vaughn turned right on Culver Boulevard and headed toward the station. "Yeah, she wasn't happy, but she finally copped to selling pictures from her surveillance jobs. I asked if she shot any at Blasdel's gunstore. At first she said no, but I used my super powers and she finally admitted staking out the store and taking pictures in the area. Some of them she sold to an online photo service. She gave me copies."

"See anything of value?"

"Hard to say. I don't know all the details of the case. Some pics were of people going in and out of the store. Others were arty shots, the mean streets of L.A. and all that. They're on a disc on your desk. You can look when we get back to the station."

Davie retrieved her travel bag from the back seat as Vaughn pulled up to the station's gate. "How's the cooking class?"

Vaughn swept his ID over the sensor and waited for the gate to open. "I'm studying for the midterm—*pesce per sico alla comasca*. My first attempt was a disaster. Had to dump the whole thing in the garbage." He paused before continuing. "So, tell me about your trip. Did Lacy Gillen tie up the loose ends with a tidy little bow?"

"Assume nothing, Jason. That's my new motto. This case is way more convoluted than I imagined. Every time I peel off a layer I find another and another."

"Just like Italian cooking."

After they'd parked, she stowed her overnight bag in the trunk of her Camaro and went into the station to look at the Natalie Salinas photos. It was Saturday evening and the squad room was quiet except for a night detective reading through warrant packages and an officer from Long Beach PD using the Robbery coordinator's computer. A Juvenile-Car P-2 sat at a desk behind her, taking a telephonic report. From what she could tell from his side of the conversation, a school security guard had discovered basketballs missing from a storage unit.

Her partner stood at his desk looking at her over the partition wall. "When do you report to RHD?"

"Not sure. I have to talk to Giordano first."

Her partner's expression looked strained as he walked around the workstation to her desk. "You want to tell me what's going on?"

"Maybe later. After I look at these photos."

"Okay," he said, stretching out the word. "You might want to check your email, too. Van Nuys Homicide dicks emailed you a report and copied me. The fire at Blasdel's place was definitely arson. They found a crude igniting device near the electrical outlet."

Davie slipped the disc into the side of her computer monitor. "Have they done the autopsy yet?"

"The morgue is backed up, but the arson investigator agrees with you. Blasdel was alive when the fire started, possibly unconscious. He won't know for sure until he gets the toxicology report and that won't be available for weeks."

"Do me a favor," Davie said. "Forward the Van Nuys email to Detective Striker."

Vaughn placed his palms on her desk and lowered his face to within inches of hers. "Why can't you do it yourself?"

She put her index finger on his forehead and pushed him away. "Because you're my partner and I asked you to do it for me."

"I get it now," he said, his voice low. "Look, Davie, I've got your back. If you have a problem with Striker, just let me know. I'll straighten him out."

She smiled, genuinely heartened by his show of support. "Thanks, but I can handle him myself. What's happening with the fires?"

"Malibu is partially contained, but Santa Paula keeps growing. It's already eaten thousands of acres and a bunch of houses. Hundreds more people had to be evacuated. Before I picked you up I heard a new fire just broke out near the Skirball Center. They think it started in a homeless encampment."

Davie massaged her temples to relieve the stress. While she'd been drinking champagne on the beach in Tortola, wildfires had been destroying lives and real estate in Southern California. She opened an online news site and learned that the Getty Museum had closed to protect the art from smoke billowing over the hills above Brentwood. The fire hadn't shifted toward Bel Air, but it was too close to ignore.

Davie did her best to tune out the noise in her head as she clicked on Natalie Salinas's photos. They were all date stamped, so she zeroed in on those taken in the days before Sabine Ponti's death. Most appeared to be establishing shots worthy of a magazine spread or a blog post, arty shots of utility lines crisscrossing above the street, and pictures of strip malls. There was one shot of a homeless man slumped against a graffiti-covered wall that would have made a good cover for a noir novel. Salinas had told her she didn't sit in her car surveilling Black Jack Guns & Ammo with a pair of binoculars. That part was true. She'd used a camera.

There were random pictures taken from different angles of an old Toyota parked in an alley next to a beat-up garbage bin. The name on the license plate holder advertised a low-budget rental agency. Davie recognized the location because of the faded sign on the wall of Nazarian's upholstery shop. She checked the date stamp and felt a chill along her spine. The picture had been taken at 10:08 a.m., an hour before Sabine Ponti had entered the gunstore.

There was one more shot of the Toyota taken around that same time. It was from a distance, possibly with a telephoto lens. It included a bulked-up man leaning against the car. Wide-set eyes squinted against the smoke of his cigarette. His hair was cut close to the scalp exposing small ears that resembled sliced mushrooms glued to the side of his head. It was clear from his furtive gaze that he was unaware he was being photographed. Davie zoomed in on the man's face and thought she saw an earring in his right ear.

She dug out the photo of the two men standing on that Florida street corner with Nate Gillen. Pulling a magnifying glass from her desk drawer, she focused on the man whose back was to the camera. He had the same close-cropped hair and unusually small ears. Her eyes drew closer as they focused on his right ear to confirm what she'd noticed when she first saw the picture: a hoop earring hanging from his earlobe. It appeared to be the same man.

Davie clenched her fists. She printed out the photo and called the car agency to find out the name of the customer who'd rented the car, using the license plate number and the date the picture was taken. She waited on the line listening to the guy clicking away on the computer keyboard.

"Here it is," he said a moment later. "He rented the car a year ago under the name John W. Booth."

Davie noted the name's similarity to John Wilkes Booth, the actor and assassin who killed President Abraham Lincoln in Ford Theatre in Washington, D.C. Either John W. Booth was the guy's real name or it was his idea of a joke. If it was the latter, he'd gone to a lot of work and expense to forge his driver's license.

"How did he pay?" Davie asked.

"Cash."

The agent hadn't kept a copy of Booth's ID, and claimed he hadn't seen the guy before or since, but he gave Davie the man's cell number. She asked him to fax the rental agreement and ended the call. When she called Booth's cell, his number was no longer in service.

She ran the name through department databases and found many John Booths, but only a handful with that middle initial. She made a list, but locating and interviewing each one of them seemed fruitless, because she believed the name was an alias.

She studied the photo again, focusing on the cigarette in the man's hand. She thought back to the smell of cigarette smoke in her house a few days ago and felt a chill.

51

DAVIE STUDIED BOTH PHOTOS she had of Mushroom Ears. Salinas's picture had been taken a year ago, but if Ears was back in L.A., he might have rented other cars. Striker already had a copy of the street corner picture. She would scan Natalie Salinas's shot near the Toyota and email it to Striker, as well.

She made a list of budget rental agencies on the Westside. First, she would map out the addresses to allow as little backtracking as possible and then visit the places on the list, hoping for a lucky break.

Before leaving the station, she picked up the car rental agreement from the fax machine. They might want to have a handwriting examiner look at the signatures if she could find a comparison. Then she picked up the keys to the Jetta and headed out.

An hour later she'd met with zero success. She sat in the car outside the fifth and last budget agency on her list and crossed her fingers before going inside. If this didn't pan out, she'd have to start checking with big-name agencies.

The man at the counter wore a company sports jacket that was two sizes too large for his slight frame. His complexion had the ghostly pallor of a recently paroled convict. She identified herself and held up Salinas's photo of the man standing by the Toyota. "Has this guy ever rented a vehicle from you? He may have used the name John W. Booth or possibly just John Booth."

The man studied the photo and shook his head. "Nope."

Davie slipped the picture back inside her notebook. "Thanks for your time."

"No, I mean he rented a car from me, but that's not the name he used. Can't remember what it was, but I'll look it up for you. The guy paid cash and he was a total jerk. I told him not to smoke in the car but it reeked of cigarettes when he brought it back. It was also a mess—empty Oreo bags and crumbs everywhere. The guy copped an attitude when I called him on it. After he left, I flagged his file as DNR—do not rent. He called me again a few days ago, but I told him I didn't have any cars available."

The desk agent disappeared into the back room and returned a moment later with a piece of paper with a name written on it in blocky capitals—MILES STANDISH.

"Miles Standish?" she said. "That name didn't ring any alarm bells?"

"Why should it? Who is he?"

"He's …" Davie paused. The name *was* pretty obscure. She couldn't expect a desk agent to also be a student of *Mayflower* history. "Never mind."

"Since you refused to do business with Mr. Standish, do you know any other agencies who might rent a car to a jerk for cash?"

His expression turned suspicious. "I know all kinds of people. Some of them wouldn't appreciate me giving their names to the cops."

"Even if those people never found out how I got the information?"

He hesitated. "You expect me to take your word?"

"That's exactly what I expect."

"What's in it for me?"

"The satisfaction of knowing you did the right thing."

He let out a nervous laugh. "Okay. The guy's name is Raoul. I gave his number to Standish. Can't confirm they ever did business, but Raoul has a fleet of cars that belong to owners who need quick cash and renters who need cars, no questions asked."

"Does this Raoul have a last name?"

He swiped away beads of sweat forming on his face. "Raoul Hice. He flies under the radar. He's also an ex-con, so be careful how you approach him."

After Davie left the rental agency, she sat in the car to consider her options. If Raoul Hice had information that would identify Mushroom Ears, she had to interview him. Vaughn could go with her, but that meant involving him in a case that was no longer assigned to Pacific Homicide, which would put him in the awkward position of saying no.

Technically she should call Jon Striker and tell him what she'd discovered. She wondered how annoyed he'd be if she interviewed Raoul Hice without consulting him. Pretty annoyed, she guessed. Plus, it was risky to go alone. And it was even riskier to continue working the case without including Striker. To avoid talking to him, she emailed the information about Raoul Hice and headed home.

52

SHE GOT AS FAR as Sepulveda and Pico before her phone rang. A glance at the display panel told her it was an incoming call from Striker. If she didn't answer, he'd just call back so she pressed *accept*.

"Just got your email," he said. "Question—why are you working this case by yourself?"

"My partner developed a lead while we were out of town. I followed up. Now I've turned it over to you. You're welcome."

"I didn't say it wasn't good information." He paused before continuing. "Look, maybe I was too abrupt with you at the airport. If so, I'm sorry. But we're on this case together now, and it's going to be difficult if we don't communicate."

If the conversation had taken place after a good night's sleep, she wouldn't have felt so defensive. But she was suffering the effects of jetlag and the loss of the familiar back-and-forth she had with her partner. Vaughn would never have treated her in such a paternal way. She didn't want to talk to Striker, much less work with him. The only thing that pushed her forward was the commitment she'd made when she took this job—to stand in the shoes of the victims, protecting their interests against all others. That meant reining in any personal feelings that could jeopardize the case.

"Got it," she said.

There was a long pause before he responded. "I'll be at Pacific in fifteen minutes. We'll talk when I get there."

The line went dead.

Striker's tone sounded frustrated, maybe even angry, and it was clear the comment wasn't a suggestion. It was an order. She had no choice but to return to the station. To do otherwise would confirm the department's position that cops engaged in personal relationships shouldn't work together.

When Davie arrived at her desk, the Long Beach patrol officer and the J-Car officer were gone, but the night detective was still reading through reports. She typed her rental agency interviews on an official computer form. The notes and the Salinas's photo disc would go to Striker when he arrived.

A few minutes later Davie heard footsteps and glanced up to see Striker standing by the door of the squad room. His expression was pinched as he beckoned her to join him in the hallway. She grabbed her notes and the photos and walked toward the door, expecting him to jab his finger in her face and make some bullshit accusation about her lack of team spirit. Instead, he seemed tired and unhappy.

His voice was flat. "Is there someplace we can talk in private?"

"Outside in the parking lot or upstairs in the Roll Call room. Take your pick."

Striker nodded toward the stairs. As soon as they entered the empty room he pulled two chairs toward a back corner and took a seat. Davie remained standing. His forearms rested on his thighs, his head tilted upward, staring directly at her with those startling blue eyes of his. "Are we okay?" he asked.

This was not the time for rehashing hurt feelings, so she paused a moment to shoehorn all the memories from the previous night into a small compartment of her brain and lock the door. Maybe she'd sort it all out in the future—or maybe not.

"Sure," she said with as much nonchalance as she could muster. "We're fine."

Striker straightened his spine and nodded. "Good. Before I left the office I cross-referenced the information you had on Raoul Hice and found an address in South Gate. He has an arrest record that goes back to his teens, including a conviction for Grand Theft Auto. According to our records, he's on parole. I think we should drive over and see what he has to say."

"Now?" Davie asked. "It's almost seven thirty."

"You have something better to do?"

As a condition of his parole, Hice's property could be searched any time of the day or night without a warrant as long as law enforcement had a suspicion he was engaged in criminal conduct. His dodgy car rental business was cause enough. With his conviction for auto theft, it was possible at least some of the vehicles in his fleet were stolen.

They took Striker's car to South Gate, a city with its own police department and one of the highest crime rates in the country. It would be dangerous enough for the two of them to go there. Going alone would have been reckless.

The address led them down a narrow street to a building surrounded by a tall metal fence topped with spearlike points. The area was tangled with power and telephone lines strung from wooden poles. A faded sign over the door read BODY SHOP • FREE RENTAL CAR • INSURANCE WORK.

As Davie got out of the passenger door she felt wary and boxed in by the stucco buildings lining both sides of the street, all with barred windows and graffiti-covered walls. An older Chevy Impala with tinted windows drove past, loud music blasting from an open window. Her hand covered her weapon as the car slowed a moment, then accelerated, disappearing around the corner.

As they reached the gate, Davie held her flashlight like a javelin, ready to use it as a weapon. The beam of light revealed a padlock hanging unsecured from a metal loop. Before entering, Striker whistled to see if that brought any dogs, but no snarling Dobermans or Rottweilers answered his call.

The gate creaked as Striker pushed it open. Several cars were parked on the property, all older models. At the side of the building was a white van similar to the one Davie had seen speeding away from Robert Montaine's storage facility. There were thousands of similar vehicles in L.A., but seeing this one on this particular lot spiked Davie's pulse. Through the dim light from a security spotlight on a neighboring building, she could make out two bays in the garage. One side was vacant. On the other side was a Prius sitting atop an automotive lift raised to the ceiling.

The place looked quiet except for a light beaming from the office window. Davie kept her flashlight on as they made their way across the uneven concrete, scanning the area for signs of movement. She peeked through the grimy glass and saw a man in his mid-thirties sitting at a desk, talking on his cell. He had olive skin and dark brown hair greased back, a flat nose, and full lips that any Hollywood starlet would envy. Sparse facial hair lined his jaw and upper lip and bushy eyebrows fell onto his lids, creating a hooded look.

Striker tapped on the door and then turned the knob. The intrusion startled the man. He jumped out of the chair and slipped the phone into his pants pocket. "Do I know you?"

"LAPD," Davie said, holding up her badge. "Are you Raoul Hice?"

He wiped his hands down the sides of his pants and sprinted over to them with a grin and an outstretched hand. "Come in, Detectives. Welcome. Are you collecting for the policeman's ball? I gave last year. Glad to help out again."

Hice knew they were detectives because she and Striker weren't in uniform. Plus, his past run-ins with law enforcement were numerous enough for him to figure it out even without seeing the word *detective* spelled out on her badge. She ignored his outstretched hand. Instead, she slipped the flashlight into the loop of her belt, surprised to see that Hice's eyes were blue. "The LAPD doesn't have a policeman's ball. That's a scam."

Striker's voice was low but steely. "We understand you run a car rental hustle out of this shop."

Hice flashed a look of fake surprise. "Here? No way. You heard wrong."

"Lots of cars on the lot," Striker said, glancing around. "None of them appear to need bodywork."

Hice's demeanor was cool, his tone affable. Davie had interviewed a lot of witnesses, from cooperative to hostile. Hice had the confidence and easy patter of a conman.

"Most of them are in for minor repairs. The rest are done. Just waiting for the owners to pick them up."

She took out her phone. "So if I contact the registered owners, they'll back up your story, right?"

He shifted his weight from foot to foot as if his cool was wearing thin. "Yeah, sure. Go ahead."

"Good to know." She turned toward the door. "Be right back, partner. I'll run the plates."

"We know you're on parole, Mr. Hice," Striker said. "We don't need a warrant to tear this place apart looking for contraband. I'm sure the South Gate PD would back us up."

"Okay, okay, stop. Just so you know, what I'm doing isn't illegal. If people with cars need extra cash, I match them with customers who have a need. Everybody wins."

"That's not what you advertise. Your sign says free rental cars." Davie held up the photo of Mushroom Ears standing by the Toyota. "Has this man used one of your vehicles?"

Hice glanced at the year-old date stamp and laughed. "A year ago? Who do you think I am, Hertz? I don't keep records that far back."

"We think he may have contacted you recently," she said. "He uses various names, including Miles Standish and John Booth."

Hice squinted at the image. "You're kidding me. This picture is crap. I can't even tell what he looks like."

"Look again," Davie said.

He returned his focus to the photo and frowned. "What did this guy do anyway?"

"Maybe nothing," Striker said. "We just want to talk to him. Has he ever rented a car from you?"

Hice's eyes darted from Davie to Striker. "Am I in trouble over this?"

"That's between you and your conscience." Davie tapped the photo with her finger. "We just want to know this man's name."

Hice sat on the edge of his desk, rubbing the back of his neck. "He called almost a week ago, looking for a rental. Said an associate of mine referred him. I only saw him once but I remember those weird ears. Don't know how the dude can hear out of them."

Davie couldn't hide her impatience. "His name?"

"Andrew Jackson."

She gave Striker a side glance and rolled her eyes. "You have an address for Mr. Jackson?"

"I didn't ask for one. He didn't want a paper trail."

"What happens if he wrecks the car?"

"The first time I rented to him, he paid in person and in cash. I charged him for the rental, a security deposit, plus he wanted to pay a retainer for the next car. After that, we had an arrangement. I drop off a new car at the address he gives me and I pick up the old one. It's never the same place. The money for the next rental is in the glove compartment, and there's always a nice tip for the extra service."

Striker picked up an invoice from Hice's desk and looked it over. "What happens if Andrew Jackson doesn't bring the car back?"

"The junkers I give him aren't worth much. If he doesn't bring it back, I still have the retainer. I reimburse the owner more than the car is worth. Everybody's happy. But that hasn't happened."

"I guess money is no object with this guy," Striker said, returning the invoice to the desk. "When was the last time he used one of your cars?"

"I picked up an SUV this morning and dropped off a Honda."

"Where?"

"Some hooker motel in Palms called the Beach Bum."

"Where's the SUV?" she said.

He hesitated then pointed to a Nissan parked along the side of the fence. Davie walked over and tried the door. It was locked. "It has a navigation system. Mind if I check it out?"

Raoul ran his hand through his greasy hair. "Yeah, okay."

Striker followed him into the office and returned with Hice and the keys to the Nissan. Davie started the engine to activate the navigation system but was disappointed to find that all past addresses had been wiped clean.

She pointed to the white van. "Did he ever rent that?"

"A few days ago, but only for a couple of hours."

Davie thought back to all the times she'd sensed somebody watching her—behind the garbage bin at Mar Vista Gardens, the Nissan hanging back on the freeway, and the white van at the storage unit. Mushroom Ears was following her, and probably had been for some time. She wondered what would have happened at the storage unit if she hadn't seen his shadow and called out.

Striker noticed her silence and filled the void with another question. "Did Mr. Jackson say when he'd need another car?"

"He prefers to mix things up. He'll call me when he's ready."

"We need the make, model, and license plate number of the vehicle he has now."

Hice told them it was a 2005 Honda Civic. Davie jotted down the license plate number while Striker handed him a business card.

"Do us a favor," he said. "Don't tell Mr. Jackson we're looking for him. And if he calls, let me know."

"Sure. No problem."

As they walked back to the car, Davie turned toward Striker. "You think he's on the phone right now warning old Andy that we're on his trail?"

"Bet on it."

53

THE NEIGHBORHOOD OF PALMS was in Pacific's jurisdiction. Since she'd been assigned to the division, Davie had driven by the Beach Bum Motel many times. On the way there, she told Striker about the van and her belief that Mushroom Ears had been following her. He sat silently for a moment and then said, "Okay." She was glad he hadn't overreacted, but at a minimum a mild expletive would have been appreciated.

The Beach Bum was a two-story rectangular building located midblock with a strip of parking slots straddling both sides of a driveway. She assumed the yellow paint had once been cheery, but it had faded into the ashen hue of a jaundice victim. At one time, the motel had been a place for families seeking a budget vacation close to the beach, but over the years it had become party central for hookers and junkies, the perfect place to cook heroin without repercussions if your cheap lighter burned a hole in the carpet.

It was dark and the parking lot was almost full. Striker pulled the car into one of the few remaining spaces close to the office. "Do we have a plan?"

"Ask uncomfortable questions," she said. "Isn't that what we do best?"

Striker gave her a knowing glance before shouldering open the car door and heading toward the office. Through the glass door, Davie saw a male wearing a thin white dress shirt with the sleeves rolled up to his elbows. He had dark hair, small features, and skin the color of raw umber, a shade she remembered from her childhood box of crayons. If she had to guess his nationality, she'd say Pakistani.

Contrary to Raoul Hice, the man didn't seem a bit startled when they walked in. He'd probably been watching them since they rolled into the lot. Considering the motel's clientele, hyper-vigilance seemed an important bullet point on any employee's resume.

Davie flashed her ID. "We're looking for information about one of your guests." She placed the photo of Mushroom Ears on the counter. "He was last seen driving a 2005 Honda Civic."

Striker stepped up to the desk. "He may have been using the name Andrew Jackson."

The desk clerk studied the snapshot and handed it back to Davie. "Mr. Jackson checked out this morning."

"How did he pay?"

"Cash. He claimed he'd lost his credit card. I told him I needed a security deposit in case he damaged the room. He gave me a thousand dollars. Good thing, too. After he checked out I found a hole in the wall. I know he did it because he didn't ask for his deposit back."

"Did he give an address?"

The man pulled out an old-fashioned ledger and slid his finger down the columns. Given their lack of technology, Davie guessed the motel didn't want to keep too close tabs on the clientele. When the desk clerk found the entry for A. Jackson, he rotated the book so Davie and Striker could see. He had used a familiar address—the LAPD's Police Administration Building in downtown L.A.

Mushroom Ears was turning out to be a real comedian.

"We want to look in his room if that's okay," said Striker.

The clerk shrugged and handed him a key from a pegboard on the back wall. "Ground floor. Last unit. But you're not going to find anything. I cleaned it already."

The hinges of the room's frail wooden door creaked open and the strong odor of disinfectant invaded Davie's nose. "Too bad the department doesn't issue gas masks."

Striker reached into his pocket for a tube of menthol rub similar to the one Vaughn always carried. She smeared a dab under her nose and handed it back as she stepped inside the room. The damage to the wall was more a dent than a hole but could have been made by a fist. It appeared Mushroom Ears had anger-management issues. She searched the floor behind the cabinet and saw an accumulation of dust and at least one used tissue—so much for the manager's cleaning ability. It was dangerous to touch anything you couldn't see, especially in a room used by junkies. A used syringe might be concealed under the tissue.

She could hear Striker in the bathroom opening the top of the toilet tank, so she put on latex gloves and used a motel emergency placard to herd the debris out into the open. She probed the tissue with the card and detected an odor that was familiar and unsurprising, given that the motel was hooker haven. She also found a piece of thin rounded plastic that could have once been a protective cover surrounding a cell phone.

Under the bed was more dust, a ball of tinfoil the size of an egg, and a half-eaten Oreo.

Striker appeared in the bathroom doorway. "Find anything?"

"Maybe," she said. "The first car-rental agent I spoke with said our guy had a thing for Oreos. This may have enough saliva for DNA analysis."

She showed Striker the cell cover and the tissue. "Hard to say how long these things have been here. The manager's cleaning skills aren't worth crap."

Striker went out to the car and came back carrying three evidence envelopes and a plastic bag with the room number scrawled on it with a black marker pen. "I found this on the cleaning cart by the office. The clerk says it was collected today."

Davie opened the bag and looked inside. There were several food wrappers and a crumpled piece of notepaper bearing the Beach Bum logo. Scrawled across the surface were a two-digit number and the letters *Bay Ln.*

Davie showed it to Striker "What do you make of this?"

He glanced at the paper. "Ln might stand for lane. Could be an address."

While Striker wrote on the evidence bags, Davie searched the Internet on her cell. The address wasn't in L.A. or Santa Monica or any of the half dozen cities in the area that she searched. She finally found it in Palos Verdes, an affluent off-the-beaten-track community with panoramic views of the San Pedro Channel, Santa Catalina Island, and gray whales migrating to and from Mexico.

"You want to go for a drive?" she asked.

54

THE WHITE STUCCO HOUSE in Palos Verdes was around 5,000 square feet and reminded Davie of pictures she'd seen of the Greek island of Santorini. Perched on the hillside, it had a gorgeous view of city lights with a patio facing the Pacific Ocean, a perfect venue for entertaining on warm Southern California evenings. They parked on the street and walked up a circular motor court to the front door. No lights were on in the house and nobody responded to the bell.

Striker pointed to the house next door. "Let's door-knock the neighbors."

They made their way to a pale blue Cape Cod. Davie heard footsteps inside and then the static of an intercom.

The woman's voice was slow and drawn out, tinged with a faint Southern accent. "How can I help you?"

Davie glanced up and saw the camera. She held her badge up. "LAPD. We're looking for your neighbor."

A woman in her fifties, wearing a polar-fleece bathrobe and sheep-skin boots opened the door. Her tawny bobbed hair, round brown eyes, and slow manner of speech reminded Davie of a cuddly sloth.

"They're at their house in Cabo," she said, drawing out each word. "Not sure when they'll be back."

Striker stepped forward. "Sorry to bother you so late. We were under the impression a man lived there, possibly alone."

The neighbor glanced toward the stucco and frowned. "They rent the place out short-term through one of those online services. The neighbors disapprove. Just because people pay a lot of money to stay there doesn't mean they're good people."

"Is the house rented at the moment?"

"A man has been staying there for the past few days. He parks in the garage so I haven't seen him to say hello."

"Is he there now?"

"I wouldn't know. If you walk around back, you can look in the garage window. The Carlsons' Jaguar is parked on one side. The renter parks on the other. He drives several different cars. My husband and I think he's up to no good."

"We need to call the Carlsons to get the man's name. Do you have their cell number?"

"Not necessary. Before they left, they told me his name. It's Al De-Salvo."

Davie decided against telling her that Albert DeSalvo was the name of the infamous serial killer known as the Boston Stranger. "You think the Carlsons would mind if we walked to the back of the house?"

She brushed the tawny bangs off her forehead as she considered the request. "I'll go with you. I've been wondering myself what's going on over there."

Davie led the way with her flashlight through an unlocked gate along a narrow side yard to the garage. Striker looked over Davie's shoulder as she beamed light though the window. There was only one car parked inside: the Jaguar. It seemed to take forever to get the slow-walking neighbor back to her front door, where Striker handed her a business card.

"If he comes back, would you let me know?"

She read the card. "Homicide? Should I be worried?"

"We have no reason to believe he'd be a danger to you or your family," Striker said, "but don't approach him or question him about anything. If you see him come back to the house, please call me. My cell number is on the card. If you think it's an emergency, call 911."

Davie and Striker watched the woman go inside the house and heard the audible sound of a deadbolt clicking into place.

They returned to the car and sat in the darkness. Davie stared out the window, willing Mushroom Ears to pull into the circular driveway.

"Without searching the house, we don't know if the guy moved out."

Striker glanced at her. "I know what you're thinking but there's no way I'm going to let you go in there without a warrant."

She looked at him and smiled. "Of course not."

They watched the house for another thirty minutes but saw no signs of life. Davie noticed Striker's head leaning against the window. His eyes were closed and his breathing was steady and rhythmic. She nudged his arm. He jolted awake.

"Sorry," he said, raking his hands through his hair. "Guess the day is catching up with me."

"Yeah, I need to crash for a few hours. Take me back to Pacific. We can start again tomorrow."

Striker dropped her off in the station's parking lot and pulled away with barely a "goodnight." She was opening her car door when her cell squawked and vibrated with a force she'd never felt before. A message appeared on the screen from the Office of Emergency Services to residents of Bel Air: INCREASED WINDS CREATING EXTREME FIRE HAZARD. STAY ALERT. LISTEN TO AUTHORITIES. PREPARE TO EVACUATE. Davie's thoughts swirled with fear and disbelief as she called Alex Camden's number.

He answered without prelude. "I got the alert, too. I'm in Laguna Beach, dining with a client. I'm heading home right now, but it'll take me at least an hour to get there. Leo and Vinny are alone inside the house. Can you stay with them?"

"On my way. What about the art?"

"All I care about is you and the dogs. If the fire comes anywhere near the house, get out. You won't have time to save anything."

She sped north on the 405 behind a stream of red taillights moving toward an inferno, people heading home as she was, preparing to save what they could before evacuating. Red flames with pockets of white and yellow devoured the hillsides and sent plumes of smoke into the night sky. She was still two miles from the Sunset Boulevard exit when, for the first time, she feared she wouldn't make it home. Her heart ached as she thought about Leo and Vinny trapped inside Alex Camden's house. The place was hermetically sealed because of his artwork, so she doubted the dogs could smell the smoke, but they might sense the disturbance in the atmosphere.

Finally her exit appeared and she tore up the ramp. After she drove through Alex's gate, she parked the Camaro to the side of his driveway and used her key to open the French doors by the swimming pool. There was no security in the cottage, but the main house was Fort Knox, complete with an alarm system and an armed response from a rent-a-cop company. Alex kept an inventory of expensive art objects in the house, so she understood his concern. Other houses in the neighborhood had been broken into. Valuables had been stolen, but never from his place as far as she knew.

The sound of barking and the clicking of toenails on hardwood floors met her as she turned off the alarm. She called to the golden retrievers, but that was hardly necessary. Leo and Vinny barreled around the corner and scooted to a stop when they recognized her. She ran her hand over their soft coats to calm them and maybe to calm herself, as well.

Their leashes were hanging in the mudroom. She pulled them off the hooks and set them by the French doors in case it became necessary to load the dogs into the Camaro and leave. She grabbed a bag of kibble and filled their bowls and refreshed their water dish, all the while monitoring her phone for updates.

The TV was tuned to Channel 4 for the latest news as she collapsed on the couch with the dogs at her side. The wind was fluky. No one could predict which way the blaze would turn next. All she knew was the Skirball wildfire was burning out of control and heading her way.

Davie was exhausted from stress, travel, and the time change. She closed her eyes. The next thing she heard was the sound of barking. She glanced toward the French doors and saw Alex Camden standing on the patio. As soon as he opened the door, the dogs ran to him and smothered him with love.

"Thank you, Davina. I'm so grateful you're all safe."

Davie glanced at the TV and saw a Bel Air home not far from them, fully engulfed in flames.

Alex saw it, too. "I have a friend with a loft in downtown L.A. He's invited me to stay with him until things settle down. I just need to pack a few things and put the dogs in the car."

Davie spent the next twenty minutes helping to crate Alex's most valuable pieces of artwork and loading them into his SUV, keeping an eye on fire updates on the TV and her phone.

"I think we've done all we can for now," Alex said. "I'm going to my friend's place. You're welcome to come with me."

"I can bunk with Bear if I have to leave. For now, I'll stay and keep an eye on things here."

After Alex drove away, Davie located the garden hoses, for all the good that would do, and retrieved her overnight bag from the trunk of her car. She left the Camaro parked in Alex's driveway—closer to the street in case she had to evacuate in a hurry, but mostly because she was too exhausted to move it.

Once inside her cottage, she peeled off her travel clothes and showered but didn't dress for bed. Instead, she put on a pair of jeans, a long-sleeved T-shirt, and her running shoes. If an evacuation notice was issued in the middle of the night, Davie had to be ready to go. She called Bear to let him know she was safe before grabbing her gunbelt and climbing up the spiral staircase to the loft where she had better visibility in case the fire moved closer.

She'd always thought about people in a disaster who were given fifteen minutes to decide what they'd choose to save before fleeing their homes. She'd never considered that in the context of her life—until tonight. The cottage contained no family photos. The ones from her early years were at her mother's house. Those taken as a teen were in a box in Bear's bedroom closet. None of the furniture in the cottage belonged to her except for Celeste, her grandmother's rocking chair. It made her sad to think if she had to evacuate, the chair would be too bulky to take with her.

She collapsed on the futon with a feather comforter wrapped around her body. Her hand touched her most cherished possession— her grandmother's earrings—before drifting off to sleep.

55

CODE RED.

His client was still dithering about eliminating Detective Saffron. She was no match for his skills but appeared to be a good investigator. That was the problem—she was too good. He couldn't take the risk of her learning his identity. Acting on his own would break his rule not to kill anyone he wasn't paid to kill, but if his client didn't make a decision soon, he would be forced to take her out without authorization.

Working with the client over the years had been lucrative, and at the rate his cat Gizmo was powering through kibble he could use the extra money. So, for now, he waited. In a year or two he would retire and go on a long vacation in Europe. Maybe he'd go back to the restaurant in Zaragoza for his favorite paella with Spanish saffron. The more he thought about it, the more the idea appealed to him. It would be a fitting nod to the sexy detective. Truth was, he'd grown attached to her. They would never be friends, of course, but he had grudging admiration for her style.

His St. Christopher medal was still missing, causing him a sense of pervasive distress. The medal had kept three generations of male family members safe. He had to find it before he left town. He'd searched through all of the cars he'd rented and the restaurants where he'd eaten. He even went back to the house in Palos Verdes. No luck. There was only one place he hadn't looked: Detective Saffron's place. He doubted he'd lost the medal there but had to make sure. He'd wait until she was away from the house and have a look.

He poured an inch of Talisker into a glass and stared out the hotel window to the ocean view, wishing Gizmo were in his lap, raking his rough cat tongue across his cheek with his foul breath smelling of fish. As soon as he found the medal and tied up a few loose ends, he'd be finished with this assignment and on his way home. That moment couldn't come fast enough for him.

56

Just after midnight, Davie was jolted awake by metallic scraping sounds coming from the front of the house. Her breathing became slow and shallow as she listened, wondering if Alex Camden had changed his mind about evacuating and had returned to the house with the dogs.

She grabbed her cell and the .45 from her gunbelt, creeping to the loft's dormer window. Her back was pressed against the wall with her head turned toward the patio. In the darkness, a glint of light caught her eye. Her hands felt clammy when she saw a man wearing black clothing, sweeping a flashlight near the metal patio furniture where she'd found the St. Christopher medal. She realized she'd never mentioned it to Alex to see if it belonged to a yard worker. Well, coming to look in the middle of the night didn't make that seem likely.

If the man was indeed looking for the necklace, he wasn't going to find it. The medal was inside the house on the Chippendale table. The man moved to the front door and began tinkering with the lock.

Her cottage had only one exterior door yet she'd always felt safe—until now. Given all its private security, Bel Air was one of the most protected neighborhoods in the city, but with residents fleeing the inferno in the nearby foothills, thieves might see this as their golden opportunity. But a burglar would target the main residence before bothering with the contents of the guesthouse. She watched him quietly move another chair and peer at the ground. This guy wasn't any run-of-the-mill burglar. He was looking for something specific—the St. Christopher medal.

She assumed he was armed and, as she'd learned in training, all guns were always loaded. If he were successful in breaking into the cottage, there were several options. She could turn on all the lights and hope he'd run away. Except in the loft she had no access to the light switches downstairs. Once he was inside her house, she was justified in shooting him, but she preferred to arrest him instead. The last option was cover and concealment.

She slipped the flashlight from her gunbelt and pressed her body against the wall at the top of the spiral staircase, just out of sight. The front door rattled and creaked open. The man stepped inside and beamed his flashlight around the room and then disappeared into her bedroom. Moments later, he reappeared and headed for the door, and then stopped at the Chippendale table. He paused for a moment before scooping up the St. Christopher medal and slipping the chain around his neck.

Davie powered on her flashlight with the beam pointed directly into his eyes. "I have a .45 pointed at your temple. Get down on the ground and put your hands behind your head."

The man looked up, startled. He was in his late thirties with a military-style haircut and a well-defined jaw, medium complexion, and a dark spot on his upper right lip that could have been a mole. His ears were unusually small and close to his head. There was no earring, but that didn't matter. She knew who he was—John W. Booth, Miles Standish, Andrew Jackson, or whatever alias he was using today. She believed he'd killed Sabine Ponti and probably Jack Blasdel, as well.

For an instant her breathing stopped while her thoughts continued to swirl. She was alone and not sure what would happen next. She kept herself calm by focusing on the things she *did* know—keep your finger off the trigger until your sights are aligned with the target and you intend to shoot.

Davie waited until Mushroom Ears was on the ground before creeping midway down the spiral stairs, just out of his reach. She was alone. It was too dangerous to try to cuff him. She wedged the flashlight in her armpit to leave her hands free to juggle her gun and the cell to call 911. Because of the fire, cops had to be close by. If evacuation orders were issued, they'd have to be in the neighborhood to knock on doors.

She kept one eye on Mushroom Ears while she accessed the numbers on her keypad. It was only one distracted moment, but that was enough. He shot off the ground and grabbed her ankle, pulling her to the floor.

By the time she got back to her feet, he was gone.

She ran to the door but couldn't open it. Looking out the window she saw him lodging a metal patio chair under the doorknob, shutting off her escape. He sprinted toward the wall surrounding the property.

Davie recovered her gun and cell and bounded up the stairs to the loft. Bear's ladder was lying by the futon. She grabbed it. Her father's concern that she'd be trapped in the house with no means of escape seemed prescient.

The loft's side window opened with little effort. Davie held the ladder away from the siding to control the noise and manage its fall. She threw her leg over the windowsill, caught the first rung with the toe of her running shoe, and descended to the ground. Before calling 911 she wanted to know the direction he'd taken, so she headed toward the wall.

Her shoe got a toehold in the uneven stones and she hefted herself up. Her shoulder ached as she climbed. Her fingers felt scratched and raw. She stopped. If he was waiting on the other side with a gun, he could pick her off once she poked her head over the top. She hesitated for only a moment and then dropped back down into the night-blooming jasmine bushes below. She extricated herself from the vines and called 911. The call was directed to the California Highway Patrol's central communication division in downtown L.A. An operator asked her name, her location, and the nature of her call.

"I'm an off-duty LAPD detective," she said, adding the other information. Before they could transfer her to LAPD Communications, an arm wrapped around her neck and squeezed.

——————

She awoke in darkness. Sensed movement. Smelled rubber and motor oil. Heard the hum of a vehicle engine. She was in the trunk of a moving car.

Davie had no idea how long she'd been unconscious or where she was, but her tongue tasted of lighter fluid, her eyes burned, and she felt nauseated. She assumed Mushroom Ears had used a chokehold to render her unconscious but didn't know what he'd done afterward to keep her that way.

Her hands weren't tied. Big mistake. She patted the carpet around her, careful to avoid cutting herself on any sharp objects. She touched plastic—a grocery bag—and smelled sweet and chocolate. Oreos. She wondered if Mushroom Ears was still driving Raoul's 2005 Honda Civic.

Back when she was a boot fresh out of the academy, her first training officer had told her if she was ever abducted she should fight like hell at the beginning, even at the risk of dying quickly, because what came later was often much worse. She had no idea what this dipshit had planned for her. Maybe he'd just drive to the desert and shoot her. She didn't intend to wait around to find out.

There had to be an emergency release for the trunk. Those had been in cars for decades. But she didn't know the location of the one in her Camaro much less where it was on a Civic. She swept her hand across the lid of the trunk, hoping to find a lever or a loop. Sharp twisted metal raked her fingers where the release might have been. She felt for a latch on the back of the seat to see if it folded down but hesitated. If he knew she'd regained consciousness, he'd kill her for sure.

Davie pried loose the carpet, looking for an emergency tool kit. She felt around the tire well but found nothing. In the darkness her hands brushed across several cables that led from the trunk to the vehicle's interior. She didn't know what they controlled but one of them might be attached to the driver's-side trunk release.

It was dark inside the trunk but not airless. She kept her breathing steady to avoid claustrophobia. The first cable yanked free. The road noise covered the sound. The trunk didn't open but she heard a click on the side of the car. Gas cover. Tick tock. She had to get away. She tugged the second cable. It was almost free when she felt the car stop and the engine go silent.

A door opened and closed. Gravel crunched under shoes as he walked around to the rear of the car. Davie's heart pounded as the vehicle began to rock back and forth. Her body slammed into the back of the seat as the Honda began to roll downhill. The car picked up speed. She yanked the second cable hard. The trunk lid released just as the car lurched into a nosedive, bouncing Davie against the rear of the backseat. There was a splash. Cold water surged in around her.

57

FUBAR.

In his haste to recover the St. Christopher medal he hadn't noticed Detective Saffron's Camaro parked by the main house and was surprised to find her at home. To make matters worse, he hadn't killed her in the house when he had the chance. Those were the mistakes of an amateur. He'd planned to retire when he turned forty, still a couple of years away. Now he had to consider moving up that date. He'd just have to make do with the money he'd saved.

He watched as the Honda sank below the waterline of the reservoir, knowing she'd be dead soon. Even Houdini couldn't have escaped this. He had mixed emotions about her demise, but she'd seen his face. Could identify him. He had to eliminate the threat. The chokehold was just enough pressure for her to lose consciousness, but he'd known that wouldn't last more than a minute or two. Someone would be coming for her. He'd had to move the body.

She didn't weigh much, so he'd thrown her over his shoulder and carried her down the drive through the gate to the Honda. Touching her for the first time made him feel powerful and more excited than he'd wanted to admit.

He applied ether to a cloth and placed it over her nose and mouth, just as he'd done with Blasdel. That would keep her unconscious for a while longer, but he had to move quickly.

Raoul Hice wouldn't be getting the Honda back. The last retainer he'd left should cover the replacement cost. If there were hard feelings, it didn't matter. Hice had no idea of his real identity, and he wouldn't be using his services again. Soon he'd disappear. Nobody would ever find him, including either of Detective Saffron's clueless partners.

He reached for the chain around his neck and clutched his grandfather's St. Christopher medal. All his bad luck had happened when it was out of his possession. It was a miracle he'd found it. He wouldn't be that careless again.

The airline tickets were in his jacket pocket, but he couldn't use them now. Once the car was completely submerged, he checked his phone to summon one of the ride-share services he'd used in the past, but there was no cell service. In the distance he saw a light and headed for it.

58

DAVIE STRUGGLED TO OPEN the Honda's trunk, but the weight of the water forced it closed. The car was sinking and she was trapped. Bear had always told her panic killed. He was probably right: at the moment, it was squeezing all the air from her lungs. She fought terror as she sucked up the last remaining air. She held her breath and waited as water closed in on her.

In her mind's eye she saw her father's face. Wondered if she was about to die and how sad he'd feel about that. An eerie calm came over her as she waited for the vehicle to fully submerge and the pressure to equalize. She kicked off her shoes. They would only weigh her down. When she applied pressure to the trunk, it opened.

The water was black. Davie couldn't see the surface or tell which way was up. She blew out some air and followed the bubbles. Her lungs felt as if they were about to explode as she swam upward until she broke the surface, gasping for air, choking. Water entered her nose and mouth. Fresh water. She looked around and saw nothing but blackness.

It was a short swim to shore and a fifteen-yard crawl up a dirt bank. She fought her way through brush and reeds to a narrow dirt road sheltered by an umbrella of pine and sycamore trees. She walked for what seemed like miles, carefully avoiding potholes and uneven pavement on the dark road. In the distance, she saw the familiar flashing blue lights of a police cruiser. Shoeless and dripping wet, Davie staggered toward the car.

59

DAVIE STUMBLED UP THE street and found a Beverly Hills patrol car and two officers, one sitting in the black-and-white and one standing on the front porch of a McMansion, talking to a man in his fifties. She padded up to the car and identified herself.

The officer stared at the soggy socks on her feet, her stringy red hair dripping water, and her sodden clothes. "You got some ID?"

Davie brushed chunks of mud from her clothes. "Call my partner. He'll vouch for me."

"Wait here." The officer walked up to the porch and pulled his partner aside, pointing to Davie standing on the street. Then he beckoned for her to join them.

When the homeowner saw Davie's condition, he invited all three of them into the house. His wife offered her towels to dry her hair. As it turned out, the couple had reported a suspicious man walking back and forth in front of the house and had called the police. The officers responded but the man had left the area. Davie suspected Mushroom

Ears had used the couple's address to hail a cab or a ride-share and was just waiting for his transportation.

She ran her fingers through her wet hair. "Where am I?"

"Franklin Canyon. Beverly Hills."

"I need to use your phone," she said.

One of the officers handed her his cell.

Vaughn answered the call. "Are you okay? The whole effin' department is looking for you."

"What's going on?"

"When you lost contact with 911, all hell broke loose. Cops swarmed your house and the neighborhood looking for you. Where are you?"

"Somewhere in Beverly Hills." She gave him the address and told him to have somebody check ride-share and cab companies for a recent pick up. "I'm with a couple of Beverly Hills patrol officers. They volunteered to drive me to Pacific. I should be there in about twenty minutes."

"I'll tell Striker." He chuckled. "Boy is he pissed at you."

"What's happening with the wildfire?"

"It changed direction. The evacuation notice was lifted in Bel Air. People can go home, at least for now."

Davie's clothes were still damp when she arrived at Pacific station, so she went upstairs to wash up and change. She always kept a uniform in her locker in case of a tactical alert or UO—an unusual occurrence such as a fire or flood that required maximum deployment. But her badge was at home, so she put on the only other clothes available to her: running tights and shoes, along with a blue sweatshirt, logoed with a cartoon shark and the words PAC-14. Her personal weapon was missing, but the department-issued Smith & Wesson was in her locker.

She hooked her uniform belt around her hips, slipped the gun into the holster, and twisted her damp hair into a knot on her neck.

Ten minutes after returning to her desk, Davie was talking to Vaughn when Striker burst through the door of the squad room. His face looked pale and drawn and dark circles were visible under his eyes. She guessed it had been a stressful past few hours for him, too.

He walked to her desk and leaned on the partition wall. "You okay?"

"I'm fine. Any luck with the taxi companies?"

Tension drained from his face. "Not yet, but while we were in the BVIs, your facial ID request came back. The man wearing the suit on that street corner is a Miami billionaire named Al Benito. I assume he's the guy Jack Blasdel claimed to freelance for. The other person is Roland Ducey—at least, that's the name on his military records. We also got warrant returns for Sara Montaine's phone records and those for Black Jack Guns & Ammo. The day before she was killed, she called the gunstore and spoke to someone for fifteen minutes. That had to be Blasdel. Five minutes after that conversation ended, Blasdel called a number in Miami that belongs to a business controlled by Al Benito. I'm guessing he told Benito that Sabine was alive in exchange for a finder's fee. Loyalty meant nothing to him. It was all about the money."

"Except June Nakamura claimed Sabine was afraid in the days before she died," Davie said. "Doesn't that suggest somebody had already tipped off Benito and that's why she needed a gun?"

Striker drummed his fingers on her desk. "Good point. Blasdel's recent cell records show he called Benito again the day you interviewed Gerda Pittman, so they were definitely still in touch."

"Blasdel admitted Pittman told him I was looking into Sabine's death," Davie said.

307

Vaughn had been standing in the background, listening, but jumped into the conversation. "If he was still working with Benito, that might explain how he could afford to buy all those businesses."

Davie nodded and turned toward Striker. "Any of the bank records come back?"

Striker grabbed a chair from a J-Car cubicle and sat. "No, but remember my contact at the Florida Department of Law Enforcement? I called him an hour ago. He confirmed Valerie Ferrick is Benito's chief financial officer. Apparently, they launder money through their own enterprises, but they also target willing partners in the business community. FDLE has been investigating both of them for multiple felonies, including online gambling, racketeering, and money laundering. The case is before a Grand Jury right now. I asked if the Seaglass Cafe was part of the mix. He said no, but he asked me to send him details of our investigation."

"So, who is Roland Ducey?" Davie asked.

"Benito's hired gun," Striker said. "My contact believes Benito would have paid Ducey to kill Nate Gillen, Sabine Ponti, *and* Jack Blasdel if they threatened his business. One of our detectives is knocking on Arman Nazarian's door as we speak to show him Ducey's photo. If we catch a break, he'll ID Ducey as the guy he saw running from the gunstore after Ponti was shot."

Davie had started this investigation vowing to look at every piece of evidence no matter how obvious or farfetched it seemed. That's how she'd discovered Sara was Sabine. Harebrained as it seemed, there was one thing that hadn't been checked—the Four Paws email list. It was a long shot that it would produce any relevant information, but she felt compelled to look. She located the USB drive and slipped it into the computer monitor.

Vaughn watched over her shoulder. "What are you doing?"

"Being thorough." She clicked on the newsletter mailing list file. First, she plugged in the names of all former employees of the Seaglass Cafe who were listed on Detective Brooks's witness statements. One of them might have been an animal lover, recognized Sabine's photo, and told the wrong person. Nothing. Next she typed Lacy Gillen, Nate Gillen, Valerie Ferrick, and Al Benito. No hits. It was difficult to imagine a conman was also a cat lover, but she searched Jack Blasdel's name, but he wasn't there. As a last resort, she typed in Roland Ducey.

She was elated when she found him. Trevor Lofaro had told her Four Paws purchased names from other lists. Ducey's was among them. She looked forward to finding out why.

Vaughn sat on the edge of her desk, staring at the screen. "You think Ducey saw her picture in that newsletter and recognized her even with the plastic surgery and the dyed hair?"

"It's plausible," Davie said. "Benito may have hired Ducey to kill Sabine for stealing his hundred grand from the restaurant, but cancelled the contract once he thought she'd died in that boating accident."

"Why would Blasdel rat her out?" Vaughn asked. "He helped her disappear."

"Gerda Pittman said Blasdel had a crush on the woman he helped disappear," Davie said, "but she told him to go pound sand. His Don Juan image must have taken a hit, because Pittman said he was bitter about the rejection."

"So, when Sabine called him again to ask for his help," Striker said, "he figured he could monetize her troubles and also get a measure of revenge."

"Ducey may have already been following her, but I'm guessing Blasdel negotiated with Benito to stage her death as a suicide in his gunstore." Davie closed the file and removed the USB drive. "I wonder where Ducey is now," she said.

"We distributed his photo," Striker said, "and alerted border patrol, train stations, the Coast Guard, and airports, including Ontario and Long Beach."

Davie stood to relieve her stiffness. "Flying out of a major airport is a nonstarter. He's smart enough to know he'll never make it on a flight. He's got money. There's nothing stopping him from paying a taxi driver to take him all the way to Patagonia."

Striker's cell buzzed. He glanced at the screen and walked into the hall to take the call.

"Ducey's not actually under pressure to leave town," Vaughn said. "He thinks you're dead. That gives him some breathing room. He may be holed up nearby waiting until it's safe to get away."

Striker returned to the squad room. "I assigned Detective Presser from Homicide Special to call ride-share services and taxi companies. He just got a hit. A cab driver picked up a fare near Franklin Canyon Reservoir. He said the guy paid him a thousand dollars to take him to a street corner in Oxnard. From his description, we think it was Ducey. Presser is on his way. Should be here in a few minutes."

Even given how little she knew about Ducey, Oxnard didn't make sense. It wasn't exactly a Southern California transportation hub. There were private yachts but no major port or international airport. It was possible he had a safehouse there, but it still seemed an odd stopping point for a man on the run. Davie plugged the cross-streets into her phone map but found nothing of interest in the area. She adjusted the map with her fingers so she could see the broader picture. The only landmark nearby was the US Naval Air Station at Point Mugu.

She held out the map for Striker to see. "What do you make of this? It's an air station. That means flights are going in and out of the base, right? Ducey was in the service. Any idea what it means?"

Striker's eyes widened. "Space A, space available. If you're retired military and you qualify, you can take any open seat on any Department of Defense aircraft. Mugu moves people in and out of there for training, so Ducey might be able to find a flight."

"How do you know all that?"

"My dad is retired Navy."

"Seal?"

A man Davie didn't recognize entered the squad room and looked around the room. Striker stood and walked toward him. Over his shoulder, he said, "Admiral."

That was the last thing she'd expected to hear. Striker had told her his mom, not his dad, taught him how to sail and that she'd dismissed his dad from the Striker Navy early on because he was a busy man. There was definitely a story behind that but there was no time to discuss it now, because Striker led the man to Davie's desk and introduced him to the group as Detective Presser from Homicide Special.

"Everybody vest up," Striker said. "I'm going to interrupt some judge's dinner to get an arrest warrant for Roland Ducey—Abduction and Attempted Murder of a Police Officer. We'll put the rest of the case together once we have him in custody. Let's take two cars. I'll drive the unmarked. Vaughn, can you get the keys to a black-and-white? I'll meet everybody in the parking lot."

Davie ran upstairs to her locker, grabbed the Kevlar vest and her raid jacket, and headed out the back door. A few minutes later, Striker slid into his unmarked detective vehicle and beckoned Davie to join him in the passenger seat. Vaughn and Presser got into the patrol car.

Before transitioning from the 405 to the 101 North for the sixty-mile drive to Oxnard, Striker gave her a few factoids about Point Mugu. It was difficult to access, the terminal was remote from the main gate, flights could be delayed or cancelled without notice, and there were no reservations accepted. Ducey would just have to show up and hope for the best.

They went over the details for several miles until a lull in the conversation left Davie feeling reflective. She'd always strived to know as much as possible about her victims and felt she could now construct a narrative of the last two years of Sabine Ponti's life from what she'd learned in her investigation, along with a little speculative putty.

Sabine had experienced major emotional trauma during that time: loss of a relationship and a job she loved, her parents' approval, and her old life in Connecticut. Her effort to restart her life in Florida was met with tragedy and failure. After all that upheaval, Sabine must have felt grateful to Charles Montaine for his kindness and devotion to her, which from most accounts she'd returned in kind. It had to be a shock to lose him to cancer so soon after their marriage.

Davie thought of something Sabine's sister-in-law had said during her interview—that Sabine's death in that gunstore was the second goodbye. True, but to Davie, the second goodbye was even sadder than the first because it was the final goodbye. It was Davie's nature to view all victims' stories as tragic, but Sabine's life and death seemed like a tangle of unforced errors and bad luck.

"Why so quiet?" Striker said, bursting her thought bubble.

She glanced at him and noticed his short hair was in disarray, with spikes shooting off in every direction. She'd maintained her professionalism toward him since returning from the BVIs, but seeing that messy hair transformed Striker the detective into Striker the man who'd made love to her in a tropical paradise in the presence of geckos. She took deep breaths to chase away the memories. This was not the time to indulge those thoughts.

She picked up her cell. "Just checking the map."

"I know where Oxnard is."

"You don't know the exit."

Davie unbuckled her seatbelt so she could face Striker without craning her neck. Normally, she didn't wear a belt, unless she was in a high-speed chase, because they restricted her movements. Back in her patrol days, she and her partner had taken fire from gang members. When she drew her weapon, the butt got tangled in the seatbelt and delayed her response. She would never make that mistake again.

"Just curious," Striker said. "Why did Nate Gillen risk partnering with Benito? He must have known the guy was trouble."

"You want logic or my wild side?"

His voice was low and even in the dark car she could tell he was smiling. "I've seen your wild side, so hit me with some logic."

She looked at the map on her cell. They were still miles from the exit, with plenty of time to fill. "For sure, he wasn't Benito's dupe. Gillen had to know what he was getting into. Lacy said he wasn't good with money, but after his pact with Benito he started making buckets of it. I don't care how clueless he was about the finance side of the restaurant business, all that extra cash didn't come from hawking logoed coffee mugs. He not only bought into Benito's scam but he got greedy enough to divert five million of the man's greenbacks into a private offshore account. His luck ran out when Benito busted him."

Striker checked the rearview mirror and nosed the car into the fast lane. "So, what evidence have we missed?"

Davie leaned her head against the side window and watched the taillights of the passing cars. "When I spoke to Blasdel he told me Sabine came in to buy a Smith & Wesson .38. He seemed sure about the make. But the crime report stated the weapon was a Colt .38 Special. I thought it was weird because he remembered everything about that day in minute detail except for that. When I asked about the discrepancy, he got jumpy."

"So your theory is Ducey shot Sabine with—what—his own gun? The Colt?"

Davie's tone sounded defensive even to her. "Well, you don't seem to buy that, but why not? Blasdel lures Ponti to his shop on the pretext of selling her a gun. Ducey is waiting. The twenty-minute gap between the time of the gunshot and the arrival of patrol officers leaves time for Ducey to stage the scene and get away. There were fingerprints on the Colt but they were smudged and couldn't be identified. I think we should take a closer look."

Striker drummed his fingers on the steering wheel. "Ducey is a hitman. Blasdel was only a minor player in the murder plot and not exactly trustworthy. Why didn't he kill Blasdel at the same time he killed Sabine? Seems tidier to eliminate the lone witness. Stage it as a murder-suicide."

"Hopefully, we can ask him that question."

Striker's phone rang. His side of the conversation went something like, "Hmm...no kidding...that's great...thanks." Then he ended the call.

Davie glanced at him. "Who was that?"

"My boss. He said Nazarian just identified Roland Ducey as the man he saw running down the alley the day Ponti was killed."

"Perfect."

"That's not all. Remember that generic deposit slip you found in the storage unit? We now have the bank records. The account belonged to Sara Rice, apparently the name Ponti used before she married Charles Montaine. She opened the account with nine grand cash.

After that, she made a series of cash deposits for similar amounts until the balance reached around eighty-four thousand and then continued to make deposits for smaller sums. Our people also found employment records. Before her marriage to Charles Montaine, she worked as a waitress at a couple of restaurants. There may have been other sources of income, too."

"Is the money still there?"

"Nope. Two weeks before Ponti died, she closed the account. The bank issued a cashier's check made out to Four Paws for a hundred thousand dollars."

It took a moment for the information to register. Davie had known the donation to Four Paws was the same amount as the money missing from the Seaglass Cafe. It appeared Sabine deposited the money she'd stolen in small increments, minus what it took to establish herself in L.A., and kept adding to the balance with money she'd earned.

"Sabine wanted to make amends for her theft," Davie said, "and at the same time honor a man who truly loved her."

Striker flashed a skeptical frown. "Amends with stolen money."

"Okay, so it was stolen. The point is it was *her* stolen money. Her stepson forced Four Paws to return a donation dedicated to his father, and it wasn't even his money."

"Sometimes life isn't fair."

Davie wasn't interested in platitudes. She checked the map again. "Take the next exit and then turn right."

Striker steered the car into the right lane. "One more complication. My boss also says the Point Mugu terminal is closed on weekends. If Ducey plans to take a military flight, he has to find someplace nearby to lay low until Monday."

Davie grimaced. "Needle, meet haystack."

60

THE INTERSECTION WHERE THE cabbie had dropped off Ducey comprised rows of light industrial warehouses. Striker turned the unmarked police car into a quiet parking lot of a shipping company that was closed at this late hour. Presser and Vaughn followed behind in their black-and-white. They stepped out of the patrol car and into the backseat of Striker's car, listening as he called Oxnard PD to let them know the LAPD was in the area and might need backup.

"This place is in the middle of nowhere," Vaughn said. "I bet he caught another taxi to cover his tracks."

"We passed a motel about a mile away," Davie said. "Let's see if he's there."

Ducey wasn't at that motel or any other likely places in the vicinity. Next, they searched outside the immediate area. Nothing. Bars were open until four a.m. Davie made a list and found the closest one was only a quarter mile away from the drop site. Since Ducey would recognize Davie, Vaughn and Presser took turns casing the first three bars on the list, but found no sign of him.

It was Vaughn's turn to sweep the fourth bar. Davie's sense of alarm spiked when her partner didn't come out right away. She was about to go in after him when she spotted him pushing open the door with his foot while juggling something in his hands. Four paper bags of French fries. The smell of grease in the closed car turned Davie's stomach. She donated her bag to her partner and dropped her window until the French fries were consumed.

Presser went into the fifth bar. Vaughn took the sixth. About five minutes later, he appeared from around the back of the building and jogged to the detective car.

His breathing was shallow and fast as he slid into the backseat. "Ducey is sitting at the end of the bar facing the front door. With a woman."

Striker reached for his radio. "How many people inside?"

"It's packed. I'd say fifty or more. There are two entrances, the one in the front and one in the back at the end of a hallway past the restrooms. It opens onto an alley. I left through the rear door. I doubt he noticed but even if he did, I'm guessing he thinks I'm in the can."

"What's Ducey doing?" Davie asked.

Vaughn wiped sweat from his forehead. "Drinking and chatting up his lady friend. He could be in there until the place closes."

Davie turned toward Striker. "Maybe there's a Plan B."

He kept his focus on the front door of the bar. "What did you have in mind?"

"I could go inside and—"

Striker interrupted. "Not just no, but hell no."

Davie felt her cheeks flush. "Hear me out. He thinks I'm dead. Seeing me might throw him off his game. If I can convince him there's no getting out of this, he might surrender."

Vaughn slapped his palm to his forehead. "What are you smoking, Davie? He's already tried to kill you once. What's stopping him from popping you and walking out the door before anybody notices?"

"Listen up," Striker said, raising his voice to get their attention. "There's no way we're going inside a crowded bar with guns blazing. First, we have to assume Ducey is armed but he may not be the only one. There could be customers who're also strapped. If somebody gets nervous and overreacts, too many people will die."

"Yeah," Vaughn said. "Think of the paperwork."

Striker ignored the flippant comment. "Here's what's going to happen. I'll have Oxnard PD meet us a couple blocks away. Ducey is still inside so we need to cover the exits. Presser, you take the rear door. Richards will take the front. Vaughn, you go back inside through the back door. Text me if he makes a move to leave. Whatever you do, do not confront him inside the bar. Once he exits and moves away from the entrance, we'll approach him from behind and take him down."

Davie knew if they'd had advance notice of Ducey's whereabouts, there would be multipage tactical plans with diagrams, assignment rosters, and a list of the closest hospitals in case things went sideways. But even if they had all that, there were still a million ways things could go wrong.

"What if he comes out with the woman?" Davie said. "He could take her hostage."

Striker looked away. "I'll ask Oxnard to bring a plainclothes female officer. We can pose as a couple and distract Ducey long enough to separate him from the woman. We'll discuss details when she gets here."

Presser and Vaughn took positions. Davie opened the door to get out, stopping when Striker grabbed her arm. His voice was low and steely. "Be careful. If anything happens to you, I'll have to kill somebody."

Davie nodded and got out of the car. She took a position behind a parked vehicle and watched as Striker drove to the staging area to brief Oxnard PD. It took fifteen minutes before he returned and backed the car into a vacant parking spot. Davie joined him in the car.

"Oxnard doesn't have a female officer available," he said. "If he comes out with the woman, I'll pose as a customer and find some way to separate them once Ducey is on the street."

They sat in silence for nearly twenty minutes before Striker's cell lit up with an incoming text. It was from Vaughn. Ducey was on the move and the woman was with him. Striker radioed everyone to get into position.

Davie and Striker drew their weapons and got out of the car. They had no idea where Ducey would go next, but if he went to a vehicle they would jam him up before he opened the car door.

Davie squeezed Striker's elbow and pointed to the entrance. Ducey paused as he held the door open for the woman. They moved forward in a supportive embrace. The woman looked to be in her early fifties, wearing a low-cut sweater and tight jeans with sky-high heels. She was staggering, as if she was drunk.

"Shit," Striker whispered. "This could get tricky."

Ducey continued bracing the woman with his arm as they headed toward the parking lot. There was no indication he knew anyone was watching him.

"I'm going to distract him," Striker said, starting to rise.

Davie grabbed his arm and pulled him down. "Wait." She pointed toward the front door. Vaughn was walking out of the bar.

"Hey, Sheila," he yelled.

The woman turned. "Yeah. Whaddaya want?"

"Beau says come back inside. You got a phone call."

Ducey's expression soured. "Sheila's busy. Tell Beau to take a message."

Sheila broke free from Ducey's grip. "Beau's the bartender, asshole. He's my friend." She turned to Vaughn. "Tell him I'll be right there."

Ducey reached for her purse and said matter-of-factly, "Give me the key. I'll wait for you in the car."

Sheila struggled with him for possession of her handbag. She teetered on her high heels, lost her balance, and fell to the asphalt on one knee.

What came next was a shitstorm.

Ducey grabbed the car key from Sheila's bag and pressed the button to unlock her car door. The headlights flashed on a nearby VW Passat. Ducey walked quickly toward the car. Vaughn dragged Sheila to safety behind a parked vehicle. Davie and Striker advanced to within twenty feet of Ducey.

"Roland Ducey!" Davie shouted. "LAPD, get down on the ground!"

Ducey looked up, startled as a raccoon in a garbage can. He bent over. For an instant she thought he would actually comply. Then he reached into his jacket and pulled out what looked like a Sig Sauer P365 and fired off a round in her general direction and two more that went wild.

A thousand emotions flashed through her mind about the two men she'd killed and how tortured she'd felt afterward. A blink of an eye was all the time Davie had to decide if she could do it again. Her target was sighted. Her finger left the barrel of the weapon and slid into position on the trigger. Muzzle flashes lit the night sky. Spent shell casings clinked on the hard asphalt. Gunpowder polluted the air around her. Ducey crumpled to the ground. The gun fell out of his hand. Sirens blared. Davie ran toward him, kicking the weapon out of his reach.

Ducey was bleeding from a chest wound. His voice was weak but he was still breathing. "You're alive."

Davie tilted her head and smiled. "Surprise."

He coughed up a trickle of blood but managed a faint smile in return. "How did you find me?"

"Shoe leather and minutiae."

"I screwed up."

"Good thing for Sabine Ponti that you did."

He struggled for air, sensing he was in bad shape. "She was just a job, like all the others."

"Tell that to her family."

Something she'd said seemed to trigger his alarm. He grimaced in pain as he reached out toward her. "Gizmo."

She didn't understand what he was talking about and didn't have time to ask because just then she became aware of Sheila's screams.

Blue-suits flooded the parking lot. Striker motioned for her to go. Davie ran toward the screaming woman. She found her pale and covered in blood, hovering over Vaughn's still body.

Davie shouted, "Officer down!" and then fell to her knees beside him. He was trying to sit up, bleeding heavily from a wound to his thigh. He moaned in pain.

She jerked her head toward Sheila. "You hurt?"

The woman abruptly stopped screaming and managed a mute zombie-like shake of her head.

Davie pressed her fingers just above Vaughn's wound and sensed a pulse. She unbuckled his belt and used it as a tourniquet to staunch the bleeding.

"Jason, it's Davie. Can you hear me?"

His eyes fluttered and then closed. He was obviously in shock.

She was barely aware of boots pounding the ground and the flashing lights of an EMT vehicle. At some point, a paramedic yanked her away from Vaughn's side. She sat on the hard ground a short distance away, paralyzed with dread and only vaguely aware of the tears spilling down her cheeks.

Sometime later, Striker guided her to her feet, his voice cracking with emotion. "Paramedics have taken Vaughn to the ER. The Watch Commander called his parents. They're on the way. I can wrap things up here by myself if you want to head over to the hospital."

"What about Ducey?"

His voice was flat. "Looks bad. I'm not sure he'll make it."

61

SHORTLY AFTER DAVIE HAD been accepted into the police academy, Bear warned her that cops can't remember shit about anything when they're in a gunfight, sometimes not until the next day when the shock wears off. Sometimes the facts elude them forever.

It was early morning on Saturday, a week after the takedown of Roland Ducey, and Davie still couldn't say for sure how many times she or Striker had fired their weapons, or whether one or both of them had hit the target. But knowing those details wasn't her responsibility. The LAPD's Force Investigations Division would pick apart the shooting and eventually lay out their findings in a comprehensive report.

Ducey had been airlifted to Harbor/UCLA trauma center where he remained, clinging to life. She hoped he survived. That was going to be one interesting interview.

A couple days after the shootout in Oxnard, Striker's Florida Department of Law Enforcement contact called to let him know the

Grand Jury had brought a thirty-eight-count indictment against Al Benito and Valerie Ferrick for money laundering and a host of other felonies. His team had served arrest warrants in the early morning hours and taken both of them into custody without incident. Lacy Gillen was safe and sound in her Miami home when officers came to take her statement.

Davie sat on a chaise lounge by the swimming pool with Alex Camden hovering over her. He handed her a mimosa he'd made from Dom Perignon and fresh-squeezed orange juice.

He clinked his glass against hers. "To gratitude."

"To gratitude," she echoed.

She took a sip and felt the bubbles tickle her nose. The sentiment was timely and appropriate. She *was* grateful. Dedicated fire crews had worked around the clock to contain the Skirball blaze and spare them from tragedy. Other communities had not been as lucky. Davie mourned with the families who'd lost homes and a lifetime of memories. Most of all, she was grateful Vaughn was alive and with only soft-tissue gunshot injuries. Her partner would recover from his wounds and return to Pacific Homicide.

Alex pulled the collar of his Burberry scarf around his neck to ward off the morning chill. "I trust you're feeling better, Davina."

"I'll be better once I get back to work."

A look of concern swept across his face. "Yes. That'll be any day now, I'm sure."

The phone connected to the gate intercom rang. Alex answered and then glanced at her. "Yes, of course. I'll buzz you in." He pressed a button on the phone's base.

"You have guests." Davie swung her legs off the lounge and onto the ground. "I'll head back to the cottage. I have work to do."

He held up his hand to stop her. "Stay, Davina. The visitor isn't here for me."

She swiveled toward the driveway and saw an unfamiliar black SUV drive up and park. A moment later, Jon Striker got out of the driver's seat and headed toward the pool, one hand hiding something behind his back. The other was clutching papers.

Alex summoned his dogs. "Call if you need backup." He winked and disappeared into the house.

When Striker got closer, Davie saw he was hiding a bouquet of red roses behind his back. He hesitated before handing them to her as if he were suddenly embarrassed by the gesture.

Flowers. Grammy would approve. Davie touched her grandmother's earrings, remembering they'd been an engagement gift. Someday she would tell Striker the story about her grandparents' lunch at that diner, the jukebox playing "When I Fall in Love," the proposal, and the carousel ride at the Santa Monica Pier afterward. Someday.

She studied his earnest expression for a moment before speaking. "They're beautiful. Thank you."

His gaze was soft and steady as he sat, resting his forearms on his thighs. "Glad to see you're okay. How's Vaughn?"

"He's out of the hospital and staying with his parents. His biggest beef right now is he won't graduate with his cooking class."

"That's a good sign." Striker paused for a moment. "Lieutenant Repetto told me she offered you a position at Homicide Special. She said you turned her down."

"I told you before. I'm happy at Pacific."

He dropped his head and stared at the ground. "You're a good detective, Davie Richards. It would be great to work with you, but I understand. I just want you to be happy."

She lowered her face to the roses, inhaling the perfume and feeling the velvet petals against her skin. "I want that for you, too."

He moved to the edge of the lounge until their knees were almost touching. He reached out and handed her one of the envelopes.

"What's this?" She set the bouquet in her lap, slipped her finger under the seal, and tore open the envelope. It was an official department form that cops used to request days off. She looked up, puzzled. "I don't get it."

He handed her a second envelope. Inside were two pieces of paper—a list of flights to the island of Tortola and sailboat rentals from a charter company in Road Town. "I thought you might want to take a few days off to dance on the sand at Foxy's."

"I told you, I don't know how to sail."

He gently tapped his fist on her knee similar to a judge gaveling the courtroom to order. "I know, but I do."

She tilted her head, smiling. "You?"

"Me," he said, leaning closer to her, smiling back. "I'll teach you everything you need to know."

She hooked her finger between the buttons of his blue oxford shirt and guided him closer. "About sailing?"

"Among other things. I'll bring sunscreen if you wear that see-through dress you bought at Apple Bay."

Davie felt a flush creep across her cheeks. She remembered him eyeing the dress but hadn't thought much of it at the time. "See-through? Why didn't you tell me?"

He pressed his lips together to hide his amusement. "Hmm … guess I forgot."

She glanced at the flight schedule. "I'm not sure this is a good idea."

Striker stood and pulled Davie to her feet. He put his arms around her and whispered in her ear. "Are you going to make me do this all by myself?"

She slipped her hand in his and led him toward the cottage. "Let's negotiate, see what happens."

© Marisa Q Photography

About the Author

Patricia Smiley (Los Angeles, CA) is a bestselling mystery author whose short fiction has appeared in *Ellery Queen Mystery Magazine* and *Two of the Deadliest*, an anthology edited by Elizabeth George. Patricia has taught writing classes at various conferences throughout the US and Canada, and she served on the board of directors of the Southern California Chapter of Mystery Writers of America and as president of Sisters in Crime/Los Angeles. Visit her online at www.PatriciaSmiley.com.